Hell: A love story

Hell:
A love story

Mat Bowes

HerpDerp Media
2016

First Printing: 2016

ISBN 978-0-578-17891-2

HerpDerp Media
3913 Pisa Dr, Unit G2
Panama City, Florida 32405

Edited by Sarah Stuckey

Cover design by Lucas Stuckey

Special discounts are available on quantity purchases by corporations, associations, educators, and others. For details, contact the publisher at the above listed address.

U.S. trade bookstores and wholesalers: Please contact HerpDerp Media
email Bowesmj0@gmail.com.

This book is dedicated to anybody who was ever told they can't.

Contents

Acknowledgements

Thanks
John Bowes for always believing in me
Sarah Stuckey for checking my spelling
Lucas Stuckey for mad Photoshop Skillz

And all the people, good and bad, who made me the man I am today.

Preface

Dear Reader,

I never sat down and told myself that I wanted to be a writer. I didn't write this for fame or fortune. In fact, if you're reading this and don't know me personally then I'm filled with a mix of flattery and shame at the idea you actually paid for this.

I wrote this book because I had a story to tell. This is, at least to a small point, a semi-autobiographical account of my adult life.

The benefit of being the story teller is that I get to decide what to tell you. It's a tougher job than you think. If I tell too much then it becomes unbelievable, and if I don't say enough then it becomes boring. I hope that I've put enough into this story that you walk away with a better understanding of me and maybe a better understanding of yourself.

Just limit the hate mail please.

Part 1

Take a deep breath and count backwards from 10. It was one of the few pieces of advice his father had ever given him that he could really understand. Close your eyes and start counting. Inhale on the evens, exhale on the odds. All his life he had been a light sleeper. Doctors had told him for years to eat better and get more exercise and maybe it would help him, advice he frequently disregarded.

10. Inhale. He rolled to his side and saw that she was still sleeping. Even with the darkness he could make out the curves of her face. She was pretty, pretty enough anyway. She had the look of a woman who had seen the best and the worst of life and lived to tell the tale. Now that she was here, now that he had had her, he could make out every imperfection that he had somehow overlooked. He could see the wrinkles on her forehead and the slight discoloration of her teeth from years of smoking.

9. Exhale. They worked together for almost a year before she failed a random drug test. After, they kept in touch through social media, hanging out occasionally in familiar settings, having the occasional drink or smoking the occasional bowl. It was only recently that she had been open to anything more, blaming the delay on her previous relationship, which she would only describe as having ended in disaster. Like a new car that had rolled off the lot for the first time, she had depreciated with use. Now that he had caught her and the chase was over, she was suddenly not nearly as valuable, a problem he faced often.

8. Inhale. He rolled to his other side and, with the grace of an injured elephant, climbed out of bed. He looked back and found her still sleeping and let a sigh of relief. He managed his way through the bedroom by memory before making his way down the hallway, passing the disapproving and judging eyes in the pictures from the past, family members, long dead, who stood as a reminder that he was an under achiever.

7. Exhale. He stopped and looked out the window, watching the hookers dressed grossly inappropriately for the weather, makeup running, hair matted, and clothes soaked, doing their best to look as appealing as possible in a thunder storm. Their only chance for a sale was the addicts who were so desperate for their fix that they had started propositioning people on the street for it. You end up with a war of the depraved, unappealing hookers and addicts both offering to service strangers, neither side giving in. This is why he chose to live here. Sure, the rent was cheap and easier than finding a place uptown, but if he was honest, even if it was with no one but himself, it made him feel better about being him.

6. Inhale. He stopped for a glass of water and then headed back to the bedroom. By now his eyes had adjusted, and he navigated the bedroom with ease, avoiding unnecessary noise in an effort not to wake his guest. As he lay in bed, he watched the lights from the passing cars and lightening dance across the ceiling. He told himself that tomorrow would be a new day. He told himself that he would make life changes. He would eat better and exercise more. He would go back to school and make something of himself. He gave the same speech he had given himself so many times before, and in the back of his mind, he knew it was a lie. His eyes became heavy, and in the light show on the ceiling, he saw memories of better times, summers and first loves. As he drifted off to sleep with false plans of better tomorrows, he was happy.

As his eyes opened, he found himself sitting at the bar in a room that could only be described as late 80s tacky. In one corner was an empty stage with an unplugged and antiquated jukebox sitting next to it. In another, he saw electronic dart boards and a foosball table. Mismatched tables and chairs filled the middle of the room, and the bar took up a whole wall. Aside from the few wall-mounted lights, most of which were burnt out, the only light came from the neon signs for beers and liquors he had never heard of. Through the dim lights, he could make out odd paintings scattered on the wall with no real sense of uniformity. On the far wall, by the stage, was a mural of a civil war battle, troops from both the North and the South preparing to attack each other. Behind the bar was a pack of wolves hunting a man through the snow, on the left side of the room was a picture of a woman in a dark dress spinning in the rain, and on the right side was a painting of a single man, but the left and right halves of his body were different, and he appeared to be trying to pull himself apart to go in opposite directions. Mark was alone in the room with the exception of the bartender, who stood at the far side of the bar in a trance-like state cleaning the same glass over and over.

"Hello?" Mark asked in a confused and trembling voice.

With a start, the bartender looked up. The hurry in his step and smile on his face gave the impression that he had not seen a customer in some time. "Good evening! I am so sorry; I didn't see you there. It's not normally the night we have guests. Welcome to Smitty's! What can I get you?"

Mark ordered whiskey, neat, and a glass of soda, something his father drank and one of the few things he could remember about the man. It wasn't until the drink was poured and he had taken his first sip that he realized that he had no idea where he was. The bartender had vanished through a curtain behind the bar. For the first time, Mark noticed that this appeared to be the only entrance or exit to the room.

He sipped his drinks, alternating between the whiskey and soda while he sat in silence and tried to make sense of his surroundings. He heard thunder, and it reminded him of waking up, but that seemed so long ago. Another sip, the room felt like it was expanding. The stage and the dartboards felt so far away. Another sip, the silence was deafening and broken up only by the familiar sound of thunder. The lights dimmed slightly for a moment with the boom.

He finished his drinks and sat in silence for what felt like an eternity, just staring at the curtain and wondering if the bartender would ever come back. He called out, at first a weak "Hello?" and waited but found no answer. He called again, this time a little louder, "Hello?" but still no response. Curiosity got the better of him, and he stood from the bar stool. He found his legs weak and wobbly from what he could only assume was the drink.

After balancing himself, he made his way to the far end of the bar where he lifted the counter and stepped behind it.

"Hello?" he called with a little more confidence, "I'd like to pay for my drink please?"

The thunder was his only answer, booming loudly enough to cause him to jump. He slowly made his way to the curtain, and with his right hand trembling, he reached across to the left side to grip it. He took a deep breath and called out, "Hello?" one more time but to no avail. He closed his eyes and pulled the curtain, and when he opened them, he was awake.

Dripping sweat, he rolled to his side. Nicole was gone, the smell of her body wash and a note saying "thanks" written in pink lipstick on a napkin the only proof she was ever there. He rolled to his back and stared at the ceiling while trying to focus his mind. He had always had trouble remembering his dreams and found it strange that this was so vivid, so real.

He pulled himself out of bed and stumbled to the bathroom, pausing for a moment to check his reflection in the mirror. The bags under his eyes betrayed him as the only sign of age on an otherwise youthful face for a man in his 30s. He was slightly taller than average and had a build that Nicole had lovingly referred to as doughy, not obese but by no means fit either. He wore his brown hair cut in a style of what could be called "conservative rebellion". It was just long and disheveled enough to be a giant fuck you to the older generation, but short enough that he blended well with the rest of the working professionals and drones in the office. The few abstract tattoos from when he was younger covered his arms, all easily concealable in case one day he had to get a "real" job, but strange enough that in a couple of years he would feel uncomfortable explaining them. He bathed and dressed before sitting down for a bowl of cereal that had clearly been created for children. The cartoon squirrel's thought bubbles told him not to be fooled by the marshmallow—this was still a great source of vitamins and minerals. Full of sugar, he would then take the number seven bus for almost an hour uptown. On the ride, he would zone out and watch the slums pass and transition into ranch-style housing and finally into the hustle of a big city.

Work was a fly-by-night loan company called Loans4You on the 15th floor of the Phillips Building, a towering behemoth of a building that had once been considered the fresh start for the city. When the building started seven years ago, Mayor Greenburg, the mayor at the time, announced that it would be a new beginning and that the 20 stories of office space would be used to rejuvenate the economy for the city. He would shout, "No more waste, no more pollution, no more crime!" through whatever microphone was closest to him before explaining that this would be the shining beacon in the city. He announced that he planned to revamp the city to match the new structure, a monument of steel and glass, and focus on changing the city into a futuristic world, and then he used this promise for the next three elections before the city collectively called bullshit. The new mayor immediately scrapped the plan and wrote it off as ill-conceived and wasteful. By then, the construction was complete and with it came low cost office space which, in turn, brought shady telemarketers and pyramid schemes. For all its outward majesty, the building quickly gained a reputation for chop shop companies. Every week a new one would show up, and a few months later, they would suddenly shut down leaving most of their staff unaware until they showed up for work and found the doors locked. What was once a symbol for change was now a towering reminder that people will say and do pretty much anything to get what they want.

Loans4You specialized in providing high interest loans for the elderly and barely legal and was one of the few businesses that seemed to have any longevity in the building. What they did was not technically illegal as much as it was morally irresponsible. The majority of their customers had no real need for a financial loan, and most of them had no real means of ever paying it back. The genius of the company was that it was simply a middleman. It was neither responsible for the financial risk nor the collections. The loans were fulfilled by struggling banks that paid a percentage for each loan created. When the loan was defaulted, Loans4You would buy the loan for pennies on the dollar from the bank and then sell it for half its worth to collection agencies. It was a system where, with the exception of Miles Trubuck, the owner of Loans4You, everybody lost.

Mark had been working for Loans4You for 3 years. What had started as a throwaway job had turned into a career. Sales came natural to him. He was just charming and confident enough to be likable without being considered cocky and arrogant, a fine line to walk.

"Plans tonight?" the voice from the next cube came across loud and intrusive.

"The same thing I do every night," Mark responded.

Wayne started in the same class as Mark so many years ago. As time passed, their class graduates dwindled, and now they were the only two left. A short man, Wayne stood 5'4 and owned every inch of it. He wore glasses over his very Jewish nose, and his hair was dark and frequently a mess.

"Discovering immortality using quantum physics and burnt toast?" They both smirked at the nostalgia of the inside joke that nobody else in the office would understand. Outside of Nicole, Wayne was the only person with a reasonably similar personality as Mark. Neither of their social circles really accepted the other, leading to few meetings outside of the building, but for eight hours a day they were inseparable.

"I think I'm going to hit the Lounge for a few drinks and see what kind of trouble I can get into."

Wayne sighed. "That place is so depressing. I just do not get why you go there. Nothing but desperate and lonely people."

Mark smiled as he placed a hand on Wayne's shoulder. "That, my friend, is exactly why I go there."

After work, the majority of the building would head to the basement level to visit The Lounge. During the day, The Lounge was a meeting place for young professionals. People would negotiate business deals over drinks at 2 in the afternoon or take an investor to brunch at 10 am. Like so many things, normal business hours were completely different than after hours. At 6 pm, the kitchen closed and some local band would set up where the salad bar stood just a few hours beforehand. The restaurant/bar catered to people in their late 20s and early 30s who were trying to forget that they had given up their dreams of being a musician or an artist and instead took a job for corporate America. People with hidden half-sleeve tattoos and piercings most people would never see sat around and enjoyed the company of other people in their same situation. Most conversations never graduated past the first name stage. You never walked out feeling that you had made a real and true connection with someone; instead, you got just enough of a connection to make you feel alive in a way that no drink or drug could do. At the end of the night, you would say your goodbyes and shake hands or offer a quick hug, anything to tell yourself that this meant something. Then you would go your separate ways. At the end of the night Mark would walk the four blocks to the bus stop where he would take the number seven bus home and feel something strange. He wasn't sure, but if he had to call it something, he would tell you that he thinks it is what satisfied feels like.

As the elevator lowered from the 15th floor, Mark took off his tie, rolled up his sleeves, and unbuttoned the top two buttons on his shirt. The elevator ride at the end of the day was always long as it stopped every other floor to pick up more and more people ready to blow off steam. After what felt like an eternity, the doors slid open for the final time and the cab was immediately filled with music and the smell of debauchery.

Mark exited the elevator and made his way through the crowd to the bar. He felt at home, like he was with his people. College drop-outs or people who quit after an AA degree and now jump from job to job desperately searching for what TV and movies have told them life should be like: the work life balance from family sitcoms where you never have to worry about money and still have plenty of time to build a family. The Cosby effect.

In the golden years of television, you had sitcoms about everyday Joes who worked hard and came home to a housewife like the *Honeymooners* or *I Love Lucy*. It gave you a sense that the lives these people are living are like your own; it gave you a sense that this was as good as it gets. Mark's generation grew up with the *Cosby Show* and *Full House* where everybody was a Doctor or Lawyer, Architect or famous News Anchor, worlds where people barely worked a 6-hour day and still paid their bills and lived in large houses. Even shows that focused on the poor ended up giving unrealistic expectations. Even Roseanne won the lottery.

Mark quickly guzzled back his first drink and ordered a second before venturing out into the crowd. In the distance, he could see a bachelorette party and then by the pool table a group of people watching a game. Of course there was the dance floor, but with the music it was hard to interact with people. Just as he was about to give up, he noticed a woman coming out of the ladies room.

Conditioned by 80s teen comedies, if ever asked about it later he would say that time slowed down and from across the bar, their eyes met. He would say that if he had to call it something, he would call it love at first sight. The streaks of purple and blonde highlighted her brown hair as it framed her face and accented her small, upturned nose. Looking at her, he couldn't tell if she had horrible taste, or was just trying to be ironic. In a sea of business attire, she stood out in thick-rimmed glasses, a black, floor-length skirt, and a t-shirt several sizes too big for her that had been creatively cut and tied to be more form fitting and show off her back, which was covered in a single large tattoo of flaming angel wings.

She walked from the restroom to the crowd surrounding the pool table tournament, standing in the back and peering between the onlookers. Mark watched for signs that she was with someone, but it seemed as if the whole place had blinders on and looked right past her. It felt like they were saving her for him.

He retreated to the bar and restocked his drink before making his way to the pool table and taking the spot next to her. He took a deep breath in; she smelled of cotton candy and cigarettes. The game was a furious game of cock blockery. The first player would place the cue ball where the second player had few shot options, and the second player responded the same way. They both seemed very skilled, and either could have finished the game at any time, but it was more fun toying with each other, seeing who would break first. It became apparent that this was not about the tournament, but about who could force the other to make a mistake. Mark was familiar with the game; he had played it with almost every woman he had ever been with.

"How long have they been at it?" he asked his prey.

Without looking from the table, she responded, "I've only been here for an hour, so longer than that. I think they are just fucking with each other at this point."

He smiled; it was nice to know he wasn't the only person who thought like he did. "You kind of look out of place around here. Do you work in the building? Most of the companies have pretty strict dress codes."

With her eyes still glued on the game, she responded, "No, I'm just fucking the bassist. The closest I usually get to this far north is this sushi place on 96th."

"Norris on 96th?"

She turned with a smile, and for the first time, and their eyes met. "You know the place?"

Then in unison, they both said, "HIYA!" and made a karate chopping motion with their right hands.

"I love their octopus salad. Don't tell anybody, but I kind of have a thing for tentacles.," she said with a wink. He couldn't tell if she was joking. Her eyes darted up and down his body. "You don't look like you belong here much either." She grabbed his wrist and pulled it towards her to get a better look at the tattoo on his forearm. "In a sea of yuppies, the guy with a smiley face and cross bones on his forearm tends to stick out."

The music stopped, and from the PA came the announcement that the band would be taking a short break.

"Well that's my que," she said as she let go of his wrist. "I'll see you around," she finished with a smile before pushing her way to the opposite side of the bar where she threw her arms around some skinny guy in way-too-tight jeans.

Discouraged, Mark finished his drink in one swallow and left the bar. As he walked through the parking area, he thumbed through his phone until he came to Nicole and sent the one-word text "busy?" just in time to make it to the bus stop where he sat. His phone buzzed with her response. "Yeah, sorry. Tomorrow?" A typical response. All too often, Nicole was off doing her own thing, only interested when it was convenient to her. He chose not to reply.

The worst part of working in the city was the commute home. It felt like leaving life behind. Mark would look behind him and watch the city slowly disappear from sight as it was replaced with the suburbs full of families sitting down and sharing dinner until they too were gone. Much like the morning commute let him believe that he was heading to a better place, the trip home only stood as a reminder of everything he did not have.

From the bus stop to his apartment was only a few blocks, but they were filled with the homeless looking for change and hookers looking for johns. With every few steps came another request for help or an offer for a good time. Mark walked by in silence. His only thought was that of cotton candy and cigarettes. He climbed the three stories to his apartment, and once inside took a hot shower in the hopes it would clear his head. As he lay down for the night, he made himself the same promises. Tomorrow would be a new day. He would make life changes. He would eat better and exercise more. He would go back to school and make something of himself. His eyes became heavy as he watched the lights from passing cars on his ceiling. He saw the outline of a man gliding across the floor.

Mark's nostrils filled with the stench of stale beer. He opened his eyes and found himself sitting on a barstool in the familiar bar from his previous dream. The room looked and felt different, smaller and hotter. In the mirror behind the bar, he could see the empty stage and the jukebox that now seemed to have power. The mirror itself looked different, no longer a picture but a regular mirror, and the murals that covered the walls were gone. The neon signs that had been the main source of light were now dimmer as some had stopped working. There were now other patrons sitting both at the bar and at the tables, all of them looking just as confused as Mark felt. The same bartender greeted him, "Good evening, welcome to Smitty's! Whiskey neat and a glass of soda, right?" Before Mark could answer, the bartender started pouring the drinks.

He understood that this was a dream, and knowing that, he tried his best to take control of it. He asked the bartender his name, and in response, the bartender simply pointed to a nametag that read Jimmy. "Where am I? Why am I here, Jimmy?"

With a polite but confused smile, Jimmy said, "Well, you are at Smitty's, sir. I cannot speak for why you are here, but it is my pleasure to provide you with the best service possible while you are."

Mark could feel his face warm, and he didn't know if it was his frustration showing, or if it was just the heat from the room. "How do I get out of here, Jimmy?"

His polite smile turned to one of caution, the smile of an authority figure giving a final warning. "Normally people come here because they want something, sir. You can leave anytime you want, but you are here for a reason, and because of that, you will only keep coming back."

Mark's head was spinning. His vision became blurry.

"You don't look so great, sir. Have your drink and enjoy the show. Maybe you will feel better if you stop thinking so much."

10. Inhale. As fast as he had appeared, Jimmy had ducked back behind the curtain. The lights dimmed, and a spot light hit the stage. A roar of applause began, and a man dressed in a black pin stripe suit made his way to the stage. He had the body language of a game show host, not walking as much as gliding on air.

9. Exhale. Mark attempted to stand, but his legs gave way, and he only just caught himself on the chair. His body was numb to every feeling but temperature, which only seemed to rise. He tried to focus his eyes to the man on stage.

8. Inhale. "Ladies and gentlemen, boys and girls of all ages, welcome!" He opened his arms to the crowd and continued. "You are here because you have a need, a desire. You are here because you would give anything to get what you want and lucky for you, I am here to help!"

7. Exhale. The room erupted in cheers as the presenter raised his hands in the air. Mark could feel his arms give way. He felt like he was falling through the floor. The heat was overtaking him. He couldn't be certain, but he thought that this was what dying felt like.

6. Inhale. "You all know Jimmy, right?" The crowd responded in agreement. "Well, Jimmy was a client and now just look at him, owner and operator of his own pub!" The crowd offered him a round of applause to which he responded with a small bow. "Jimmy here had a desire, and I helped him gain it!" The crowd again erupted in applause.

5. Exhale. Mark felt as if his lungs would explode from the pressure. He could not take air in or let out the little bit he had stored. His vision had gone black, and the noise from the presenter and crowd faded out. For a moment, he was alone, floating in nothingness. His mind was empty aside from the sole thought of how alone he really was.

Thursday, September 11th

He woke up in a sweat, his head pounding and his body on fire. In his sleep, he had kicked and thrown the covers and pillows from the bed. His room looked as though it had been ransacked. He swung his legs over the side of his bed and sat up, doing his best to remember his entire dream. It was not as vivid as before. He knew it was the same location, but the fine details had escaped him.

He pulled himself out of bed and stumbled to the bathroom, pausing for a moment to check his reflection in the mirror. His face looked old and wrinkled compared to just yesterday. It felt like he had not slept at all. He stumbled through his apartment and finally crashed on his couch. On his coffee table was his phone with a blue blinking light. He picked it up and unlocked it in a single swift motion to find that Nicole had texted him 8 times. The first 3 were a single question mark. The fourth and fifth were his name followed by a question mark. The sixth read:

(11:08pm) Are you mad at me?

The seventh read:

(11:43pm) I'm coming over.

The eighth and final message read:

(1:19am) What happened? I stood outside your apartment and I could hear you screaming for like an hour!?! Are you ok? Call me please.

"Hello, Mark?" She sounded out of breath. "What the hell happened last night?"

He thought for a moment, not totally sure how to answer the question. "I honestly don't know. I had a strange dream, but I don't remember what about." He thought better of telling her about the reoccurring setting as the hippy side of her put a lot of stock into dreams, and he had neither the time nor attention to devote to a lecture about his drinking problems. "All I know is it must have been a pretty bad dream as my bedroom was torn apart this morning."

Silence came through the phone's speaker for what felt like an awkward amount of time. "So I have to tell you that Jimmy is going to come stay with me."

Jimmy... Mark lost himself in thought. Why does that name sound familiar? Jimmy... Had he recently met a Jimmy?

"I know you never signed up for a woman with a kid, and you know I really care about you, and I get the feeling you really care for me, so I wanted to make sure you know about him."

Jimmy... Was that the new guy at work?

"It just means I may not be as available as I have been, but if you need someone to talk to, then please don't hesitate to call me. Promise you won't forget about me." This statement snapped him back to attention and gave him a warm feeling in his chest, something he normally only felt watching the conclusion of family movies. As he spotted the number seven bus round the corner, all he could muster as a response was "Thanks, I will."

Floor 15 was known for its air conditioner. When stepping off the elevator, you were often hit by the chill of the air. Management, Loans4You in particular, reasoned that keeping the offices cold would promote alertness, but it was commonly discussed by the employees that it was a way to foster illness, which in turn generated absenteeism and lead to denial of bonuses. An auto-dialer was programed with customer information bought from late night infomercial and pizza delivery websites, the prime customers for unneeded loans. It read the recipient a message letting them know that they and they alone may be eligible for a new loan that could be used to help pay for college or fulfilling the dream that had already passed. Mark sat in his 3 by 3 cube while waiting for the next call, and counted the minutes to the end of the day.

"You look like shit there, buddy." Wayne remarked as they found a seat in the Lounge.

"I didn't sleep so well last night," Mark confessed. "I had a strange dream, but I don't recall too much what it was about. This morning, I woke up and found my bedroom looking like it had been ransacked in the night."

"Strange," Wayne halfheartedly mused as he reviewed the menu knowing it never changes.

From across the room, they heard a woman shouting about the quality of her meal to a meek man in a dingy white button up shirt and a crooked bow tie. Even from a distance, Mark could hear every complaint shouted. "How stupid can you be? I said medium rare and this is clearly medium! Do you not know the difference? Don't they teach you anything here?" The meek waiter could only sputter a series of apologies while the woman went on and on.

"And you thought your job was bad." Wayne offered.

A stout woman in a similarly dingy white shirt and bow tie came to their table. "Hello, my name is Annie. Would you like to hear our specials?" she asked in a mellow and board tone. Her hair was pulled back in a tight bun, and she wore the many years she had been in the service industry in every wrinkle and frown line on her face. Wayne ordered a French dip and Mark an order of fried pickles and a pitcher of beer with a straw, the waitress rolling her eyes on every other word spoken to her.

"So I would like you to come to this group with me tonight." It was an odd request given their history as friends. "Before you say no, let me say it is not some weird cult thing or pyramid scheme." Mark felt the urge to do his own eye roll. "It is more of a social gathering thing; a lot of people from our generation working through their own problems."

Mark smiled. "That's exactly what we do at the Lounge!" he laughed. "Why don't you come with me there and at least we can drink."

Wayne seemed prepared for the conversation. "I am just trying to look out for you, man. When I look at you, I do not see a happy person, and if that is the case then maybe you should consider steps to change where you are in life."

Mark considered Wayne's words as Annie arrived with the drinks.

In a moment of seriousness, something he dreaded, Mark replied, "Look man, I appreciate you looking out for me, I really do, but I'm confident that this is as good as it gets. I don't reckon we are supposed to be happy 24/7. Happiness should come in small bites because if it was constant, then we would build a tolerance and then it would never be enough."

Wayne offered an exhausted sigh as they sat in silence for the rest of the meal, looking at their phones and exchanging only small talk about current events. Their food quickly came and went almost as fast and before he knew it, Mark was back at his desk. Because of the several cups of coffee before lunch and the beer during lunch, he was physically feeling much better, but mentally he was blocked by strange images of a man who looked like he had been pulled from a gameshow gliding across a stage.

The rest of the afternoon passed without incident, and Mark decided to pass up the Lounge in favor of a bowl of cereal and some prescription pain killers he had scored from a woman in the breakroom. From habit, he removed his tie, rolled up his sleeves, and unbuttoned the top two buttons on his shirt; but instead of the basement button, his finger moved to the button for the lobby. As the elevator lowered, Mark could hear the music grow louder from below him as he thought about his decision. He told himself that he was probably just burnt out on the Lounge and he should get some sleep after the previous night's wild dreams, but in his mind, in thoughts he knew he would never share with anybody, he thought back to lunch and his conversation with Wayne.

As the doors opened into the lobby, he could hear the music stop, followed by the muffled announcement that the band would be taking a short break. The lobby felt cold and empty as the majority of people who used it had already left, and most of the remaining people would be going to the basement. A single security guard sat behind a half-circle desk and casually flipped through a dirty magazine. Through the front windows of the lobby, the sky looked the pink and purple of a fresh bruise, a sight Mark had not seen in quite some time. His footsteps echoed through the room, forcing the security guard to look up from his magazine with an awkward smile and slight nod of acknowledgement.

Outside the air was cool and damp, typically the signs of a nighttime storm. Walking through the parking lot, he felt the familiar vibration of his phone receiving a signal for the first time in 4 hours. He glanced at the messages from Nicole.

(1:23pm) Hey Mark, are you ok?

(1:25pm) I was thinking about you.

It was the same game his mother had played for years with assorted men. She was looking for validation and attention on her terms, and Mark decided that he would not be the one to give it. He shut off the phone and placed it in his pocket as he took a seat at the bus stop. The number seven bus ran on a 2-hour loop and would not be there for half an hour. His eyes closed, and he tried to think of better times and happier places, but nothing came to mind. For several minutes, he was alone with his thoughts filled with images of neon signs and mismatched table and chair sets.

The silence was broken by a slamming door as an argument emerged from the side entrance into the Lounge. From across the parking lot it was hard to make out the fine details, but the cursing and name-calling came through as clear as a bell. She was yelling and he was defensive. She was a prude and he would fuck anything that has a pulse. She was selfish and he was arrogant. Mark thought to himself that this must be what love is like. Keeping his eyes shut, he listened to the yelling get closer as it got more incoherent. It came to a point where the voice of the woman was getting louder, but the voice of the man had leveled off: she kept walking and he stopped following. After a short time, she was standing within feet of Mark where the last message came out perfectly. "Fuck you! I'll just take a bus home, or hell, I might go home with this guy! At least he looks like he has a fucking job!"

Mark opened his eyes but avoided eye contact. The voice was familiar, but the last thing he wanted was to be dragged into some fight. She sat down next to him, the slight wind blowing through her brown hair causing the purple and blonde streaks to flutter in the wind. She reached down the neck of her dark 1950s style dress and pulled out a pack of cigarettes, took one out and paused before letting out a frustrated sigh.

"I don't suppose you have a light?" Her voice was shaky and frightened.

He patted his pockets, as if something he has never carried before would suddenly appear in one of them, before shaking his head no.

In a poetic moment, a tear formed in her left eye and rolled down her cheek as the rain started causing the tear to blend in as if it was never there. She looked at him and smiled, "I guess when it rains it pours, right?" She got up and moved out of the slight awning that offered a little protection from the weather and started spinning in a circle.

Thoroughly drenched, she sat back down before reaching out her hand. "My name is Julie, by the way. We met last night, didn't we?"

Mark smiled and nodded. She reached across him and grabbed his left wrist.

"I remember. Smiley face and cross bones!" Mark nodded again and the smile washed away from Julie's face. "Geez, you don't say a whole lot when it's quiet enough for people have a conversation, do you?"

It took a moment to process, but he just realized he had not said anything through the whole encounter. "I'm sorry. "He started, "I was just kind of taken aback for a moment. The way you danced around in the rain reminded me of something and I don't exactly know what."

Her smiled returned. "You wouldn't believe how often that happens."

He took a deep breath. "So I know we don't really know each other, but since it looks like we are both not doing anything this evening, want to not do something together?"

The pause in conversation seemed to last forever, as it tends to do in these situations. Time seemed to slow down, possibly because his heart had started moving in double speed. She smiled and said, "Sure, I've got a knife just in case you turn out to be some sort of psycho." They both laughed, and before he could blink, she pulled a butterfly knife and stabbed it into the bench between them.

Norris on 96th was a regular eatery for young professionals in the city. Norris's real name was Hanzo, but he changed it upon arriving from Japan in the late 80s. With a young bride and a dream of being the next big American action film star, he came to the states in search of fortune and fame. After 10 years and 3 low budget direct-to-home video releases (Chung Norris 1, 2, and 3), his young bride demanded that he give up his silly dream and support his ever-growing family. They brought over her father who had been a sushi chef and sold the movie rights and character of Chung Norris to build a sushi bar. Unfortunately, with the invention of the internet, Chung Norris became an underground sensation and developed a cult following. Norris attempted to cash in on the name by naming the sushi bar after himself, but the shrewd 22-year-old who bought the rights took him to court. What started as Kimiko's Sushi bar, named for his wife, became Chung

Norris Sushi, which became Norris on 96th. Norris became very aware that they could not stop him from playing the movies in the bar, nor could they stop him from having a karate yell door chime. He had taken on a host job and welcomed customers to his restaurant, billing it as "owned by the guy in those movies you love."

"HIYA!" rang the bell as Mark and Julie entered. "Welcome Norris on 96!" Norris greeted them. "Plea Sit wheve you lie!" His smile and energy was infectious.

They both took a seat at the bar and ordered; him a Dynamite and California roll, her Tuna and Yellowtail. They made the typical small talk you make when you first meet someone: the "who, what, when, where, and whys" of your life. She told him the story of a lonely girl with a history of poor choices in men. She grew up with a used car salesman for a father, always putting on a show and making promises he couldn't keep. She would watch him work, telling anybody that would listen anything he could get them to believe it if meant a sale. Her mother was a lush; always at the tail-end of a bender. She was nice and attentive enough on the few occasions Julie could remember her sober. Her parents were swingers and very open about their lifestyle. They did not try to protect or hide their little girl from the strange world of sex, often introducing her to uncles and aunts who would be around for a few weeks and then never come back.

She told him of the last "uncle" she had met. She was 17 and he was grey-haired and ancient. His belly hung several inches over his belt, to the point you could see it hanging out from under his shirt. "He smelled like peppermint and had tan leather skin. It was like he had spent his whole life outside; you know?" As she told her story, her face remained emotionless, as if she had trained herself not to take it personally. Like she taught herself not to let it get the best of her. "My father met him when selling his company cargo vans, and apparently daddy's little girl was part of the deal. Daddy introduced to him as Uncle Chad and left us alone in the basement. I never thought anything of it really, it was all part of the ceremony. He seemed like a nice enough man, placing his arm around me as we sat on the couch. I was confused, but not frightened. Like I said, keeping random people company during the prep stages was not a new concept, but this felt different than every time before. I remember sitting there and waiting for dad to come back and collect Uncle Chad, but after a half-hour we were still alone. It was bout that time that Uncle Chad moved his hand to my thigh, and it was only then when i realized what her father expected her to do. I tried to talk my way out of it and back away but he was bigger and stronger than me. Finally, I asked him to turn out the lights, and as he turned around, I hit him over the head with a lamp before climbing out the small basement window. The next day, I found out that Uncle Chad required 26 stitches and may never have full function of his left eye again. Dad beat me for causing him to lose the big sale, and later that night I packed a bag and took off for the city."

Mark was floored by the honest conversation. He found that the majority of people gloss over the bad things and only focus on the good. Most people only give you the best parts, the things they want you to see. It was refreshing to meet someone who was so open about everything, even the horrible things in their own life.

Finishing her last piece of sushi, Julie went on. She told him about arriving in the city and having no real education. She told him how she took the only things her parents had taught her; lying, alcohol, and sex, and used them to become a stripper. And then, as casually as asking someone about the weather, she turned to Mark and with a smile said, "Your turn."

"HIYA!" the door chimed as they left Norris on 96th. The rain had slowed to a steady mist as they walked back to the bus stop. Mark thought for a while, wishing she was as brave as she was. The only trauma he could think of was learning that TV and movies had lied to him about what being an adult is, but honestly, that was true for his whole generation, and not all of them shared his self-loathing narcissistic traits. Sure, he had his own demons and traumas, nothing that compared to hers. He told Julie a heavily edited version of about his father passing away when he was young and tried his best to convince her that it really did not bother him.

"He was a good man, a great man. He was wise and kind. A few months after his death, mom decided we needed to move, which started a string of new locations and men which she went through like tissue paper." It felt strange. He normally said very little about his past but she made him comfortable. "Sometimes it was a month and sometimes a year, but we would eventually pack up and she would introduce me to a new guy who would call me buddy or kiddo. They were nice enough and they all taught me something new. Engine maintenance, home repair, computer programing; each one was different from the last and was egger to share their knowledge in an attempt to bond."

Julie listened to his story with what he considered to be great interest. They talked on the way to the bus stop, then the hour-long bus ride, and finally the 10 minute walk to his apartment. Before he knew it, they were sitting on the couch, her head resting on a pillow on his lap, and it was almost midnight.

Acting on the courage that had been slowly building within him all night, he bent over and kissed her lips. She responded by grabbing the back of his head and kissing him back. She then sat up as he pulled her on top of his lap where he kissed her again. Her hair fell, framing both his and her face, and he was stunned by just how beautiful she was in this moment. Her hands moved to his neck and his to her hips. He pulled her close, feeling the weight of her on his chest. She broke the kiss and pulled away and said "I won't sleep with you. Not tonight." before leaning back in to kiss him again.

The feeling of intrigue that came from the chase was replaced with a strange disappointment. It was hard to describe, not the kind of disappointment that came from being denied sex, but the disappointment that came with the understanding that it was better to go without.

She shifted her weight and climbed off his lap, making it to her own feet before breaking the kiss. Taking his left arm, she pulled him to his feet and led him down the hallway to his bedroom. She navigated the apartment like she had been there a million times, walking backwards and pulling him along. In the hallway, she stopped and immediately found the one photo of him as a child. Her eyes went wide as a smile crossed her face. "You were so cute! What happened?" she asked in a teasing manner. In his bedroom, she headed into the closet, and when she came out, she was wearing one of his t-shirts. She had taken the hanger and hung her still damp dress on the door handle to the closet. She climbed into bed and under the covers as naturally and comfortably as if it was something she had been doing for years. Mark stripped to his boxers, turned out the light, and climbed into the empty side of the bed. She rolled over and positioned him so she could cradle in the crook of his arm. It felt strangely natural. Her light breathing was hypnotic and before long, Mark too found himself drifting to sleep.

Slow motion images of Julie spinning in the rain fogged Mark's mind. The whole evening replayed itself from a third person perspective where he could watch it all. Now they were outside of Norris on 96th where she first took his hand. He felt the warmth wash over him. He opened the door to the familiar "HIYA!" chime only inside was not a sushi bar, but instead the familiar interior of Smitty's. Mark quickly turned around, but the door was gone and in its place the mural of a man whose two sides were trying to pull himself apart.

"Like trains passing in the night, I was wondering when I would get to see you."

Mark spun towards the bar, towards the familiar voice. A man in a black suit sat at the bar patting the empty seat next to him. "Please, sit down. We have much to talk about."

His body seemed to move without his consent. He felt like he was only along for the ride and in no real control. With each step, his mind shouted to stop to no avail until finally Mark took his place upon the bar stool.

In a swift motion, the man grabbed Mark's hand, gripped it tightly, and said, "My name is Jack."

His voice was calm and confident. He spoke as if you should already know who he is. Mesmerized, Mark smiled politely and noticed his drink of choice already poured and set on the bar front of him. Looking back, he found the stranger still facing him, but now holding his own glass in front of him. He appeared to be in his late 20s and wore a rugged and handsome face. His features seemed flawless, from his teeth being almost too white to his bright blue and inviting eyes. He was the kind of handsome you only see on TV. His smile, his posture, his whole presence; everything about the man could only be described as perfect. "What should we drink to? How about new friends!"

They both took a sip, and finally the words, "Who are you exactly?" slipped past Mark's already numbing lips.

Jack smiled his bright white smile and spun in his chair like a child. At the end of his spin, he was facing Mark head-on and replied, "Me? I am just a friendly stranger, looking for a good conversation over some fine drinks. I cannot help but notice that the options in this bar are a bit slim, but you seem like the kind of guy I could have a good chat with."

Mark noticed his lack of conjunctions and found it a distracting and glaring blemish on the rest of his perfection, making him seem something either more or less than human. He unbuttoned the top button of his jacket and pulled on his tie, loosening it slightly.

"So tell me Mark, what do you do?" Before he could answer, Jack went on, "I bet you work in an office somewhere, probably entry level work. Maybe you make calls, or receive them, either way you probably hate it, am I right?" Mark said nothing, more confused than anything else, and Jack continued, "Let me ask you something, Mark. Where do you see yourself in five years? I know you know how easy it is to remain stagnant. Do you want to still be living alone in a shitty apartment? Working at a job you hate for too little money and no recognition? Sure, at the end of the day, you can partake in some promiscuous sex and recreational drug use, hoping to pass the time until you go home and fall asleep, promising yourself that tomorrow is the day you will change, but the truth is that nothing really changes until you change. "

Mark's head was swimming. He took a large sip from his glass and considered what he had just heard, subconsciously ignoring the fact that this stranger knew his name and instead focusing on the detailed retelling of his daily activities. Sure, it could be that his sorry excuse for a life is not exactly what you would call original. Hundreds of thousands of people probably felt the way he did. His eyes darted around the room but found no way to leave.

Even the curtain behind the bar had disappeared and only a red brick wall stood in its place.

"Hit a little too close to home, did I?" Jack said between his toothy grin. "You probably think this is as good as it gets, right? You probably run around thinking that this is as happy as you need to be. You have a job and your bills get paid. As boring and lack Luster as your life is at the end of the day, you fall asleep content. I mean it has worked out well so far, right? But what if you are wrong?"

Mark thought back to his conversation with Wayne. As his own argument was used against him, questions flooded his mind. Wasn't he just with Julie? How did he get here? Was this a dream? If it was a dream, then wasn't he in control?

Mark responded, "And what if I'm not? What if this is all I need?" Jack's perfect face twitched at his indifference.

He felt a smug sense of accomplishment. In his mind, he had told off this stranger who seemed to know him too well. He had put him in his place and told him that he was ok living his shitty little life, even though it was a bald faced lie. Mark took a big gulp and finished his glass before slamming it down on the counter. He shook the cobwebs from his mind and made his plan to stand up when he was stopped by Jack's hand on his arm.

"Please, sit. Hear me out," He said as he reached in his jacket pocket and produced a card. "See, I am a recruiter."

Mark sat and looked at the card, which had raised gold print reading:

Jack Darby
Acquisitions and Recruiting

"I have heard good things about you and come a long way to meet you." Jack explained. "It has been a long time since I was told to contact someone with such a high priority."

This idea intrigued Mark. As far as he could tell, he had never really done anything well enough for someone to take this much notice, at least not to his knowledge. "Who do you work for?" Mark asked.

Jack cautiously looked around in an exaggerated display of paranoia. "It is all very confidential, very hush-hush if you know what I mean. Right now, all you need to know is that my employers are very interested in you."

The vagueness of the statement was the nail in the coffin. The whole encounter had turned Mark off, but this had gone on just a bit too long. He told himself again that he was in control. He told himself that this wasn't real before turning to Jack who was taking another long sip.

"Look, I appreciate the drink and your time but I'm really not interested." He smiled politely and backed away from the bar.

It was then that he heard a loud crack and a booming voice scream, "This is not a negotiation!"

Frozen with fear, Mark did his best to remain calm as the walls had begun to melt and fire bellowed from the light fixtures. He felt a hot hand on his shoulder, and he turned to face Jack. When he did, the face that he found was not the same one he had seen all night. The contour of his face had formed peaks and valleys while his jaw line dropped, elongating his face. The handsome and face had turned into what could only be loosely be called the face of a man.

Mark took a deep breath.

10. Inhale. In a swift move, Jack kicked the chair from beneath Mark and caught him with a firm grip, placing him on his feet. The already dim lights lowered, and the crack of lightning could be heard through the walls. "No!" He shouted as he grabbed Mark by the shoulders. "You have two options. You calm down, relax, and listen to what I have to say, or you keep coming back here over and over again until it is too late."

9. Exhale. Jack's face started to contort. His eyes became yellow, and his white teeth started to blacken. "You cannot run away from this. It is going to happen. Stop all this petty bullshit and man the fuck up!"

8. Inhale. "This is your chance to live up to your potential!"

The sentence broke Mark's concentration. He couldn't think of the next number or remember how to exhale. All he could hear was his mother reminding him that his father was a great man, reminding him to live up to his potential. Mark sat down on the stool and the lights came up. The disfigured look on Jack's face had vanished as both men sat with their drinks raised in the air.

Mark shook the fuzzy feeling from his head and then surveyed the room. For the first time this evening, he couldn't tell if this was a dream or not. The walls were no longer melting, and the lights were no longer flames. His eyes made contact with Jack's, and for a moment he felt safe, as if that one glance was enough to convince him that none of it had happened. For a brief moment, he was happy. And then Jack spoke and said, "I can do it again..." before smiling and taking another long sip from his drink.

With an exasperated sigh, Jack started, "Did you know that thousands of years ago, representatives from both what you call Heaven and Hell met in what is now Las Vegas, and the 37 percent rule was made effective? According to this law, if 37.9 percent of your life was worthless, or was used for ill gains, then you do not get a trial, there is no jury of your peers, no talk or plea bargains. When you die, you go directly to the Underworld where you will be punished for your sins, and it will happen sooner than you think. Within the next few months, in fact."

Mark struggled to follow along. The information came quickly and didn't make much sense. He attempted to ask a question but was quickly silenced as Jack continued. "I know, I know. You have questions but do not ask me how I know all this or when it will happen. A lot of the future is unwritten, and the fine details can be a bit foggy. All that matters is that within a matter of months you will shed your mortal body and spend eternity serving in the Underworld, one way or another."

Jack took a long sip of his drink while Mark tried to process what he had just been told. The tone of Jack's voice briefly changed into something kind and almost thoughtful as he said, "I wish I could tell you more, I honestly do," before returning to its usual exaggerated confident tone. "You know, it used to be a lot of Wrath and Envy, but now a days it is mostly Greed and Pride. It is funny how things change. Most of what you hear is true, fire and brimstone, ironic punishments to suit the crime. Irony is big there. For what it is worth, I am sorry I have to be the one to tell you this. It is always the hardest part of the conversation, so I am just going to hit you with facts. This is about the numbers. At this point, you have been alive for 32 years, 3 months, and 3 weeks; which is a total of 11801 days. We subtract 12 years because the first 12 years never count for anybody. Do not ask me why, I do not make the rules. Minus 12 years leaves you 7421 days, 2793 of which were spent performing selfish acts for self-serving reasons."

Mark thought about the past year, jumping from woman to woman, living paycheck to paycheck, making poor and destructive life decisions. He tried to think of the last selfless thing he had done, but his train of thought was interrupted by Jack's words. "Right now, you are trying to think of the last good thing you did, right? Let me help. Three weeks ago, you gave your seat on the bus to a pregnant woman. Do you remember that?" Mark shook his head "no," but as he did, the scene replaced the etching of wolves in the mirror. "Good, because that did not count. Sure, to that woman you seemed like a gentleman, but you and I both know that you only did it because you would have rather stood than sit next to the homeless guy behind you. Two months ago, you gave to a paraplegic but only to impress Nicole. How did that work out for you?" The etching in the mirror changed to that of a scene in Mark's bedroom, Nicole naked on top of him, her head thrown back in ecstasy. "The last thing you did that was truly selfless was you gave a man named John a slice of pizza you had ordered for lunch at work. You were not full and you had planned on saving it for later, but for some reason you offered anyways. How pathetic is that?"

Mark swallowed his drink in one gulp. He had no memory of anything he was being told, but the etchings in the mirror showed him in great detail. He hung his head in shame. "No, that couldn't be. I'm not a bad guy..."

Jack cut him off. "This is not about being a good guy or a bad guy. Do not take it personally. You are a Special Case. We are in need of people like you Mark, people who are dedicated, capable, and follow orders without question." Jack then reached for a briefcase that had appeared in front of him and opened it slowly to build suspense. Inside sat an ancient looking document that seemed to shimmer and shine under the dim neon lights of the room. "If you sign this document willingly and submit your soul, then you will be put to work in our acquisition office. You will be given a shitty apartment to live in when you are not at a job you hate finding people who might be open to signing contracts that do not benefit them. Sound familiar?" he asked with a smile.

Mark was speechless. He hated to admit it, but what Jack was saying made a great deal of sense. If this was real, then he would much rather spend eternity in an office doing menial work than spend an eternity in torment and pain. Jack spun in his chair like a child before stopping to take a long sip of his drink. The contract sat in the open, drawing his eyes to it.

"How do I know this is real?" he asked. "This is a dream for Christ's sake."

But before he could finish the sentence, he felt Jack's leathery hand come across his face hard.

"Firstly, do not use that name in front of me. Secondly, you will see how real this is when you wake up with stinging pain in your cheek." Mark could tell that Jack received a sick sense of pleasure from the exchange.

He said, "Look, I've listened to what you have to say, and now I would like to go. I want to wake up. I understand that you say I'll only come back, but I don't care. I want to leave this bar right now," as he emphatically pounded his fist on the counter, causing the glasses to shake slightly. The volume of his voice increased with each word, and his eyes locked on the bright blue pools that were Jack's eyes. "I don't care who you are or what you are saying. I have listened to what you had to say, and now I want to leave. It's my choice, dammit!"

Jack sat in silence, his face echoing his polite smile. "The only thing keeping you here is your own mind. If you want to leave, then you walk through that door anytime you wish." Mark followed Jack's finger as he pointed to the wall across the bar and next to the jukebox to a wooden door, and when he looked back, Jack, the briefcase, and the drinks were gone. He sat alone at the bar with only Jimmy for company, who appeared out of nowhere politely smiling and cleaning a glass. Mark stood, wobbly on his feet, and struggled to cross the bar.

He stopped in front of the wooden door that had magically appeared before looking back at Jimmy, who offered a wave and a pleasant "Please come again!" He turned back to the wooden door and slowly reached out for the door knob. His hand trembled with each inch until he securely grasped the knob like it was the only thing he knew was real. With a deep breath, he turned and pulled the door towards him and stepped into the blackness on the other side.

"Mark!" He felt small hands on his chest. "Mark!" They were pushing him, shaking his body. "Wake up!" His eyes opened to see Julie leaning over him. Her worried face changed to a smile, and she wrapped her arms around him. "You had me so worried. You were shouting and tossing like a you were possessed!" Mark attempted to sit up, and Julie released her grip on him so he could do so. His body was slick with sweat and the sheets damp. She touched the side of his face, which caused him to jump slightly due to a burning pain, before saying, "Take a deep breath and count backwards from 10." He turned to look at her, his eyes adjusting to the darkness. "It was something I learned when I was little. Inhale on the evens, exhale on the odds."

With a feeling of total calm, he fell into her arms as they both lay down. He could feel her heart beat through her chest as her breasts cushioned his head. He would later confess to her that he had never felt this comfortable with anyone, a feeling that she said she shared.

Friday, September 12th

Hours passed and before long, it was morning. The remainder of the night was peaceful and without incident. Mark had awoken first, his arm draped over Julie's waist with her back pressed to his chest. Even with her makeup caked, smeared, and smudged, he found her attractive. He rolled, attempting to pull away without waking up his bedmate. After quietly moving to the living room, he found his phone on the coffee table, the same place he had left it the night before. The blue blinking light told him there was a message, and he felt a sudden sense of deja vu. As he picked up the phone, it rang, startling him.

Nicole's picture and phone number flashed across the screen. "Hello?" he answered.

"Hey! I didn't hear from you last night." She sounded nervous.

From down the hallway, he could hear his door open and then close and then the door to the bathroom open and close. "Is everything alright?" he asked.

"Oh yeah." she paused. "Everything is fine. Listen, I want to see you tonight. I feel like you've been pretty distant because of Jimmy, and I want to make sure you and I are ok."

From down the hallway, he could hear the sound of the shower start. Mark thought for a moment, searching for a reason to decline but came up empty. "Ok, come by when you get off of work. I'll be home."

Her voice perked up. "Ok, see you tonight!" and the call ended.

By the time the sound of the shower stopped, Mark had made some toast and scrambled eggs for two. Julie came from around the corner wearing only the shirt she slept in last night; her hair was wet and combed straight back and her face was bare of the battle paint she had woken with, causing her to look several shades paler. She confidently walked to the fridge and pulled from it a bottle of orange juice. As if she had organized the kitchen herself, she quickly found a glass and poured herself a drink before sitting down at the folding table.

"So what were you dreaming about?" she asked as she stuck her fork into the eggs. "Do you have a lot of nightmares?"

Mark shook his head. "I don't know, it's not often I remember dreams." As he spoke, the image of Smitty's bar flashed in his mind. Had he dreamt about it again?

"That's strange.," she said through a mouth full of eggs.

Mark offered a soft chuckle as he wasn't sure if he should be offended or not. "How so?"

Julie shrugged as she swallowed a mouthful of orange juice. "I've never met someone who doesn't remember their dreams, and I think it's weird because I remember all of my dreams."

"Even the bad ones?" he asked.

She smiled and said, "When I was little, my dad told me that dreams are just warnings. It's our mind telling us to focus on one subject or another. I don't know if it's true or not, but I've always thought that the bad dreams were the most important because it's your mind telling you something has got to change."

She told the story with such respect and care for her father, an action that he envied. Mark had always held grudges, some far longer than needed. To hear her still show care and understanding for a man after the abuse she said she had experienced spoke volumes. He watched as she devoured the meal in front of her and smiled when she broke away from breakfast only long enough to say, "You know what I like about you? You're not afraid to use pepper in your eggs."

They finished their meal in silence, and when she was done, she got up, washed her dishes, kissed Mark on the cheek, and walked back to the bedroom leaving him in a state of shock and confusion from the whole ordeal. She emerged a short time later dressed in the dark grey dress she had worn the night before. Mark had just finished his own dishes and met her at the table where she sat down and picked up his phone. After a few quick taps, her breast began to ring and she smiled. She placed his phone by his hand, and then placed her hand over his saying, "I expect you to use it," Before standing and walking out of his apartment.

The commute up town seemed to drag as he compared the mundane task to the morning's activities. Mark tried his best to zone out while watching the speeding images as they changed between the slums to the suburbs to finally the city. At the stop before his, an old woman got on the bus. As she passed him, their eyes met. He couldn't help but notice her bright blue eyes and felt a sense of déjà vu like a negative energy making him so uncomfortable that he completely forget about the emotions Julie had stirred within him. The morning passed with a series of similar encounters in the lobby, in the elevator, even in the restroom. It seemed every stranger he met had the same bright blue eyes and they all caused an unknown sense of dread within him. By the afternoon, his distracted behavior had gained Wayne's attention.

"What is going on with you? You have been acting strange all day," he asked.

Mark did his best to act indifferent but felt totally transparent. "I don't know," he lied. "Just not feeling great. Must have been something I ate that disagreed with me."

Wayne did his best to engage him several more times before the end of the day, but it always ended with a distraction or flat out dismissal of the original question. After work, they rode the elevator down together. The small space between them might as well have been miles. It was easy to see that Mark could not wait to get home. Outside, he called a cab which changed the hour-long commute to one of less than twenty minutes at the cost of almost 30 bucks. The transition made him question just how valuable his time was. The cab stopped in front of his building, which was a nice change from the 3 block walk to the bus stop. Mark climbed the stairs to his apartment, kicked off his shoes by the door, and then stumbled to his own room where he crawled into bed and pulled out his phone, looking at his new contact and trying to think of something to say. A casual greeting felt too informal and diving right into something deeper felt too rushed.

"You don't have to call, I'm right here," a voice called from the door way. Excited, he looked only to find Nicole standing there in a baby blue skirt and white tank top. Her hair framed the smile on her face as she walked towards the bed, dropping her purse on the way. "I really enjoyed our time together the other night. Sorry I've been kind of tied up until now."

She placed her right knee on the bed and then swung her left over him and straddled his crotch. He attempted to ask how she got into his apartment, but before he could get past the first word, she leaned down and kissed him, sucking in and biting on his lower lip in the process. She knew his buttons and appeared to be trying her best to press them all.

After the kiss, she answered his partially asked question, "The door was unlocked," before going back in for another kiss. He tried his best to focus, but with the stimulation, he found it almost impossible. A rush of energy engulfed him as she slid her hand down his body. With all his will power, he pulled away from her kiss and pushed her back into a sitting position. "What's wrong?" she asked as she bucked her hips and grinded against him.

"Stop," He pleaded. "I don't want this right now."

She smiled. "I don't know about that," she began. "It certainly feels like something you want." She reached down for the button on his jeans, and his hands met hers. The smile rushed away from her face. Frustrated, she sat back and asked, "What is with you? First you want me and then you ignore me. It's not something physical." She bucked her hips, grinding into his stiff cock. "I know you are into it, so what gives?"

He rolled to his side, causing her to slide off him and land on the other side of the bed. "It's not you." He couldn't tell if the statement was a lie or not. "Last night I had another crazy dream, and today was super weird and long." He placed his hand on hers in an attempt to offer some reassurance. "I'm just not up for it right now." He asked himself if he would feel the same way if it was Julie but couldn't answer.

Nicole swung her legs over the side of the bed and crossed her arms, doing as best she could to show her disappointment. It wasn't just his sexual buttons she knew how to press. Her voice waivered and cracked as she asked, "Is this because of Jimmy? Or are you fucking someone else?"

He knew what she meant, but instead chose to answer the question she asked. "No, I'm not fucking anybody else, and no, the fact you have a child in your life does not matter to me."

She stood and walked around the bed to her dropped purse. "I've got to go," she explained, the makeup running from her eyes. She fumbled through her purse trying to find her phone as she spoke. "I forgot that my landlord is coming to fix my shower." Her voice was rushed and emotional. It was hard to tell, but Mark was confident she was lying. He had hurt her and, as he usually did, he felt like an asshole.

"I'll text you later and we can go get a bite, ok?" she said as she backed out of the doorway before turning and rushing down the hallway, leaving him feeling alone and selfish.

Lying back on the bed, Mark shut his eyes. He tried to empty his mind, but all he could think of was the image of Julie spinning in the rain. He opened his eyes and picked up his phone as it buzzed in his hand with a new message from Julie:

(5:36pm) Busy tonight? 86th and Jackson, after 7.

wear your red shirt

He did a quick search for the address, but found nothing online. He responded:

(5:40pm) What exactly am I looking for?

His phone buzzed again with her response:

(5:41pm) ☺

He changed into jeans and found the single red button up shirt she must have seen in his closet. He checked the time, 5:50; he had ten minutes. He rushed down the steps and ran the 3 blocks to the bus stop just as the number 7 bus pulled up. The whole ride he thought about the message. The address she sent, 86th and Jackson, was uptown and on ten blocks south of Norris on 96th. That was the easy part, but what was it exactly? The bus pulled to his regular stop around 7pm, and Mark started heading north on foot.

Walking north on 78thSt, the area was lifeless like a scene from a movie or TV show. The whole area was commercial real estate. Looking up, he could still see the lights shining on the steel and glass centerpiece that was the Philips Building. As he walked north, the skyline changed to that of other modern buildings, and finally into the large brick buildings that filled the remainder of the city.

Crossing onto 83rdst started the investment firm and collection company sector. It was known to many as Debt Row and earned its reputation. Rumors about how the City Council pressured the building owners to withdraw the long term leases these companies held were always popular and spreading. Cleaning up this part of the city was the last goal of the former Mayor Greenburg that had not been written off, but few people believed it would ever happen

By 86th street, he started seeing mom and pop shops, bodegas, and restaurants. Mark took a left on 86th and passed the sports bars and Chinese restaurants that flooded the first floor of antique apartment buildings. Life had picked up, and with it, the seedy underbelly of drug dealers and prostitutes. The neon lights gave him a feeling of déjà vu, but he couldn't tell why.

He passed block by block until he could see the corner of 86th and Jackson. Pink neon from a sign that proudly read "The Pretty Kitty" flooded the street. As he got closer, he could see a large, intimidating black man holding a clip board and dressed in a grey suit wearing sunglasses in the near dark. To the left of him and the door stood a line of people, both men and woman, behind velvet ropes that wrapped around the building.

He opened his phone and sent the message:

(7:43pm) The Pretty Kitty?

And waited several minutes but received no response.

Mark approached the building where he was flagged down by the bouncer. He pointed to himself and mouthed the word "me?" to which the bouncer nodded while maintaining his look of disgust.

"Name?" he asked, looking at his clipboard. Mark stated his name, which came out more like a question through his shaky and unconfident voice. "Are you asking me or telling?" boomed the bouncer. "Man the fuck up Red Shirt Mark. You're on the list." And with an exaggerated motion, he made a check on the board and opened the door.

An announcer called over the pulsing music, "Savanna and Diamond to the main stage. Rose to stage 1, Zantha to stage 2," as the noise flooded out into the street. Mark stepped into the club, blinded by the neon and black lighting that filled the entryway and led into the main room. On the left wall stood a bar with a glass top and three stages filled the rest of the room, the largest in the form of an "L" in the middle and two smaller ones on the north and west walls. Two entryways closed only by curtains were next to each of the smaller stages, and every inch of the remaining open floor was covered by standing people and small tables. On the main "L" stage, two women danced around poles, gyrating to the pulsing music as a crowd surrounded them offering singles for their attention. The two remaining stages held one dancer each. The crowds surrounding them were smaller than the one at the main stage. Every table was filled with gawking and drooling strangers.

His phone buzzed. As he pulled it out and raised it up, the light from the screen illuminating his face, a large man in a dark suit grabbed his arm. Through the music, Mark could make out the bouncer's booming voice yell, "No photos!" as he started to pull Mark towards the entrance. He tried to explain through the music and noise that he was only trying to check his messages, but the bouncer either couldn't or wouldn't hear him.

"Bobby!" a shrill voice yelled from behind him. The bouncer stopped and looked through the crowd. "Bobby! He's with me!" the voice yelled. Julie was pushing herself through the crowd, her sheer white robe open at the top revealing glimpses of a red corset, the purple and blonde streaked brown hair falling on her shoulders in waves. "It's cool Bobby." She offered a smile as she placed her hand on Mark's arm, causing the bouncer to release his grip.

"Sorry darling, I was just helping your boy out." Bobby grabbed Mark by the collar, adjusting it as he offered the warning "If you start any trouble, you'll be eating through a fuckin straw, get me?" Mark nervously nodded. Bobby released him before turning to Julie with a smile. "You give me the word, baby girl, and I'll make sure he never walks again."

"Oh, Bobby." she smirked. "You know I can take care of myself."

Bobby's smile widened. "I know it girl, but just because you can, doesn't mean you have to." He winked at her and then turned and cut his large frame through the rest of the crowd.

"His bark is worse than his bite." Julie offered, but it did little to ease his mind. She pulled him to a couch on the wall next to one of the stages and said, "Stay here for a few minutes," before winking and walking away.

Mark surveyed the room. He had been in a few strip clubs before, but never one so nice. If not for the naked women swinging around polls, it could have passed for a high-end night club. She returned at the beginning of the next song with a drink and said, "I paid for a three song dance so we can talk for a bit." She handed him the drink. He took a long sip and found that she had chosen his mixed drink of choice, whiskey and coke. She placed her right heel between his legs and unfastened her robe, dropping it from her shoulders and throwing it on the couch next to him. "This doesn't freak you out, does it?" she asked as she straddled his left leg and gyrated back and forth on it.

"No," he lied, trying to sound confident. "This isn't my first rodeo."

She whipped her hair in time with the beat and asked, "How's the drink? I saw your brand in your kitchen."

Her actions and movements had caused him to momentarily forget that he was even holding a drink. "It's perfect, thanks."

She smiled, causing her teeth to pop under the black lights. She spun around and found herself between his split legs, rubbing her backside against his crotch. "So here's the thing," she started, "I'm not the kind of chick to jump from guy to guy. I'm not some whore." With the word whore, she pushed hard to his crotch, his erection betraying him. "But ever since that first night at the Lounge, I have kind of felt something for you, something I don't quite understand." She laid back against him and threw an arm up and around his neck as she bucked against him. The first song ended and quickly transitioned into the second as she stood and turned towards him. She planted her feet, both legs at a 45-degree angle. Between her red panties and the bottom of her corset, he could see part of what could only be tattoos of pistols, one on each hip, pointing inwards to her crotch. She leaned in, arching her back and sliding up his chest. "So I like you." She pressed her body against his. "And it feels like you like me too," she added with a smirk. She flipped around so her back was to him and continued to grind against him, grabbing his hands and placing them on her hips. With a sense of fear, Mark looked around and spotted Bobby by the bar glaring at him.

"I'm not the best at being in relationships," Mark confessed.

"It's ok," she reassured him. "Neither am I." The song changed, and she stood up, turned around, closed his legs, and straddled his crotch. She placed his hands back on her hips and continued to grind. "I understand how stupid this sounds considering our current position, but let's start slow, ok?" she asked with a smile. Mark was confused by the situation: he had never been positioned in such a way. All he could think to do was nod. "I need you to be ok with this, with my job. Know it's only a job and that I'm never unfaithful." He nodded again, and she smiled. She then slid off his lap and landed in front of him on her knees, leaning forward, pushing his legs apart and pressing her breasts against him, sliding upward until they were face to face, until he could feel her breath on his face. He felt her hand move down his side and slide something into his pocket. "Have a few drinks and enjoy the show." And as the last song ended, she leaned in and kissed him on the cheek. Grabbed her robe and walked away.

Mark headed to the restroom and into a stall where he adjusted the erection before leaving the stall and checking himself in the mirror. As he splashed water on his face and gave it a quick rub, he remembered that she had given him something. He reached deep into his pocket and found a stack of ten thin plastic chips, each a one inch square. He held one at eye level, and imprinted in pink were three lines of text:

Pretty Kitty
VIP
Good for one drink

Mark pocketed the chips and exited the restroom as he heard the announcer say, "Mariah and Zelda to the main stage. Lucy to stage one and Janet to stage two." The contrast in lighting threw him off, the florescent in the restroom and the black light and neon of the rest of the club. He let his eyes adjust and made his way to the back of the club and took a seat at the only empty table he could find. Before long, a waitress found him and asked for his order. He held up a chip and asked for a whiskey and Coke, which she promptly returned with. He surveyed the club and its patrons. Every stereotype was there: blue collar men with t-shirts tucked in jeans to look classier crowded around the stages broken up by the occasional young kid looking for his first adventure into the world of adult hood and the odd woman who was either there to support her man's admiration for scantily clad women or to make sure that everybody she was with knew that she was cool and ok with being there to begin with. On stage one, Julie was hanging upside down on a poll while simultaneously unlacing her corset. Spaced out, Mark didn't notice Bobby the bouncer pull up a chair and join him.

"You know, I've been doing this a long time," his voice boomed. Mark was startled and immediately pulled back. "Sometimes, I'll go for months without seeing it, and sometimes, it's a nightly or weekly event. These girls, these women, sometimes you can tell what they are thinking as they perform." Mark thought it was classy that he shared his thought without using the word dance or strip in any variation. "That girl," Bobby nodded at Lucy, at Julie, "that woman has been on stage for five minutes, and the whole time she's been watching you, waiting on you to watch her." Mark looked up at Julie, who had her back to the audience as men from all walks of life watched her rub against a pole. In the mirror their eyes met, and she smiled.

"So what did you get up to last night?" Wayne asked through a mouth full of pizza-flavored snacks. "I cannot remember ever seeing you smile for this long. It is a pretty drastic change from yesterday."

Mark was leaning back in his office chair, staring at the ceiling, and thinking about the previous night. Once his shift ended, he and Bobby had shared several drinks as they watched Julie perform. As the night wore on, he could tell what she had meant in their private talk. Men approached her and she offered them lap dances, but never as enthusiastic as the one he received. Bobby could tell he was starting to get uncomfortable and always offered the same advice. "It doesn't matter because she's not looking at him, she's looking at you." And she was, and it always made him feel better.

Mark gave a vague description of his adventure. The lack of details made it feel much dirtier than it really was. "And then at 2am or so, Bobby put me in a cab, and the next thing I know, I was lying in bed and my alarm was going off this morning."

"Alone?" Wayne asked with a childish smirk.

"Yes, alone," Mark answered.

"Man, as much shit as I give you for your piss poor life decisions, every once in a while I am really envious of you. I think I would have much rather had a few drinks with a bouncer in a strip club than play Trivial Pursuit for four hours." It was a sentiment that had been offered many times before, but this time it made him feel a strange kind of proud.

"You never had a wild and crazy phase growing up?" he asked.

Wayne smiled as he shook his head. "Not really. I mean, every kid has a few small acts of rebellion, but nothing you would ever write a book about."

Mark thought back to his own childhood. "I guess I was pretty normal until I hit my teens. It wasn't until my late teens that I really found myself."

Wayne laughed. "They say that the first 12 years never count anyway. You never do anything worth much in your first 12 years."

Mark locked his computer and took off his headset. "Lunch time, you coming?" He asked as he pulled away from his desk.

Wayne sighed in frustration. "No can do, promised this woman a call back in 15. I can meet you down there if anything changes."

On the elevator ride down, Mark's phone buzzed with a new message from Julie:

(11:06am) Good morning sunshine.

(11:06am) Hey, how did you sleep?

(11:07am) Pretty good, Bobby told me he put you in a cab and I wanted to make sure you got home safe.

(11:07am) Yeah I woke up in bed this morning but don't really recall how I got there. I remember Bobby putting me in the cab but after that I have no clue. Plans tonight?

(11:07am) Yeah, sorry, but I'll text you when I'm done and see if you're still up.

(11:08am) Ok.

He slid his phone back in his pocket as the doors slid open. He stepped out and into Smitty's. He quickly turned around, but found only a mural of a woman dancing in the rain. Panic set in as he searched the bar for signs of life but found it empty. He walked to the bar and called out "Hello?!?" but received no answer. Walking behind the bar, he pulled the curtains to reveal a brick wall. Spinning around to the empty room he called out again "Hello!?" but received only silence in answer. In an act fueled by desperation and frustration, Mark grabbed the first bottle he could find and flung it out into the middle of the bar, causing it to shatter on an empty table.

"Hey buddy," a familiar voice called out. "I work hard to keep this bar open and in order. Let's not destroy my livelihood please." Mark turned to see Jimmy, who was standing by the sink cleaning a glass mug with an agitated look on his face before looking back to the previously empty bar with a confused look.

"What the fuck is going on here?" he asked, taking a step towards Jimmy.

"Hey now," he said as he took a step back and raised his hands in a surrendering pose.

Mark slammed a glass on the counter, breaking it and slightly cutting his palm, before shouting, "Why do I keep coming back here!"

Jimmy smiled. "Come on man, you're a smart guy. You should have figured this out by now. I mean, you talked with Jack, you know what they want. Everybody wants something, and this is where they come to negotiate."

Frustrated, Mark leaned on the bar and put his face in his hands. "I never wanted to make a deal. I don't want this so why do I keep coming back?"

Jimmy's face changed, and for the first time, he sounded sympathetic. "Look, my job is to provide a warm and inviting atmosphere. It makes the transition easier to understand. I have seen this before. Sometimes they want specific people, people who are damned either way. I've seen them have their one-on-one meetings, but I can't tell you why you're so special or why they chose you." Special, Mark remembered Jack had told him he was a Special Case. "I can tell you that it's not all bad. I mean, I spent a good part of my life working for people and dreaming that one day I'd own my own place. It's not a perfect situation, but I gave them what they wanted, and I got what I want; call it a compromise. I'm not one of them," he continued. "I am just a regular guy like you. If they have made you an offer, then I'd take it because the alternative is eternity paying for your sins, and chances are if you are here, you have a lot of repayment ahead of you."

"Mark!" He felt a pair of hands on his shoulders shaking him. "Mark!" His eyes opened to find Miles Trubuck. He was back in the elevator at what appeared to be the top floor. "Mark, are you ok? You left 20 minutes ago and someone found you sleeping in the elevator. Is everything alright? Maybe you should take the rest of the day."

Mark looked past Miles' shoulder and saw a group of people staring at him and the owner of the company, all with concerned looks on their faces.

"No, I'm good. I just had a long night," Mark explained. "I'll be fine once I get some lunch in me."

Miles turned towards the crowd that had formed. "Ok, show's over. Everybody needs to get back to work." The crowd murmured to themselves and dispersed.

"You sure you're ok? I don't need a law suit on my hands." The concern in his voice was undermined by his words.

Mark stood and dusted himself off. "I'll be fine," he said as he pressed the button for the lounge.

On the elevator ride down, Mark's phone buzzed with a new message from Nicole:

(11:06am) Good morning babe.

(11:06am) Hey, how did you sleep?

(11:07am) Pretty good, just wanted to apologize for the quick leave last night. Wanted to make sure you were ok.

Mark felt a strange sense of Deja vu.

(11:07am) Yeah, I didn't sleep that well last night, went out and met this nice guy named Bobby and had a few drinks with him.

(11:07am) Cool, plans tonight?

(11:08am) Nothing solid.

(11:08am) Mind if I come by?

The elevator doors opened to Wayne. Mark put his phone in his pocket without responding to Nicole's message. "What are you doing here?" he asked.

Wayne smiled. "I could ask you the same question. You said you were going to lunch almost a half hour ago."

They found an open table, and Wayne reached for a menu while Mark put his head in his hands. "I think I may be going crazy."

"Well, that is not good," Wayne commented with indifference in his voice.

Mark lifted his head and leaned back into the chair. "Apparently I just fell asleep in the elevator. Mr. Trubuck woke me up after someone found me."

"Well, you were out drinking all night, so maybe falling asleep is not really that strange." He put the menu down and gave Mark a puzzled look and asked, "Are you bleeding?" while motioning to his own forehead.

Mark reached up and felt the wet spot on his forehead with his fingertips and doing so noticed a small cut on the palm of his hand. The sight caused his dream to come flooding into his mind, and for the first time since his first dream, he could remember everything in great detail. He considered telling Wayne but stopped as he wondered how you tell someone that you're eternally damned? He wasn't even really sure he believed it himself. "I don't know, man. I must have fallen and cut my palm in the elevator." It seemed like a good enough excuse. "Maybe you're right. Maybe I'm just tired."

After lunch, Mark decided to take the afternoon off. He rode the elevator to the lobby and passed the guard who was diligently pretending to do his duties while there were people who mattered in the building. Once outside, he pulled his phone from his pocket. It was still on the conversation with Nicole, who had sent an additional message of only a question mark as if she was waiting for the answer.

(12:04pm) Taking off of work early, need to do some running around; Ill message you later.

Short, sweet, and to the point. She responded immediately:

(12:04pm) ☺

He closed the message and searched the internet for "church," causing a map to populate with letters "A" through "F" in various locations on it. He stopped for a moment and tried to remember the last time he had been in a church; : his father's funeral. His family had never been really religious growing up, but when his father died, his grandmother insisted on a traditional service. A bunch of people whom he had never met filled the pews and listened to chapters from the Bible as a big picture of his father stared at him from six feet away. Through his smile, the picture seemed to silently judge him, remind him of his failed potential. It was easy to feel like he had let the old man down, as living in the shadow of greatness can make anybody feel inadequate.

The closest option, St. Luke's, was only a few blocks from work, so Mark headed in that direction. He was not totally sure what he was looking for or hoping to find. The building was a monument to gothic architecture, towering over the cemetery ground surrounding it. The wooden doors were large, at least ten feet tall, and stood atop a set of stone steps menacingly looking down on the street. Mark climbed the steps and pushed the door on the left, causing it to swing open with ease. Inside, he found an unsettling quiet. Candles were sporadically set up throughout the hallways and archway which lead into a large room. A small bit of light made it through the stained glass windows, which had depictions of the most iconic scenes from the Bible, stories that even Mark had known. The only other source of light came from even more candles spread throughout the room at the end of each row of benches and behind the podium on the stage. A warm voice called out from behind him, "Can I help you?" causing him to jump and knock a Bible off the arm of one of the benches. He spun around to see an older woman wearing a smile that quickly ran from her face when they made eye contact. Her hair was pulled back in a tight bun on the back of her head, and her face showed years of experience. Her hands were folded behind her waist, and she stood uncomfortably straight.

Mark bent to pick up the book and handed it to the woman, who did not attempt to take it. "I don't know if you can or not. I'm not really sure what I'm looking for. I guess I'd like to talk to someone about religion and stuff."

The woman nodded. "Religion and stuff?" she repeated. Mark smiled. "Young man, regardless of what you may have seen in movies and television, most churches do not take walk-ins. If you would like to speak with the pastor, then you will have to make an appointment, or you can speak with him briefly after services."

The news was deflating. He had come here looking for answers or some piece of mind, he had come here concerned for his immortal soul, and he was being turned away.

"Sister Shannon? Who is it?" asked a voice from around the corner. A young man came up from behind her, placing his hand on her shoulder. "Who is our visitor?" he asked again.

Without taking her eyes from Mark, she responded, "Father, this young man has come in without an appointment and asked for counsel. I have advised him that you are busy and that he should make an appointment, and now he is leaving."

The young man looked at Mark with a warm and inviting smile. "While it is true we ask that you make an appointment, I do happen to have some free time if you would like to come with me to my office. I will be happy to provide you with what assistance I can."

Mark felt a sense of satisfaction in his words as the woman glared at him. She turned and in a whisper said, "Sir, I do not think it is wise for you to talk to this man. I'm sure you have something else that you must be doing."

In what Mark took as an effort to show he was not hiding anything from anyone, the father replied, "Please, Sister, we are here to help all of God's creations. I can spare a few minutes of my time for this man." He then looked at Mark and motioned for him to follow. They walked out of the large room and down a hallway to a small office.

The office was considerably modern compared to the rest of the building; had he not known any better, he would assume it was an office in someone's house or small business. Two of the walls were lined with bookcases and shelves, the third held certificates and photos, and the forth a large window looking out into the cemetery. His desk was neat, but clearly used daily. The pastor sat behind the desk and motioned for Mark to take one of the two empty chairs in front of it.

"My apologies, we never really did get introduced, my name is Father Phil." He extended his hand.

Mark quickly debated if he should give his own name as he shook his hand. "Mark. it's nice to meet you."

Phil's face was welcoming. Mark felt open, like he could talk to him without consequence.

"You as well, Mark, now what brings you to me today? How can I help you?"

Mark thought for a moment on how to express his concerns without sounding crazy. "I've been having strange dreams that take place in a bar with strange murals painted on the walls." Phil nodded as he looked on interestedly. "It's happened three, maybe four times, I can't be sure. At first, it was just this bartender named Jimmy, but the second and third time, I don't remember much of, only that I know I was there." Mark paused long enough to try and judge his reaction, but found it difficult as the man had not reacted at all. "The last time was a few hours ago. I fell asleep in an elevator. This time, Jimmy told me I met a man named Jack and that I should understand why I keep dreaming about the place. He said that they want something from me."

Phil leaned on to his desk and asked, "Who's they?"

Understanding how strange it sounded in his head, Mark took a deep breath and said, "I don't know who exactly, but Jimmy suggested I give them what they want. He said it is better than spending an eternity paying for my sins. I think they are trying to barter for my soul."

At the conclusion of the story, the Father stood and turned to look out the window, placing his arms crossed behind his back. He took a deep breath in and then exhaled before turning around. "Well, that's quite a story Mark." He began pacing behind his desk. "Did you know that selling your soul to the devil is a reasonably new story? Nowhere in the original text does it describe a situation where someone has exchanged his soul for a prize. That idea didn't really come around until the renaissance." Phil walked to the front of the desk and then sat upon it facing Mark like an authority figure trying to look cool. "The good news here is that what you are experiencing was made up by creative types during a time when putting the fear of the unknown into people was popular. Your dreams are your subconscious telling you that things need to change, and this is a good thing. This is the natural way the body and brain work. The bad news is that there is nothing I can do to help you, my child. I will be more than happy to pray for you, but until you make the decision, nothing is going to change. Take the chance. Sign the contract. See how far the rabbit hole goes. This could give your mind the message that you are willing to change."

Mark nodded to show he was listening while doing his best to hide the anger caused by this dismissal. It felt too real to be some figment of his imagination, and how could that explain the cut on his palm? "I recommend that you speak to a professional about your dreams and come to our next service, hear the good word of our lord. It is not an easy road to travel, but you will find that it very rewarding for those who make the trip." The smile never faded from his face, and it was easy to see that he was someone who has an abundance of faith in what he was saying. Mark shook his hand and thanked him for his time before showing himself to the door.

Walking down the hallway towards the door, Mark felt his phone vibrate with a new message from Nicole:

(1:12pm) How's your running around going?

As he read the message, Mark felt a hand on his shoulder, causing him to spin around defensively.

"I've seen people like you before," Shannon started. "I know why you are here."

Mark asked, "You do?" with his voice trembling.

A sinister smile formed on her face. "Yes, heathen, I could tell since you first came in. Your look betrays you." Mark's heart rate rose with each word. Could she see something others could not? Could this woman tell him if he was crazy or damned? "I have been around long enough to see this everytime we have a new pastor." A confused look spread across Mark's face. "You heathens come out to test his faith with nonsense and poppycock. Well, you failed this time. Phil's faith is unshakeable, and you should be ashamed of yourself!"

Mark's heart sank as he turned and walked through the large wooden doors. The sun was bright in the sky, and the world ran like it always had, but Mark felt as if he were moving through it in slow motion. Walking back to the Phillips Building, he pulled out his phone and texted Nicole the message:

(1:26pm) I'll be home in about 2 hours.

He sat at the bus stop with his head leaning against the glass. Afraid to sleep, he kept his eyes open and thought back on his life— the people he had met and the places he had gone. He thought about the women he had been with and how his relationships had ended. He felt as if he wasn't necessarily a bad guy, he never went around kicking puppies or starting wars, but he struggled to find anything really good or selfless that he had ever done. The ride home was filled with thoughts of self-loathing, and for the first time in his life, he wondered if the world would be better off without him.

He found Nicole sitting outside of his apartment, her back pressed against his door and her legs stretched straight. Through the earbuds blasting music, she must have sensed him as she looked up from her book just as he rounded the last flight of stairs. She was happy to see him, and he did his best to show the same, but clearly failed as her smiled turned to a face of concern.

"What's wrong babe?" she asked as she pulled the earbuds from her ears.

All he could muster was a shrug. "Just a long day I guess. I didn't sleep much last night."

She stood as he reached arm's length and embraced him tightly. "Aww, I'm sorry," she whispered in his ear before kissing his neck lightly.

Mark was torn; he desperately wanted to be alone, but the attention also felt nice. His mind, heart, and libido fought a war in the seconds it took him to decide his next move. He took a step back, and feeling his disconnect, she released her grip.

"I'm sorry, I'm feeling really down, and as much as I could use a good release, I'm just not up to it tonight."

The look on her face was one of disappointment and confusion. It was clear what she was here for, and she now knew that it wasn't going to happen. He let himself inside the apartment and held the door open for her to follow. She headed to the couch, and he to the kitchen looking for something to ease his riled mind. In the freezer, he found a quarter of a bottle of whiskey, which he took along with two glasses to the living room.

"You know a lot about dreams, don't you?" he asked.

Her gaze perked at the mention of the subject. At several points it was made clear that dreams interpretation is not a subject that interested him. "I've read a book or two," she replied as she tried her best to pose in an interested and professional posture.

He explained, "I keep having dreams where I end up in a shitty little bar, and I'm the only person there aside from the bartender." She nodded, making sounds of acknowledgement. "The only entrance is through a curtain behind the bar, but the first time there was a door way, and the last time it had changed to a brick wall. On each wall there is a mural, one of a Civil War battle, a pack of wolves hunting a man through the snow, a woman in a dark dress spinning in the rain, and a single man in two different halves trying to pull himself apart in opposite directions." In the natural pause of the story, Nicole asked if he had a note pad and a pen. He retrieved them from a drawer in the kitchen before taking a long drink straight from the bottle, completely ignoring the glass in front of him.

After a pause, Nicole's single word response was "Wow," followed by another pause while she reread and considered the information on the pad in front of her. Mark poured some whiskey into his glass and quickly drank all of it.

"Well, the only things that really stand out in your dream are the murals on the walls." Nicole tapped the pen on the pad in front of her. "In the civil war scene, was it before, during, or after the fight?"

Mark thought for a moment. "They were preparing for the fight. They were both lined up as if it was seconds before the battle."

Nicole made a quick note. "Ok, three of the murals are pretty straight forward. Your subconscious depicting two armies preparing for a great battle, two opposing forces getting ready to face off, considering it is a battle in the Civil War, you consider these two opposing forces to be old of origin." Mark poured himself another glass and stared into the whiskey, expressionless. "The wolves attacking the man typically symbolize pack mentality or many against one. The man pulling himself apart is an internal struggle or the trouble of making a decision. Three of the murals are about struggles. Have you been feeling like someone is out to get you? Or have you been feeling like there are many people attacking you?" Mark shook his head slowly and swallowed the drink before pouring himself another. "The last mural I can't really make out. If it was a man in the rain, then I would say it is about you being reborn, but with a woman, I don't know."

"I only remember the first and the last time in great detail, but every night for the last week, I have had a dream of this place. The bartender says that I've had conversations with some guy named Jack that I don't recall." Nicole's eyes went wide. "The last time the bartender told me that I was damned and that I should take what they are offering me as it would be a better option than eternal punishment."

Nicole sank back into the couch, abandoning her previously proper posture. "Did you take the deal?" She asked eagerly. "Did you sign the contact?"

The word contract burned in his ears, and a picture of a man in a black suit with bright blue eyes and actor-white teeth flashed in his mind like a picture he had seen years ago and had forgotten but suddenly remembered.

Mark shook his head. "I don't know." The excitement left Nicole's eyes.

Mark poured himself another drink, emptying the bottle which he then causally tossed it to the side, causing a loud thunk on the floor. "Do you believe in god?" The question sounded silly to him and came out with a half-laugh as he never thought he would ever ask it. Nicole seemed distracted and only offered a shrug. He finished his drink and stood up, wobbly at first, but steadying fast. His vision started to blur. "Do you think he listens to us?" He stumbled to the kitchen and dropped his glass in the sink, and then he passed out.

Mark dreamt of a time when he was younger, sitting in the front seat of a pickup truck with his father at the wheel. The road seemed to go on forever with no visible twists and turns. In the distance, he could see field after field of corn starting to peak through the ground. They might have well have been the only people on the planet. It was a lonely kind of beautiful. His father drove with one hand on the wheel and one hand on the shifter even though he had not had to change gears for almost an hour. He must have worn his feelings on his face, because without looking from the road, his father said, "Isn't it beautiful?" He was a simple man and enjoyed the simple things in life, soft spoken and gentle, nothing ever got to him. "You know Marky, the thing about land is that they don't make it anymore." He said with a half-smile. He was full of pseudo-wise advice and information.

"If it walks like a duck."

"A zebra can cover himself up, but he can't change his stripes."

"No point in painting a turd, Marky."

Mark would smile but never really understand most of what his father told him. Going 80 miles per hour made the world go by in a blur. When so much of it looks the same, the world starts to look like it's standing still. On the horizon, a speck appeared which grew with each passing second. Mark didn't notice it until his father changed gears and started to slow down.

"What's the point of having the world if you never give it?"

"Marky, the measure of a man is not what you have but what you give."

His father was like that, always willing to help. As their truck slowed, Mark could start to make out the shape of an old sedan parked on the side of the road, hazard lights flashing and white smoke pouring out from the open hood. A dirty looking man leaned against the driver's side door in a stance that said he had not a single care in the world. Mark tried to imagine how long he must have stood there to gain such composure; he looked calm, almost content, and as his father pulled to the front of the broken down car, Mark wondered how he would react in the same situation.

The rumbling engine stopped, and his dad pressed in the emergency break while unbuckling his seat belt. The look of anxiousness grew on Mark's face until it was unavoidable to discuss. His father placed his hand on his shoulder and said, "Everybody is a stranger until you meet them, son. Who knows how long this man has been out here broken down? If we don't stop, then who will?" The sentiment did little to ease Marks nerves. "Let me tell you something my father told me and someday you will tell to a son of your own. Close your eyes and count backwards from ten. Breathe in on the evens and out on the odds. Any time you are scared or nervous, you do this, and before you can get to one, it will all be better, promise." And with that, he winked and opened the driver's side door.

10. Inhale. Mark could hear his father's steps as he made his way to the back of the car. "Hello!" he shouted in a friendly and upbeat manner. His father was never afraid of talking to strangers. "Looks like you've got some car trouble here. Good thing we came along when we did." The stranger replied, but Mark couldn't make out what it was he said as his voice didn't project nearly as well as his father's.

9. Exhale. "Gotcha. Well, let's take a look and see if we can figure it out. If nothing else, I've got some chain in the back of my truck, and if all else fails, we can pull you along by the axel!" Both men laughed. The sun was starting to set, creating an orange and purple horizon.

8. Inhale. "Marky?" his father called out to him. "Marky, come on out here, son." His voice sounded strange, not the happy and positive voice Mark was used to. He unbuckled his seatbelt and opened the passenger door, climbing down from the lifted truck. From the side of the road, he couldn't see his father at all, but could hear him call out again, "Marky?"

7. Exhale. Slowly, he walked to the back of the truck, his hand tracing the painted accent lines down the body. He called out to his dad, but it came out only as a whisper. As he rounded the back passenger side, he saw his father bent over the engine bay of the broken down sedan, the stranger holding a knife in his right hand and using his left to hold his father's left arm, bent at the elbow, and pulling it to the middle of his back like some sort of move he had seen in a wrestling match.

6. Inhale. The stranger stared at him, his face in a twisted smile showing off his mix of gold and naturally yellow teeth. Without looking away from Mark, the stranger asked his father, "Where are the keys?" in a breathy and shaking voice. The answer didn't come fast enough so he asked again, this time louder and faster. "Where at the keys!" as he drove his free elbow in to Marks fathers back.

5. Exhale. His father let out a groan in pain and with the little bit of air still in his lungs, he said, "In the ignition." Mark had never seen his father in such a positon before. He waited for the moment where he would spin around and take the stranger by surprise, but the moment never came. The already twisted smile the stranger wore spread even wider as he used the butt of the knife and hit his father on the back of the head.

4. Inhale. Mark's father fell to the ground, and the stranger backed away and towards the driver's side of the truck holding his knife out at Mark until he was out of sight. Mark ran to his father, who was lifting himself using the front of the old sedan as a brace. Blood was streaming from the back of his head, but he other than the cut, he seemed no worse for wear. "Dad?" Mark asked as he placed his hand on his father's back. He turned and sat on the lip of the engine bay while he regained his composure. His truck started, and they could hear the gears grind as he struggled with the manual transmission.

3. Exhale. The white lights came on as the stranger found reverse and the truck started moving. Mark's father pushed him hard, and he flew backwards, landing in the grass. Mark watched as his father's truck backed into the sedan, pinning his father's legs between the bumpers. He let out in a scream as the stranger changed gears, causing the grinding noise to return. The truck pulled away and his father collapsed in a heap.

The shock engulfed Mark's brain as he tried his best to process this situation. An hour later, his father was sitting in front of that sedan, Mark sitting in front of him cross legged. The screaming had stopped, and it was hard to tell if he couldn't feel it anymore or if he had just gotten use to the pain.

"Mark?" his father asked, snapping the boy out of his trance-like state. "Everything happens for a reason."

Mark's eyes opened, and he was lying in bed. The dream fogged through his mind with only the mildest of details remaining. He never thought about how six months later, his father was living in an assisted living center. He never thought about the phone call that ended with his mother crying. He never thought about the time his mother told him that his father, the strongest and wisest person he had ever known, had taken his own life. Ignorance was bliss.

Sunday, September 14th

The hazy details of his dream faded as he struggled to remember how he had gotten to bed. He turned and saw the familiar outline of Nicole lying next to him. He propped himself up, his head throbbing, as he felt his pocket vibrate. He reached under the covers for his pocket and found his pants unbuttoned and open. Shock and confusion struck him as he pulled off the covers to reveal his pants still on but his flaccid cock laying out of his pants still in a condom, semen leaking out into a puddle on his pubic bone. The shock and confusion turned to anger as he lifted the covers more to reveal Nicole was not wearing anything below the waist.

Nauseous from the drinking, he got up from bed and rushed to the bathroom where he flushed the condom and then disrobed for the shower. As he washed himself, he tried to focus his anger on Nicole, but the absent memories made it hard for him. He remembered her kissing his neck and the fight between his heart, mind, and libido. It was possible that he instigated this. It was possible that this was his own fault. The heat from the shower clouded over the mirror, and for a moment, when he wiped it clear, he thought he looked like his father. Nicole had gotten up and left in the time it took him to shower. The smell of her body wash and a one-word note saying "thanks" written in pink lipstick on a napkin the only proof she was ever there.

He grabbed the jeans he was previously wearing and pulled them on. It was only then that he felt the phone in his pocket and remembered that it had vibrated before his shower. He turned on the phone and sent Nicole the message:

(6:20am) Where did you go?

He waited but received no response and sent another message:

(6:25am) I need to talk to you.

But he again received nothing. Mark attempted to occupy his time while trying not to look at his phone every few minutes. TV, reading, napping; he tried to find something, anything to pass the time as he waited for his phone buzzed with a new message. He thought about Julie but decided against sending her a message as he didn't know how to explain that he had slept with another woman. Finally, his phone vibrated and he saw a text from Wayne.

(11:03am) Busy tonight?

He could lie and say that he was, but then he would be stuck with nothing but his thoughts all night. Maybe going out would help him calm his nerves. Maybe going out would help him think of what he was going to say to Nicole or what he was going to say to Julie. "

> (11:40am) No. Nothing really going on, what do you have in mind?

(12:10pm) I'll pick you up at 4ish.

At 3:30 Mark dressing in the clothes he had previously worn the day before. He couldn't help but smell Nicole on his shirt. Waiting in front of his apartment building, he checked his phone every few minutes in case he had missed a text from her, but nothing ever came. Wayne pulled up in an early 2000's gold sedan, and Mark got in the passenger side.

"So where are we going?" he asked, hoping for the best.

Wayne quickly pulled onto the road before replying, "We are going to this group I found." Mark instantly felt regret. "Hey man, I know you are not really comfortable with this, but hey... free coffee and donuts?" Mark let out an audible sigh of displeasure. "No one is asking you to get up or speak, just hang out and listen, ok? Just have an open mind." The street lights passed as they traveled uptown. Slums turned to suburbs and that turned into the city.

With a sudden realization, Mark asked, "How did you know where I lived?"

Wayne smiled. "You have called and asked me to bring you home after a few too many drinks several times."

Mark tried his best to remember but came up empty. "What were you doing in the slums?" Another reasonable question considering Wayne lived in the suburbs.

"It was my weekly board game with my grandparents. They actually live just a few blocks from you." As his car rolled to a stop at a red light, Wayne looked at him and said, "Not everybody who lives downtown is a bad person, Mark."

A nauseous feeling he couldn't explain stirred within his stomach as Wayne spoke. He recognized it as the feeling that came from eating too fast when he was a child. Was this what having a conscience felt like?

Wayne's gold sedan pulled to a stop outside a large, unmarked building. It stood five stories tall and was made of redbrick. There was a surprising lack of windows below the top two stories, which gave the impression that it had been an old factory or warehouse. Cars littered the parking lot on both sides of the street, but there were other wise no signs of life, giving the area the same ghost town feel as the financial sector at night. Wayne waited for Mark on the sidewalk and then led him to an archway containing a single blue door, which he opened and entered. Inside, Mark followed along through hallway after hallway, a maze of sorts, until Wayne reached another door which lead to a large, open room full of people from all walks of life. He was right, a lot of them were people in their own age range, but scattered about were both younger and older people.

"Did you bring me to a self-help group?" Mark asked, shame and frustration in his voice.

"No sir, I did not!" Wayne responded, "This is a support group, not a self-help group."

Mark failed to see the difference. A large, balding man in a blue dress shirt that was far too small for him strode up to Wayne with the confidence of a used car salesman.

Shaking hands, the man said, "Wayne! So nice of you to come! And I see you've brought a friend?" Wayne smiled and introduced Mark, who was immediately forced into a hug with the large man. "Mark, it's so nice to meet you! My name is David," he said in a booming voice before pulling away and ending with a handshake. Mark politely nodded and stepped back, letting the two men talk.

Mark was less than surprised to see that the building was, in fact, at one time a small factory. Whoever owned the building had gutted the middle of the room, leaving the remains of an assembly line scattered along the walls covered in dust. On the far side of the large room stood a staircase leading to a walkway that hung from the ceiling and lead to offices along the outer perimeter of the wall. Mark moved to a table by the doorway where he found the free coffee and donuts. A small group of people stood close to the table, talking and laughing. As he poured his cup, his listened and tried his best to figure out what it was that all these people had in common.

"Can I have your attention?" David called out. "Please come find a seat. We will be starting shortly!" Mark followed and sat by Wayne while everybody in the room found a seat and formed a circle. With a smile on his face, David started, "I want to welcome you all here and thank you for coming. As you can see, each week, we are getting bigger and bigger. Each week, we are getting stronger." Positive murmurs spread around the circle as people looked for new faces and greeted the person next to them. "For the uninitiated, we are Addicts Anonymous, and we are a support group. While most people find us though churches, I want to stress that we are not a religious organization, and while all are welcome here, please be respectful of others' beliefs." Another positive murmur spread through the circle. "I started this group two years ago with the hopes of finding others like myself who have struggled with addictive tendencies that did not fit in with the strict categories of other support groups. If you are here with a chemical addiction—drugs or alcohol— then you are welcome to stay, but this may not be the group for you. A handful of people stood up and left the room, leaving odd gaps through the previously full circle. "Finally," David continued, "there is no judgment here. No matter what you hear or what is shared, please remember that we are all human and—" several people joined in for the last part of his speech chanting in unison "Humans make mistakes!" before bursting into an applause.

Mark found it hard to concentrate, His hand on his lap hoping to feel his phone vibrate and give him an excuse to leave. As David talked about upcoming events, his mind wandered and he thought about his own night's events and what had led him here. He thought about Nicole and the breakdown of his dream. He remembered her sitting on the couch trying her best to look proper and professional. He thought of the word contract, and then he thought of a man in a black suit with bright blue eyes and actor-white teeth. Finally, he thought of Julie. He thought about how different the night would have been had she not had other plans.

David finished talking and had passed an orange foam ball to someone else who was now sharing her story. "My name is Jessica and I am addicted to shopping."

The circle responded in unison, "Hi Jessica."

She was a tall woman, probably as tall as an average man. Her hair and clothes were very fashionable. She stood awkwardly and started to blush. "It all started in college. I would have a bad day or not get the grade I wanted on a test, and I would go to the store and buy something to blow off steam. The idea of instant gratification usually made everything all better." The crowd murmured positively at the mention of instant gratification. "So I didn't pass a test or so the guy I met never called me back, I would have a nice new pair of jeans and it would make me feel better about being me." That statement struck a bell with Mark. "Before long, a pair of jeans wouldn't be enough and things would get bigger and better. After college, I met my husband, and he still doesn't know I have this problem. Using his good credit, I apply for credit cards and then max them out only to apply for a new credit card to pay it off, only to turn around and max it out again. I don't even use the things I buy anymore; most of them end up in a storage unit I bought because I had run out of places to hide things in the house." The circle shared a murmur of understanding.

The sound of the door opening and closing drew the attention from the circle. Mark took notice of the familiar voice. "Sorry…" Julie stood by the door, her hair now bleached blonde with streaks of blue. Her eyes met Mark's and triggered moment of panic. She crossed the room as David silently stood to welcome her, directing her to a seat across the circle from Mark.

Jessica continued, "Now we are over 100k in debt, and my husband has no idea. I am here because I understand I have a problem and that I need help." The crowd erupted in applause as Jessica sat down. Despite her clapping, Julie's eyes never left Mark's.

"Who would like to go next?" David asked.

A young man, who looked around Mark's age, stood from his chair. His second-hand brown suit hung loose on him as he nervously swayed back and forth and said, "My name is William and I am an addict."

The circle, in unison, announced, "Hi William."

He was clearly uncomfortable, and Mark could see in his face that he was debating whether or not to continue. "I'm addicted to lying. I can't help myself sometimes. Well, that's not true. I can stop myself, but I usually choose not to." A wave of head nods spread through the group as a sign of encouragement. "It all started when I was young. I would say outlandish things when asked simple questions because it made people laugh. When asked where I was or what I was doing, I would create an elaborate story and people would just write it off as a kid with an active imagination. I liked the attention it got me." The crowd murmured positively at the mention of attention. Julie's eyes still focused on Mark's, and he found it hard to look away or even focus on Williams's story. "In high school, I kept it up and was labeled as snarky and sarcastic. People liked what I was doing, and it made me popular. It's like people knew what I was saying wasn't true, but they accepted the answer anyway because it was easier than badgering someone for the truth. By college, I had gotten so good at lying that I didn't even realize I was doing it. I would call out of work claiming to be sick, and then I would start feeling ill because I told myself I was sick." The circle mumbled a sound of understanding and acceptance. "My girlfriend doesn't know what I do for a living; she thinks I sell houses. I get up every day and put on a suit to drive my car to work where I put on my uniform and sell cheeseburgers." With this revelation, William broke down crying. For a moment, Mark felt for him. For a moment, he was reminded of his own issues with living up to expectations. The people surrounding William all stood and hugged him. He was the warm center in the circle of acceptance, possibly for the first time in his life.

"Thank you for sharing William," David started and then then addressed the rest of the circle. "Thank you for sharing and acknowledging your problem. Remember, we are all human and…" several people joined in, and in unison they chanted, "Humans make mistakes!" before bursting into applause. David continued, "Do we have any updates? Can we hear from a regular attendee?"

Silence fell over the circle. Introducing yourself was the easy part. Sure, it took courage to stand before strangers and tell them your deep, dark secrets, but it took even more courage to stand before them and tell them that even though you have acknowledged your shortcomings, you have not taken any steps to correct them. Most eyes darted left and right, looking for the first person to stand while Julie's eyes were locked on Mark's.

"Anybody have anything to share?" David asked again.

Without breaking contact, Julie stood and said, "My name is Julie, and I have been recovering for nine months."

In the natural pause, the circle responded in unison, "Hi Julie."

She continued, "I'm doing well; I haven't had an episode in almost 3 months." The circle burst into a round of applause, causing her eye contact with Mark to break for the first time since entering the room. "I recently ended things with this guy I was seeing and met another guy who one of my friends already really approves of. He says that this new guy is a step in the right direction. He says that this new guy may be good for me." The circle again burst into applause. Her eyes focused back on Mark. "But I don't know, I recently found out that maybe he hasn't been 100 percent honest with me. I mean, I like this guy, he makes me feel... I don't know, complete? But I'm afraid that he isn't all that he appears to be." A murmur of understanding came from the circle. "But it's ok, because both he and I are human..." and on que, the circle joined in, "and humans make mistakes!" Another round of applause came from the circle as Julie sat down. The people on either side of her patted her on the shoulder in an attempt to comfort her and show appreciation for her willingness to share, but her eyes never drifted from Mark's.

After the applause had died down, David stood. "I want to thank everybody who was kind enough to share with us this evening. I know it can be hard to open up and share, but by just being here, you are taking a step down the right road!" The crowd erupted into one final round of applause which ended with people leaving the circle and grouping together to chit chat before leaving.

"See, that was not nearly as bad as you thought it would be, right?" Wayne asked.

Mark's eyes were still focused on Julie's as she stood up and quickly left the room without speaking to anybody. "Yeah man, that wasn't too bad," he absentmindedly agreed. "Look, I've got to run outside. I'll meet you by the car, ok?" Wayne smiled wide and nodded.

Mark bolted through the door and down the hallway to the blue door which was just closing. He was right behind her. He pushed through the door out onto the street and looked both ways, but found them both empty.

"Julie!" he called out, but received only silence in return. People started pouring out of the building, and before long, the already silent street became even more so.

"Is everything alright?" Wayne's voice called out from behind him as he and David exited the building.

"How did you enjoy our little meeting?" asked David, clearly proud of what he had put together.

"It was different than what I expected," was the nicest thing Mark could think of to say. Now that he had a moment to think about something other than Julie, he tried to decide if he really needed this. Was he addicted to something? Did Wayne see something about him that he did not?

The ride home was quite. Mark had texted both Julie and Nicole but received no response. The dream that had caused so much distress was the last thing on his mind as he thought about his encounter with Nicole and what Julie had said.

"Recently, I found out that maybe he hasn't been 100 percent honest with me."

The phrase meant so much more to him than she could have possible known. He recognized this feeling, the feeling of regret. While it was not one he felt often, he did understand where the feeling came from. Julie made him feel alive in ways he had not felt in a long time. He felt a natural connection, and it appeared she felt the same. While that mutual connection was there, a definitive label was not. They had only been out once, maybe twice if you count visiting her at work. Two dates did not a relationship make. But if that was the case, then why did he feel so bad when he thought about Nicole?

Wayne could read the distress on his face. "Look man," He started, "I just cannot tell what is going on with you, but for the last week, you have been all kinds of distracted, and I am concerned about you."

Mark looked up from his phone and watched the suburbs pass. "You know that girl from the meeting, Julie?" Wayne nodded. "I met her a few days ago at the Lounge. I was the guy she was talking about." The silence from Wayne spoke volumes. "We went to Norris and had some sushi before heading back to my place where we talked and she spent the night."

A smile formed on Wayne's face. "Did you sleep with her?"

Mark remembered waking up in the middle of the night. He remembered her saying he was screaming. "No, we just slept. It was strange. I felt a connection with her and she said she felt the same."

Wayne nodded. "Well, that sounds great then, right?"

Mark smiled briefly. "Yeah... the problem is that tonight I met up with Nicole, and I don't know how it happened, but we had sex."

Wayne slammed on the breaks. "What do you mean you do not know how it happened but you had sex? This is pretty fucking straight forward: if you put your dick inside her, then you had sex!" The disappointment was written on his face.

"It's not like that," Mark started to explain. "I shot her down again and we talked. I had a few drinks, and I must have had more than I thought because I passed out. When I woke up, I was in bed wearing a condom lying next to a half-naked woman." They both sat in silence and understood that what was just said sounded like a ridiculous story made up by a man trying to validate and defend his actions.

The apartment felt cold and foreign. Physically, it was the same— all the same furniture in all the same places. He couldn't tell what exactly it was, but the place felt off, or maybe it was him that felt off. He headed directly for his bedroom where he laid on his bed without taking the time to disrobe. He had always had a plan, no matter how farfetched or inane it was. There was always an end game. A rhyme to his reason. For the first time since he was young, he felt lost. He checked his phone for a new message but found none, and with a sigh of defeat, he rolled to his side and closed his eyes.

He was not surprised to find that when he opened his eyes, he was standing on the stage in front of a microphone at Smitty's pub. The bar was empty save for Jimmy the bartender and Jack, who was sitting at one of the mismatched tables. From nowhere, the blaring sound of a rhythmic drum beat started, and he could hear Jack yell, "Just read the words! You will do fine!" This is right an old TV with scrolling words on it appeared.

Are you ready Steve? Uh huh.
Andy? Yeah.
Mick? Okay.
Alright fellas... let's go!

In a state of confusion, Mark was not able to hit the cues, and before he knew it, the rest of the band kicked in and started to perform Ballroom Blitz by Sweet. Mark raised his hand to his forehead in an attempt to block out the glare from the spot light. In the audience, he could see Jack yelling words of encouragement but couldn't hear him because of the volume of the music. In a fit of frustration, Mark walked down from the stage and was met by a wall of boos from an invisible audience. The spot light went off, and the music stopped with the sound of the needle being pulled from a record player. Mark looked back towards the stage and the TV was gone.

"Man, that was fucking terrible!" Jack threw himself into his seat, hitting the table and almost knocking over his drink. "I mean, why even get up there if you were never going to try?" Mark took a seat while Jack took a long sip of his drink. "A lot of people don't know it, but that song was totally written about me and a woman from New Orleans named Janice. True story."

Mark was flabbergasted at the casual nature of the conversation. He yelled, "I don't know who the fuck you are or why you keep making me come back here, but it's going to stop!" as he slammed his fist on the table.

"Yeah, that was my fault. Turns out on top of being a Special Case, our people tell us that because you have trouble sleeping, it becomes hard for you to remember dreams. The good news is we are going to fix that for you." He clicked his tongue and winked. "The bad news is you never dream in Hell, so try not to get used to it."

Mark became furious and kicked back his chair, standing up. "What the fuck are you going on about? Why do I keep dreaming about you and this…" Mark stopped mid-sentence as his focus was drawn to a small mirror with a silver frame that Jack had produced from his jacket. Within the mirror, he saw a fast-forward version of the past week's events that started with the first night he and Nicole had slept together. The thirty seconds that passed seemed to him like hours, and when the visions had stopped, Mark softly spoke the word "place," before falling backward onto the floor.

As he was lying down and staring at the dingy ceiling, all his other problems seemed trivial and petty. He struggled to accept that that he would die within months. Shock set in, and he started to think of all the things he had not done and all the things he had not seen. "I really do not understand you humans sometime. You know, I can tell what you are thinking, but every time a situation like this comes up the only thoughts you have are so cliché. Get off the floor and let's finish this." Mark pulled himself up and pulled his chair back to the table. When he sat down, he noticed a briefcase had appeared on the table. Jack slowly opened the briefcase, looking to add suspense, and inside sat an ancient looking document, withered and tattered with age that somehow seemed to shimmer and under the dim neon lights of the room, drawing his gaze to it. "When you wake up you, will remember this," Jack started. "You know why you are here, you know what we want from you, and you know that you will keep coming back until you either die or sign the contract. I have wasted enough time on you, Special Case or not. Do yourself a favor— sign it. Save yourself the hassle and pain of an eternity of torment." Mark considered the option. He thought back to the people whom he had talked to. Jimmy said to sign, but could he be trusted? He did take his own deal. Maybe convincing others is part of his job. "Sign it…" Jack's eyes changed from the pale ice blue to brown and finally to bright red as his smile grew wider. Phil the pastor said to sign the contract. What if this was all just his subconscious trying to get him to change? A red pen appeared in front of him, he reached for it and was astounded by its weight. The contract was full of legalese and small print with a cartoony big black X at the bottom next to a blank line. "Sign it…" Jack's face started to twist and expand to fit his ever growing smile which became more and more sinister as it got larger. With the pen in his hand, Mark thought about his life. He tried to think of a reason not to sign. In that moment, the years of self-doubt and disappointment of not living up to expectations caught up with him. In that moment, he thought that he wasn't worth saving. He signed the contract.

"Perfect!" Jacks voice rang out. His face had returned to normal. With one hand, he reached for the contract and with the other, he reached for and snatched the pen from Mark's hand. "Now let us talk about the final piece of business. Upon your death, you will transition, and when you wake up, you will be at your new home. The first day you should expect a car pool around 8am, so please try to be ready and prompt, ok?" Mark absentmindedly nodded. "When you wake up today, you may have a slight stinging sensation on the palm of your hand. This is due to the pen pulling blood from your hand for ink and should stop within a few hours." Jack placed the contract in the briefcase and then stood, extending his hand to Mark, who was busy contemplating what had just occurred. "Well, it has been fun Mark, see you around!" and with that he was gone.

"Wait!" Mark shouted. "Come back!"

"Sorry pal, too late." Jimmy replied from the bar. "Once they get the signature, they are off to the next appointment."

Mark stood and walked to the bar. "I think I've made a mistake. What if I can change?"

Jimmy smiled and poured a shot of whiskey, which Mark quickly swallowed. "You did good buddy. The alternative is never better. At least you are paying your debt without the torture, right? I wouldn't want to be out there in the wastes." Mark sat at the bar and hung his head. "Look buddy, I hate to say it, but it's closing time. You seem like a nice enough guy, and I wish you all the luck in the world, but chances are this is the last time we will meet."

Jimmy extended his hand to the wall to the left at a wooden door. Mark pulled himself to his feet and walked to the door. A sense of dread overcame him as he reached for the door handle and turned it. Looking back, he saw Jimmy smile and wave before saying, "Thanks for comin!" Mark opened the door to darkness and took a step out.

Monday, September 15th

Morning had come, and Mark pulled himself out of bed and stumbled to the bathroom, pausing for a moment to check his reflection in the mirror. The face looking back at him looked disappointed. Jack was right, and he could remember everything about his dream, a gift he wished he was not given. He checked his phone but still had not heard from either Julie or Nicole, so he sent them both a message asking them to call him.

"So about last night..." Wayne started. Mark had been quiet all morning, and Wayne had suspected that it was because of their conversation. "Look man, I know you do your own thing and it is not my place to judge. I am just worried about you."

Mark removed his headset. "Do you feel like taking an early lunch?"

The elevator ride down was silent, but Wayne could tell Mark had something he wanted to tell him that would be better said out of the office. They entered the Lounge and found a corner seat. Wayne reviewed the menu and waited for Mark to say whatever it was he had to say while Mark waited until the wait staff had moved away from their secluded booth.

"You believe in god, right?" Mark asked. His voice wavered with his words.

"Mostly," Wayne answered, searching for clues in his words as if it were a trick question.

Mark nervously rubbed his hands together. "So that means you believe in the devil too, right?"

Wayne shrugged. "Not necessarily. People say you cannot have one without the other, but I think that there is not one devil but several entities that rule hell." A meek waiter walked up to their table and asked for their order. "I would like an iced tea please," Wayne returned.

"I'll just have an ice water with a lemon please, and can you give us some time?" Mark added.

"What is with you?" Wayne asked in a concerned voice.

Mark sighed heavily before responding. "I think I may have sold my soul to the devil."

The look on Wayne's face clearly showed his disbelief. In a sarcastically interested way he asked, "What did you get for it?"

Mark, understanding that what he was about say sounded ridiculous, let out a deep sigh. "Have you ever heard of the 37 percent rule?" Wayne shook his head. "Well, apparently Heaven and Hell came together in what is now Las Vegas and decided that, due to overpopulation and paperwork, if a person had spent more than 37.9 percent of their life in sin, then they are deemed un-savable. They are not given a chance at redemption, and when they die, they are sentenced to be tormented for eternity." As he spoke the last line, he couldn't help but sound like a threatening parent figure scolding a small child. Wayne's face was emotionless as he listened to the story. "He told me that if I take the deal and sign the contract, then when I die, I'll be put to work in an office and my shitty little life will be the same as it is right now." Mark thought about that statement, his shitty little life. Maybe he was a horrible person.

Wayne sat speechless. What had started out as a joke had spooked him; it was clear that the conversation had made him uncomfortable. "Did they tell you when you are going to… you know…?"

Mark finished the sentence. "Die?" Wayne nodded. "No," Mark added. "He said that a lot of the future is unwritten."

"I'm kind of at a loss for words here," Wayne confessed.

"Yeah," Mark replied. "Me too."

A long silence overtook them both for the rest of the meal, broken only by the meek waiter bringing them their drinks. Neither of them spoke a word until they were both back at their 3-by-3 cubes and Wayne received a phone call.

The elevator ride at the end of the day seemed longer than usual; this was a common occurrence on days he was eager to get home. Waiting for the bus, Mark checked his messages and was surprised to find one from Julie:

(5:26pm) Shepard Park. 7pm.

Mark closed the message and searched the internet for Shepard Park, finding it downtown, only a few blocks from his home. As the number 7 bus pulled up, he responded to the message

(5:28pm) Ok

The bus was empty, not necessarily surprising considering the time of day and the destination. He sat midway down the bus aisle and felt another vibrate on his phone. Feeling a sense of urgency, he pulled out his phone, expecting a response from Julie but instead finding a video message from Nicole with only a kissy face as the text. The bus rumbled to life as it pulled away and started the next leg of its repetitive journey as Mark turned the phone sideways and pressed the play button.

The 40 second video started in a selfie view with Nicole's face filling most of the frame and the familiar background of his bedroom. "Hey babe," she started in a cutesy voice. "You're kind of drunk and passed out before we really got started, so I wanted to make sure you had a good memory, maybe something to give you some inspiration when I'm not around." Mark watched as she leaned in close and took the familiar looking head of an already erect cock into her mouth, sucking in and releasing it with a pop. "It's not nice to keep a girl waiting," she continued before using her teeth to tear open a condom wrapper.

The video paused as a new notification flashed across the screen.

New message from Julie: ☺

Mark cleared the message and continued the video. Nicole turned the camera to show an unconscious Mark lying in his bed. Despite her added commentary of "You look so handsome when you're asleep," he clearly looked like he was having a bad dream.

The bus came to a stop, and a familiar old woman came on. She slowly made her way up the steps and smiled at Mark, staring through him with piercing blue eyes, before taking the first seat behind the driver.

The camera shifted and showed only the bedspread as Nicole changed positions. When it refocused on her face, she said, "I've been looking forward to this for days," and then, slightly laughing, "it looks like you have been too." The old woman turned and made eye contact with Mark as he lowered the volume on his phone. The camera panned down to show Nicole's hand at the base of his condom-covered erect cock as the tip pushed between her lips. Off-camera, Mark could hear her moan as she squatted down and then lifted up, working him inside her until his cock had disappeared. The camera then moved back to a selfie view, and Nicole said in a breathy voice, "I love the way you feel inside me, baby," as she rocked back and forth. The camera angle changed as her phone fell onto the bed, showing several seconds of the ceiling before shutting off.

Mark sat in silence while a sense of guilt, partially from the act he had witnessed and partially from the fact it turned him on slightly, washed over him. He thought back to Saturday night and tried to recall everything he could. She was waiting for him by the door. She kissed his neck and he pulled away. He remembered telling her that he wasn't up for anything sexual, he remembered telling her no, but the video clearly showed that he was more interested than he remembered being. How many drinks did he have? One, two, three? He only found a quarter of a bottle, right? After everything he had learned and experienced in the last week, he was starting to find his own mind less and less reliable.

"It looks like it will be a nice night." Mark jumped at the sound of the voice, thinking he was alone. While he was processing his own thoughts, the old woman had moved back on the bus and took the seat across from him.

"I'm sorry, I wasn't paying attention. What did you say?" Mark asked.

The woman had a kind face, and her smile provided an instant sense of comfort. "It looks like it will be a nice night," She repeated, before nodding in the direction of the window behind Mark.

In the suburbs, you could see the night sky and all the stars, something you missed when you lived either up or down town. The crescent moon peaked over the horizon as day turned into night. The lack of clouds in the sky did indicate that it would be a nice night. Mark felt a hand on his shoulder as he looked through the window and found that the old woman had moved to share his bench seat.

"You look like you have a lot on your mind young man." Mark nodded. "Did you know that the worst advice I can give you is probably the most helpful?" Her voice was smooth and motherly. Mark fought back tears as she spoke. "That advice is that everything happens for a reason. Whatever it is that is going to keep you from enjoying this beautiful night, know that it was going to happen one way or another and try not to dwell on it, ok?" The bus pulled to a stop, and the woman got up. "This is your stop, right?" she asked.

Mark stood up from the seat and made his way to the front of the bus. He stood on the street and watched the bus pull away. The old woman sat stoically staring out the window at the sky.

As soon as the bus was out of sight, the small bit of peace of mind that the old woman had granted him was forgotten just as fast as it came. Mark pulled his phone from his pocket and opened the message from Julie and responded:

> (7:06:pm) Around the corner, on
> my way.

As he walked, he thought about what the woman had told him. "Everything happens for a reason." The words rang over and over in his head and only further cluttered his thoughts. It was too hard for him to believe that he had no control. It was easier finding blame than understanding that sometimes shitty things happen and you may never know why.

Shepard Park was a small, fenced-in piece of land in-between two slum apartments downtown. The lot was twenty-by-twenty feet and the only area with green grass and a tree for several miles in any direction. The street lights gave it plenty of visibility, even at night, making it one of the few places in the open that prostitutes and dealers avoided. The park consisted of a wooden play structure, complete with slide and monkey bars on the north east side by the fence gate, and a line of swings on the south side. Each play area was surrounded by rubber chips to ensure safety, as kids will be kids, and the remaining area was filled with lush green grass. Mark had seen the park before but never knew its name, nor had he never seen it in use.

Through the fence, he could see Julie on the swing furthest from the gate. She swayed back and forth, her feet dragging through the rubber chips, with a dazed look on her face and a cigarette hanging between her lips. The gate made a loud squeak as Mark opened it, but Julie gave no reaction. With each step, he could feel the rubber beneath the soles of his shoes giving him a slight bounce. From ten feet away, Julie looked up and took notice of him. She smiled, causing the cigarette between her lips to tilt up. Mark took the swing next to her and started to rock back and forth. She took a long drag of her cigarette and flicked her ashes, which fell to the rubber chips below her.

"So I guess I should say I'm sorry," she started without looking at him. "When I saw you at group, something in me snapped. I have been going for ages and seeing someone I just met show up and ready to hear all my problems was not something I was prepared for." Mark understood. He had not figured out his own problems yet, but thinking back to what others had shared, he couldn't imagine doing the same. She planted her feet, stopping her swing, and, for the first time since he sat down, turned to look at him. "I wasn't ready for you to see me that vulnerable. I wasn't ready for you to see how broken I am."

He took her hand and offered a smile. "In the time I've known you, including the meeting, I would have never thought of the word broken to describe you."

She smiled back, causing her face to brighten under the street lights. "That's probably the nicest thing anybody has ever said to me."

Attempting to avoid an awkward moment, Mark released her hand and kicked up his feet, breaking into a swing. "When I see you, I see a functioning human being, a productive member of society. In the most common use of the term, you may not be what people consider normal, but for us, for our generation, you are as normal as me."

She took another long drag from her cigarette before putting it out on the sole of her shoe and pocketing the butt. "So what you are saying is that you don't think I'm broken because I'm as normal as you?" Mark offered a simple nod. She continued, "So if I'm as normal as you, and I'm broken, that must mean you're broken too."

Mark laughed. "Life is all about perspective. If your life works for you, then don't let anybody call you broken or damaged."

Julie started to twist her hips in the swing, causing her swing to half turn back and forth. "So what is your vice? What makes you normal for our generation?" she asked.

It was a question Mark didn't know how to answer. "Honestly, I'm not sure I have one," He confessed. "My buddy Wayne encouraged me to go. He would never say it, but he thinks I'm addicted to sex, drugs, and alcohol."

Julie laughed. "The rock and roll trifecta?" she asked.

"I know, how cliché. I don't think I'm addicted, but I guess addicts never do, right?" They both laughed. "I don't do these things because I can't live without them; I do these things because it passes the time and there is nothing really better to do. Like right now? I have no desire for drugs or alcohol."

Julie smiled. "And what about sex?"

Mark thought of the video Nicole had sent him. "Right this moment, I'm not totally sure I want that either."

They sat on the swings for the next hour and made small talk about nonsense. They did the first date interview, asking the other's likes and dislikes and all the what if questions people use to get to know each other. Shortly before midnight, they left the park. She called a cab as they walked hand in hand back to his apartment complex where she kissed him goodnight right as her taxi pulled up and honked.

"Come see me at work tomorrow." It came out more as a command and less like a request. She could see the hesitation in his face and said, "I'll put you on the list, just in case," before giving him a final kiss on the cheek and heading toward the waiting car.

Mark climbed the stairs to his apartment while planning his next step. The contract and dream should be his first and only priority, but instead he couldn't keep Julie out of his mind. What if what Jack said was true, what if he was going to die? Even the thoughts of self-preservation turned to Julie. Was it fair to her if he would only be around for a little while longer? Then the philosophical questions kicked in: would being happy a little bit and then losing it be better than not knowing at all? His concentration was broken by a slap, hard across his face.

Mark's balance was thrown off, and his foot slipped backward off the steps. Gravity took over, causing him to fall backwards, land on his ass, and then tumble head over heels until he landed face down at the landing between floors.

"You said you weren't fucking anybody else!" Nicole shouted. "I saw you with that stripper at the park! I saw you kiss her!" Mark made it to his hands and knees in time for her to make her own way to the landing and hit him with a swift kick in the ribs. "What, wasn't I good enough for you? How many times have you fucked her?" She kicked him in the ribs again, causing him to fall to his side. She shouted again, "How many times? Tell me dammit!" Mark tried to respond but could only cough.

"And then what happened?" Wayne asked as he leaned against the counter in the breakroom.

Mark sat at the table holding a fresh icepack against his side. "I coughed again and made out the word 'none' and she backed off. She just kind of looked disgusted and left me there." He chose not to tell him about the video she had sent.

Wayne's voice came in a whisper as he muttered, "Oh wow..." before his regular voice returned. "So what are you going to do?"

Mark considered the question. "I don't know," he responded. "Avoid her, I guess. I think it is pretty clear that this is over." The finality of the statement hit him, and he silently admitted to himself that he probably wanted a way to get rid of her, and that he was glad this gave him exactly that. "I've been up all night. After she left, I took a cab to the hospital where they did some x-rays. Between the fall and the kick, I ended up bruising and cracking a few ribs, but the doctors said it could have been so much worse." The sentence made him think of the contract.

Wayne could see the distress in his face but mistook it for heart break. "Hey buddy, try not to worry about it. Some women are just crazy, you know?"

With the blessing of Miles Trubuck himself, Mark left work for the day for a follow-up with his own doctor. As he sat in the stiff chair waiting for his name to be called, his mind drifted. Colors started to blur as the lack of sleep had finally caught up with him. Each breath was a fight for air through the constant dull pain in his side, and for a moment, he thought this could be his death. After what felt like an eternity, Mark was led back to the nurse's area where they took his vitals.

Blood Pressure a little high, understandable in the situation.

Temperature 98.3, normal.

They asked what happened and he told the same lie he did at the ER; he had fallen down some stairs drunk. It seemed believable enough. With a great amount of pain, he was led back into the waiting room where he sat back down in a chair against the wall, popped a pill the ER had given him, and closed his eyes.

10 Inhale. Through foggy thoughts, Mark thought of Julie. He had seen her less than 24 hours ago but was having trouble making out the details. He thought about them sitting on the swings and laughing but could only make out her silhouette and her smell, cotton candy and cigarettes.

9 Exhale. She asked him if he could have any superpower what would it be, and he told her the ability to change shapes, to become anybody. She smiled. "Did you know that the answer to that question tells a lot about who a person is? Like if a person says they want to fly, then subconsciously they want to be free, or if they want to be strong, then subconsciously they feel weak." She didn't say it, but Mark knew she was thinking that he didn't want to be himself, and she was right.

"What would you choose?" he asked, trying to move the conversation along. She planted her feet and came to a stop, and in a serious tone said, "I would want the power to always make the perfect piece of toast."

8 Inhale. "You know the thing about doctors' offices and medical waiting rooms is that they show you the absolutely best and worst of humanity." The voice was familiar, but Mark's head was still foggy. "There is something about one's impending mortality that gives them clarity on what is important in life." Mark's eyes began to focus and he saw the waiting room again. To his left sat Jack. "You see that woman?" he asked, pointing to a heavyset brunette who was staring at a magazine. "That woman is an adulterer. She claims bi-polar disorder so she can collect social security, and while her husband is off working two jobs she is fucking three other men in their apartment building. I guess that makes her an adulterer and a thief, right?" He lightly nudged Mark in the side and even the light touch shot pain through his body. "This woman over here," he pointed to a frail looking woman with blonde and grey hair. "Watch as she looks on her child with so much love and compassion while the daughter sits there and plays with her phone. Somehow, that child does not know or realize that her mother is dying. She does not know that more than anything, her mother would love to talk to her."

"Isn't there anybody here who is not a terrible person?" Mark asked, his voice soft, almost inaudible.

Jack sighed loudly, but nobody noticed. "That old couple, both of them are loving and caring for each other. He dies in two weeks and she loses the will to live without him and dies of heart failure a month later. Their life is boring! Where is the excitement in a couple of old geezers in love?"

Love was a foreign concept to Mark. All he knew of love was from 80s teen comedies and pornography, both of which turned out to be less than reliable sources. In a sudden moment of clarity, the most important question came. "Why can you tell how long they have but not me?" Jack was uncharacteristically silent; the question had caught him off guard. "You told me before that you couldn't tell the when or how. You said a lot of the future is unwritten. How do you know their fates but not mine?"

For the first time since they had met, Mark could see a falter in Jack's face. His answer came not in the confident gameshow host voice, but one that bled with honesty like a magician being outed and being forced to tell his secrets. "Ok," he started, "I am going to level with you. I do not know why I cannot see your clock, but I think it has something to do with you being a Special Case. Your kind has been assigned to me before, and I have never figured out why but I can never see your clocks. Despite what you think, I am but a peon, a worker bee. I do not know the grand plan or where the story will go. That being said, where I am from, knowledge is power, and if someone could figure out the Special Cases then they would become powerful within the ranks."

"Mark!" a voice called to him from the distance. "It looks like our time is up, more yours than mine." Jack smiled his toothy grin. "Mark!" the voice called again, louder than before. "Before I go, I give you this." his smile disappeared as he leaned in close. With each word his face became more and more grotesque. "You got me this time. Normally I do not make these kinds of mistakes, and it will not happen again."

"Mark!" His eyes opened to find the nurse standing in front of him. "Thank god you're awake! Didn't the ER tell you not to take narcotics if you are sleep deprived?" Mark looked around the room at the faces of all the people staring at him with concern and confusion. "You must have been having some dream, Hun. You were causing quite the commotion." Mark stood and followed the nurse to a private exam room, the judging eyes in the waiting room following him every step of the way.

Mark climbed into a cab and started the trip downtown. His phone buzzed, indicating a message, but he couldn't focus on much of anything. The tall buildings of the city passed in a blur, and before long, he was in the familiar suburbs. While stopped at a red light, he watched through a large front window at a family as they sat down for dinner. The children bickered back and forth with smiles on their faces as the father, with his elbows on the table, watched his offspring. Everybody sat up straight as a mother entered the room caring a pan full of mystery food as they all looked at her with love and affection. For a moment, he couldn't tell if he was dreaming again.

Mark thumbed through his phone to find the name Helen and held his finger over the dial button. It had been years since he called. Who knows if she even had the same number? He told himself that if it had changed, he would have been notified in the yearly Christmas card but recalled no such notification. He tapped the button and waited for the line to connect and start ringing. It was possible she wouldn't answer anyways; she never was much of a phone person. It rang again and then once more. His thumb moved and held above the disconnect button. It was almost dark out, and she probably was already getting ready for bed. As the cab rolled to a stop, the last ring led into an automated message saying that the subscriber was not available. More disappointed than he thought he would be, Mark disconnected the call and exited the cab.

The sun had gone down, leaving only pools and puddles of light from the street lamps. His mind still foggy from combination of sleep deprivation and medication, he made his way step by step to his building. He paused under the streetlamp as he felt his phone buzz in his pocket, not the familiar buzz of a message, but the elongated buzz of a call. He pulled the phone from his pocket and saw the name Helen. "Mom?" he answered.

"Marky, is that you?" the line was full of static, but she sounded the way he remembered.

"Yeah, mom, it's me. I..."He didn't know how to finish the sentence. There was no real reason for his call. "I just wanted to say hi." Standing under the light in the darkness, he felt like a million miles from everything.

"It's good to hear your voice, Marky. I was just telling some people about my son in the big city." He smiled. "Judy was telling me she came out that way for some shopping, said she almost got mugged downtown!" Mark peered out into the darkness, but again saw nothing but other splashes of light on the ground from streetlights.

"It's not too bad," He offered, "I live downtown, and I've never been mugged."

Helen laughed. "You've grown up Marky. Your father would be proud." The sentence struck a chord. Would he have been? What had he really done with his life?

"I've got to go, Mom. I love you."

She sighed, "But we only just started talking! I understand. Have a good night, sweetie. I love you too." And the phone clicked off.

With Helen's name and phone number gone, Mark was left with the message notifications he had been ignoring all day. He opened them and read Wayne's first:

(3:19pm) Just wanted to make sure you got to the
Doctors and back home ok. Not sure if you are coming
in tomorrow but if you are and need a ride then let me know.

In that moment, Mark finally understood just how great a friend Wayne really was. The next text was from Nicole. It read:

(4:01pm) Can we talk? I'm so sorry babe. I've just been hurt so
much in the past. Please call me.

Mark deleted the message before reading all of it. The final two messages were from Julie.

(4:12pm) Hey stranger! I was just thinking
about you, how's your day?
(4:13pm) Are you coming to see me tonight?

>   (4:13pm) Probably not, I took a slip
>   down the stairs last night and
>   bruised some ribs.

(4:13pm) Oh no! Well I'm going to take the night off
and come take care of you.

He had never had a woman willing to come take care of him before.
The feeling was both foreign and exciting.

>   (4:14pm) Thanks.

Mark pocketed his phone and looked through the darkness to the next
pool of light splashed on the ground. He took a deep breath that made him
wince and walked into the darkness towards his apartment. Each step was a
labor as the exhaustion of the day raced through his body. At the foot of the
steps, he looked up to the first of five flights of stairs he would climb before
he was home. Using the rail to help pull him up, he conquered the steps, one
at a time, until he reached the second floor. Feeling drained of all energy, he
stopped and struggled to catch his breath before attempting the final sixteen
steps. Each step was a painful reminder that in front of him, on the landing
between the second and third floor, was where Nicole attacked him. He
rounded the corner and faced the last flight, one step at a time, bracing
himself with each step with the rail.

He had finally reached the third floor, his apartment well within sight,
but before he could take a step, an arm wrapped around his neck. He
attempted to struggle, but even with his fight or flight sense activated, he
just didn't have enough energy left in him. He felt the cold chill of metal
pressed against his throat as a man's voice whispered in his ear, "Give me
your wallet."

The smell of stale beer and piss was strong; he reasoned his attacker
was a homeless man. Mark fumbled for his wallet and stuttered, "I d-d-don't
have any c-c-cash. ," before holding it up. The attacker grabbed the wallet
with his knife hand and pushed Mark away, shoving him hard into the wall.
For the first time, Mark could see his attacker, who did not look like a
homeless man at all. His jeans and t-shirt gave him the look of just a regular
Joe.

The attacker became irate at the lack of contents in the wallet and threw
it back at Mark, shouting, "God dammit!" before rushing in and pinning his
forearm beneath Mark's chin. "Where do you live? You got anything
valuable?" Mark struggled to speak as the lack of air made him light headed.
With the little energy he could muster, Mark pointed towards his apartment.

The attacker looked to door, twisting the anger in his face into a sadistic smile.

As the knife entered his stomach, time slowed. It was not what he had expected it to feel like, being stabbed. Movies and television led him to expect a sharp pain or a burning sensation, a theory backed by previous experiences being cut by a random shard of glass or an uncovered sharp object. The pain was actually dull and hard to pin point. He could tell it was coming from his stomach, but where exactly, if it was the left or right side, was undeterminable. Mark slid down the wall as the man walked to his apartment door and rammed into it with his shoulder several times before stepping back and kicking at the area below the doorknob. Mark smiled as he realized that his attacker must have also learned much of the interaction from movies and television. In a final act of desperation, he attempted to pry open the door with his now bloody knife before giving up and hurrying to the stairwell.

Mark looked down at his bloody hand pressing hard over the wound in his stomach. Leaning against the wall, he could see his father in a similar position sitting across from him, leaning against the front of a bumper. He felt a cold chill run through his body as he looked at his father's ghost, and right before he closed his eyes, he heard his father ask "Mark?" snapping him out of his trance-like state. "Everything happens for a reason."

10. Inhale. He floated in and out of consciousness for an unknown amount of time. He would close his eyes, and when he opened them, Julie was there. He closed them again, and when he opened them, he was being carried down the stairs. The only constant was Julie telling him that it would be ok and asking him not to give up. He closed his eyes.

9. Exhale. When he next opened his eyes, he found himself in an ambulance. The bright lights blinded him at first, and when he was finally able to focus, he could see a man in a white short-sleeve button-up shirt leaning over him. The paramedic's gloved hands were pressing down on his wound, and he was surprised that he couldn't feel anything.

8. Inhale. "And then what happened?" he asked.

Through her sobs she said, "I called 911; they told me to push on the wound, so I did."

Mark could see her hands and arms covered in blood, his blood. He closed his eyes.

7. Exhale. "We have a knife wound, 5 inches deep. As best we can tell, it occurred just under an hour ago."

Mark struggled to open his eyes and, deciding he lacked the strength, gave up. Trying instead to focus on sounds, he heard a man ask, "Who's she?"

6. Inhale. Julie's panicked voice answered, "I'm his friend, his girlfriend." as it trembled with each word.

The man asked, "How old is he?" but Julie had no response. "What's his blood type?" Again, she couldn't answer. "Are you sure you're his girlfriend?" a second woman's voice asked.

Through crying eyes Julie pleaded, "I love him."

5. Exhale. "I'm sorry miss," the man's voice was stern and authoritative. "I'm going to need you to stay in the waiting room. As soon as there is an update, I'll let you know."

Mark's mind drifted off again.

4. Inhale. As his mind stirred, he found the lack of voices alarming. Mark's eyes fluttered, struggling to open, but the bright light above him fought him the whole way. With all the fight he had left within him, he finally was able to slightly open his eyes. A woman with kind eyes wearing a surgical mask looked down at him and said, "You're doing fine, keep breathing." His eyes closed again.

3. Exhale. He recalled stories of how some people see their lives flash before their eyes, and how for others, it's a bright light at the end of a tunnel. Some people say there is nothing, just a black void where you are alone with your thoughts forever, or at least until you wake up. The expectation disappointed him, as the next time he opened his eyes, he found himself in the back of a limo traveling at what felt like a high speed. The interior felt old school; the leather and wood paneling showed the vehicle's age. To his left, he found a row of switches and toggles, none of which proved responsive. "Hello?" he called toward the partition that separated the back and front, only to receive silence in return. Through the windows, he looked for a landmark or any sign but found only darkness. The seats formed to his body and were cool to the touch, the way leather tends to be until you sit for too long. The comfort lulled him in into a false sense of complacency, and before long, he no longer questioned how he had gotten here or where he was going.

After a short time, the small TV in the corner opposite of him clicked, and then the screen glowed as it came to life the way he recalled seeing older TV sets do in movies. A black and white screen showed "please stand by" for long enough that he started to ignore it, before, without notice, it changed to an upbeat song as an announcer called out, "This is your life!" as the words simultaneously came spinning onto the screen. The opening card faded, and a stage came into view as the studio audience applauded and the announcer introduced the show's host. "And now for a man who needs to introduction, Skip Mahoney!"

A man wearing a dark suit ran out onto the stage. Mark couldn't help but notice he looked a lot like Jack. They were different enough that each was still distinguishable, but shared a lot of the same facial structure, like long lost cousins. Skip walked to the front of the stage where a microphone stood as he waved and blew kisses towards the studio audience, who responded with equal affection. When the crowd died down, Skip finally spoke into the microphone. "Tonight we are going to meet the empty shell of a man who has skated through life and provided little if anything to humanity as a whole!" The crowd again erupted in cheers and applause, giving Skip another chance to again bask in the adoration. When it had died back down, Skip continued, "Let's take a look at young Mark at 9 years old." He held his hand out to a large screen behind him, and as an image appeared, it then transitioned to the whole screen.

What followed was a mix of after school special and a sitcom dramatization of the worst moments of his life. Poorly acted and complete with laugh track, he watched as people who looked like old friends acted out his poor decisions.

"Come on! What are you, a wimp?" Two children sat on swings in a park. The first child continued, "This place sucks! Let's go play in that junk car we found." The second child thought about their options while staring off into the distance at the big kids who had taken over the jungle gym. The first child started singing, "Mark is a pussy, Mark is a pussy," and laugher from the audience followed.

Reluctantly, Mark agreed to go, and as a happy tune played, the two made their way through the lightly wooded area to an abandoned and rusted car they had found the day before. The two children started arguing about who was going to drive, once again accompanied by more laughter.

They bickered back and forth until the first child was struck with a piece of child logic and said, "You can't be the driver, you don't have a license."

To which Mark replied, "Neither do you!" causing both children to look dramatically disappointed, followed by another uproar of laughs. After the final exchange, the two made their way back to the park where they once again took their seats on the swing set.

With nothing better to do and feeling defeated, Mark resumed staring off into space. The big kids had gone, and the park was now empty. Out of desire to prove he was just as good as the big kids, Mark abandoned his swing and strutted off to the jungle gym. Not wanting to be left out, the second child followed behind. All of a sudden, they were the big kids. All of a sudden, they were in charge. Hand over hand, Mark climbed to the top where he stood on shaky legs and surveyed his kingdom. He looked down and started a chorus of, "Dylan is a pussy, Dylan is a pussy," followed by laughter from the audience. Slowly, Dylan made his way up the side of the jungle gym until his knees gave out and he could climb no more. Doing his best to look more confident than he was, he slid his legs through the structure and sat on a bar. Mark wasn't fooled, and neither was the audience, who responded with more laughter.

The camera zoomed in on Mark's eyes as he first noticed something half buried in the sand under the metal webbed dome. He dropped down, hanging first by his hands and then dropping completely to the ground. Dylan, not so sure of himself, slowly turned and started to climb back down the way he came. By the time the two met under the dome, Mark had uncovered his buried treasure and was examining a brown bi-fold leather wallet.

"Where did it come from?" Dylan asked as Mark rifled through the contents.

He responded, "I'm don't know, maybe those big kids dropped it," as he pulled out two ten-dollar bills, a twenty, and an expired condom. The camera again zoomed in on Mark's faces as his eyes widened and a smile crossed his face. The next shot was one of Mark thrusting his hand into the air and clutching a small, plastic card. The camera zoomed in on the driver's license as digital effects were added to make it shine and glow as an angelic chorus accented the discovery.

The studio audience made an impressed *Ohhhh* sound, purely for the benefit of the home viewer. They had no idea what they were doing was stealing, but as quick as they could, they ran to the abandoned and rusted car. What followed was a montage of scenes showing the boys having a good time. Mark went first, climbing into the driver's seat and making racecar sounds. Dylan demanded a turn and Mark moved to the passenger seat, handing over their golden ticket as Dylan climbed behind the wheel. The scene lasted until an abrupt voice could be heard yelling, "It didn't just get up and walk away. I want my fucking wallet!"

A dramatic sting accompanied a comical shot of the boys overcome with a mix of panic and fear. The canned laughter started as the two took off towards the woods in an exaggerated style as the scene showed in fast-forward. They ditched the wallet in the weeds, having already emptied it of its money and expired condom. Finally, the screen paused on their smiling faces as they ran toward the screen, and the studio audience applauded over the rolling credits.

Mark sat back in silence. It seemed so familiar, but he wasn't sure if it was true. What he had seen was mixing with his own foggy memories, and he wasn't sure what to believe.

"That is one of my favorites!" Jack bellowed from beside him. Before Mark could think or respond, the familiar upbeat music started again, and across the TV, a banner read, "This is your life!"

Skip stood on stage again, and, addressing the audience, he said, "This was Mark's first real step toward delinquency, a slippery slope that continued into his teenage years!"

The audience applauded as the screen displayed a picture of the same two boys, only slightly older. Although they were still recognizable, the clothes and teenage angst that replaced their childlike innocence showed that this segment was years after the first. The two stood side by side, leaning against a brick wall near a lit streetlamp.

Turning to the frozen frame on the screen behind him, Skip announced, "Let's see how Mark and Dylan ended up a few years later!" The crowd offered a round of applause as the image of the boys transitioned to fill the whole screen.

"Are you sure about this guy?" Mark asked.

"Yeah man, I got his number from my brother, says he's been hooking him up for years." Dylan's trembling voice betrayed his confident pose.

The camera zoomed in on Mark's concerned face as a laugh track played. "How do you know your brother's not fucking with you?"

Dylan responded defensively. "Because I caught him and his friend playing with each other's cocks a few weeks ago. I told him that unless he's my bitch that the whole school's going to know." The boys laughed and high fived, prompting more laughter from the audience.

Headlights danced off the wall behind them as a red sports car came to a halt. The driver's side window rolled down, revealing a skinny white man with dreadlocks wearing sunglasses. Over the Ska music, which only furthered the stereotype the dealer was going for, he asked, "You that Dylan kid?" Slightly embarrassed, Dylan nodded. You could tell that being called "kid" took away all confidence he had. "Who's your lover?" referring to Mark.

"He's cool. He's with me," Dylan replied in the hopes of sounding like he knew what he was doing.

"Well, what you waiting for ladies, get in the car!" Mark and Dylan shared an exaggerated look of panic as the audience laughed, and the screen faded to black.

As it dimmed back in, the picture showed the driver and Dylan in the front with Mark in the back of what clearly looked like half of a car in front of a green screen. Trees, houses, and street lights passed in the back window as the three headed off into the night. Awkward silence filled the car, producing awkward canned laughter as the two boys shared overly dramatic, comical looks as they each tried to get the other to start the conversation.

Abruptly, the car pulled onto a dirt road and the driver killed the lights. "So I get the feeling that you little bitches are new to this, so I'm gonna make it easy. You give me 60 bucks, and I'm gonna give you a quarter. You tell anybody where you got it, then I'm gonna deny the shit out of it and then beat the fuck out of you." The audience made an *Ohhhh* sound at the threat.

Fumbling for his wallet, Dylan stammered, "I-I-I didn't know, know it would be so much. I I I only have t t twenty…" before offering it to the driver.

Before either of them could react, the driver snatched the bill from Dylan and, accompanying a suspenseful music cue, back handed him across the face. He screamed, "Who do you think you're fucking with here? Who do I look like, the fucking Good Will?". He back-handed Dylan, who was trying desperately to get out of the car, again. "This is not a joke! You two fucks have no idea what kind of trouble you're in!"

Dylan had made it out of the car, and the driver followed. They did an awkward dance, one going one way and the other going another while cartoonish music and the laugh track provided their sound. For a short time, neither of them seemed to gain or lose any ground until, as the driver rounded the front of the car, the passenger door swung open, hitting him in the stomach and crotch. As he fell to the ground in pain, the laugh track played again. Mark exited the vehicle and proceeded to kick the driver in the side several times until he stopped moving. Dylan ran to the still body and knelt down, patting his pockets and finding three quarter sacks and two hundred dollars. Dylan stood and provided a few of his own kicks before the two boys then got into the car and drove away. The audience cheered for the heroes of the story as the screen froze on the car's tail lights disappearing into the dark.

Mark clearly remembered that night. They wrecked the car, crashing it into a telephone pole a few blocks from home. The next day, it was all over the news. Jack poured himself a drink from the mini bar and said, "This last segment you might get a kick out of."

The upbeat theme song played, and the screen again displayed the words, "This is your life!" as the camera focused on Skip. "Exciting, isn't it folks?" The audience cheered. "You all know what's next. Say it with me now!"

The audience joined in and chanted as a new title card displayed the words "Where are they now?"

The title screen faded into a stage with a number of women sitting in a semicircle in front of a back drop of the city skyline. The camera panned past each of the women, pausing only slightly on them. They appeared to be sitting in order of age, starting with the youngest on the left and getting older to the right. It wasn't until the camera was close to the end of the right side before the women started looking familiar. Suddenly, the names to the faces came to him, and he could make out several women he had been with: Katie, Anna, Mary, Kim, Sandra, Sarah, and Julie. From the stage, they all looked at Skip, who sat in front of them with his back to the camera. On the second pass through, each woman's face brought back to him a memory of a place and time. Each of them had not aged since he had seen them last, and as they stood in turn, Mark could confirm everything they said was true.

The first woman in the circle stood and introduced herself. "My name's Anna, and I met Mark when he was 16. I was 14, and he use to tell me it wasn't that big of a difference. I wanted him, but he wanted someone else." The audience offered an understanding aww. "I did everything I could to make him jealous, but he only took notice of me when I put out. After that, he was too busy for me."

The remaining women and the studio audience applauded her bravery.

The next woman stood and spoke in a quick and embarrassed pace. "My name is Mary, and I met Mark when he was 16. I was a year younger, and we shared an art class. He was kind and funny, at least until the night of Junior Prom. After that, he never called me again."

She quickly took a seat while applause erupted from around her. Mark looked at Jack, who smiled and said, "You get sure do get around."

Skip looked at the camera and said, "After high school, Mark jumped from woman to woman, never sticking around for more than a month. If you asked him, I bet he wouldn't even remember some of these women's names!" The audience provided a loud boo while Mark came to terms with the fact that he was right.

"My name is Sarah, and I met Mark when he was 26. I saw him around campus, and his confidence just drew me to him. We were both creative types, and he made me want to be a better musician. We spent a night on the beach, and when I woke up, he was gone. He wouldn't return my calls after that."

The audience and the rest of the group applauded.

"My name is Kim, and I met Mark when he was 28. We worked together, and his attitude was so different than most men I'd met. I wanted him, but he was into some other girl until she wasn't around anymore. Only then did he give me a chance. I told him I had been hurt and lied to before, and he promised he would never lie." The surrounding women all nodded their heads in agreement, as if it was something they all truly understood. "One day, I couldn't take anymore and told him it was over. He tried to turn it all around and make me feel like I was the only who had been hurtful."

The surrounding women and audience applauded.

"My name is Julie, and I met Mark when he was in his early 30s. I felt an instant connection with him, although he just wanted to get into my pants. After he died, I found his phone and this video of him fucking some other woman." The audience offered an understanding aww. "I'm sure if I had given him the chance, he would have used me and tossed me aside."

Mark had heard enough. "That's a fucking lie! I would have never used her!"

Jack laughed. "It is all about perception. Just because that is not how you remember it does not mean that it is not how it happened."

Letting all of his anger show, Mark asked, "Where are we going? I don't remember anything of how I got here."

A wide smile crossed Jack's face, and the upbeat theme song came from the TV. The title screen flashed, "Breaking News!"

A woman sat behind a news desk and introduced herself. "Good evening, my name is Lucy Mays, and this is a breaking news report. We are going to take you live to Malcom Fredrick, who is live at the scene. Malcom?"

The screen cut to a man dressed in a blue suit with a yellow tie holding a microphone. Below him, a digital banner showed his name and the emblem for the local news affiliate. Behind the anchor, Mark could see police and paramedics rushing back and forth parked outside of a familiar three-story apartment building, and to the side, a crowd of bystanders standing behind a barrier.

The man spoke in a professional tone. "I'm standing here at the site of a grizzly attack at an apartment building downtown. An unknown victim was accosted when arriving home early tonight by this man," the picture of his attacker in handcuffs froze on the screen as the news reporter spoke, "Paul Shiner. The 27-year-old Shiner was found only blocks away, hiding in a nearby playground."

The screen cut to recorded footage of a body covered in a white sheet being wheeled on a stretcher into the back of an ambulance. The reporter continued in a voice over, "The victim's name has not been released, but we do know that he was taken to the Hope North Hospital in critical condition. An eye witness says that the victim appeared to be intoxicated and was having trouble making it from his cab to his apartment."

The screen cut to recorded footage of onlookers in shock. "The attack happened on the third floor of the building behind me, where it is believed that the victim lived. Though the investigation is still on-going, police suspect that this may have been a drug deal gone wrong."

The screen cut back to Lucy, who followed with, "Riveting story, Malcom. We will keep you posted on this, the latest murder in the downtown area, and all other crime notices, so stay tuned to WFXP for the only news that matters."

With a sudden and deafening click, the TV turned off.

Part 2

Day 1

The alarm rang out with a loud and steady series of beeps. Mark's eyes opened to an unfamiliar setting. This was not his room. This was not his apartment. Through the window, he could see a line of small identical buildings. The light pouring through the window looked like sunlight, only artificial, with a tint of red. He rolled to his other side and found a small digital alarm clock, still beeping and flashing the time, 6:03am.

"I always forget about the default alarm. you can change it to something subtler, if you like."

Jack's voice startled him. He had gotten used to seeing him only in dreams, but this felt real; this felt like life. The room was small and bare. Aside from the double bed, a single nightstand, and the chair where Jack sat, it was void of any decorations or furniture. He sat up and noticed that the pain in his side was gone.

"Any injuries you had before you came here do not follow. If they did, we would have to look at the aftermath of horrible and grisly murders all day."

"Where am I," He asked as if he didn't know the answer. "What are you doing here?" he followed up.

Jack smiled his gameshow host smile. "This is the last part of the recruiting process. We call it onboarding. Normally, you would take your carpool, but I wanted to bring you in myself." The casualness of his speech made Mark uneasy. He was still coping with the idea that he was no longer living, and Jack made it sound like it was the first day of school. Jack stood, pointed towards the closed door to the right of the bed, and said, "Your uniform is hanging in the closet. Get dressed and meet me in the living room," before exiting through the only other door in the room.

Mark sat up in bed and ran his hands over his stomach where he vividly remembered there being open wounds. The closet was small and held a single outfit: one white button-up shirt, one pair of tan khakis, and one belt. On the floor was a pair of black Velcro walking shoes with a sock stuffed in each. Mark dressed with the clothes provided and found it strange that they did not smell like detergent or fabric softener or have that new clothes smell. He also found that most of the clothing fit him poorly, the shirt too big, the pants to short, but the shoes were just right. Mark walked to the bed where he tried to smell the sheets, but again found nothing.

He exited the room through the same door Jack did, which led to a short hallway, which in turn led to a small living area. On the left side of the room sat a loveseat, and on the right side sat an old boxy CRT TV. Jack sat on the loveseat reading an ancient book when Mark came from the hallway.

He looked up and smiled. "Yep, you look like you work here." Mark opened his mouth to ask a question, but Jack stood and cut him off. "Let me answer all your questions because I assure you that they are not original, and this is not my first rodeo. There are two kinds of people who work here: Souls and the Fallen."

"The Fallen?" Mark interrupted.

Jack let out an annoyed sigh. "Yes, the Fallen," He confirmed. "Most of your kind still calls us demons. Now Souls, you, have either made a deal to work here instead of torment and torture or have completed your torment and torture and have moved up. Souls all wear the same outfit, white shirt and khakis. Your outfits never get dirty and never have to be maintained." Mark nodded to show he was following along. "Fallen wear suits; we are kind of the middle management. We choose to look human because we are kind of vain creatures." He leaned in and, in an exaggerated whisper, said, "Do not tell anybody," and then offered a dramatic wink.

Jack moved towards the only door in the room and opened it, leading outside. Mark took the hint and followed. The street was filled with the small houses he could see from the bedroom window. He turned and found that they were identical to his own. There were no trees or bushes, only grass in front of every house.

As Jack walked to the red compact sedan parked in front of the house, he continued, "You have no kitchen because you do not need to eat. You can if you like, but it is not a necessity. You have no bathroom because you have no need for one. You cannot even breathe, but most Souls never notice as it was more of an unconscious habit than a willful act." Mark attempted to take a deep breath and noticed the lack of swelling in his chest. He then attempted to breathe deeply from his nose, but came back with the same effect.

Jack shook his head slightly and muttered to himself, "I will never understand why they never believe me." He opened the driver's side door and entered the car as Mark did the same. "Consider this body a shell that is used to travel around. The fact that it resembles your former self is only a courtesy. We found that while Fallen cannot really tell you apart, the desire for individuality even in the afterlife is a huge motivation factor. It is all in the handbook."

Jack turned on the car and put it in gear, causing the tires to screech as he pulled out of the driveway. Acting like a teenager, he turned on the radio and energetically sang along to "Hell Bent for Leather" by Judaist Priest before saying, "This song was written about me. I had a phase in the 70s. True story."

Moving in a car felt surreal because of the familiarity of the houses. It seemed like they were traveling but getting nowhere. Jack continued, "This is what we call the Complex. It is a huge labyrinth of houses. Work hard, and you may eventually be given a carpool, but for now, just be ready in the morning and someone will get you to work." The houses started to change slightly, becoming larger with two-car driveways. Before Mark could ask, Jack explained, "This place is not without reward. You may be here for eternity, but we still want and need productive employees."

Mark realized the road had a slight curve to it as a gate started to peek around the corner in the distance. Beyond the gate, Mark could see an endless desert, all bathed in the same red-tinted sunshine.

During the lull in conversation, Mark asked, "Why do you all look the same?"

Jack was surprised by the question. "How do you mean?"

Mark thought back to the limo ride and Skip, the television host. "Both you and Skip, you both have the same angular face and features. You both have a thick head of hair. You both have a very white and bright smile. Even the way you walk is very similar."

Jack considered this, and for the first time came to the same conclusion. "I guess movies and television changed everything for us. We modeled ourselves after the images we found there, and it was successful."

Mark's mind clicked as the answer made complete sense. Imagine that the only thing you know about humans came from television and movies. Of course you would model yourself after the best -looking and most popular examples.

Jack continued, "When the Fallen started looking like humans, they were just another face in the crowd. It was hard to get someone to sign a contract when you look just like everybody else. Earlier, when I told you that we are vain, that was not a joke. Honestly, I do not think it ever occurred to me that we all share a resemblance."

Mark was startled by the humanity of his answer. "Why do the Fallen not use contractions?"

Giving a sarcastic look, Jack replied, "I do not understand what you mean?" and left it at that.

The car accelerated at great speed as it approached the gate which swung open to vast and empty plains with a single 4 lane road leading down it. "It is best if you never venture outside of the gates. The wastes are vast and filled with tormented Souls in the middle of punishment. It is all in the handbook."

Mark looked out the passenger window for any signs of Souls being tormented but saw nothing. The ride felt like a disappointing wildlife tour.

Jack sped up even more, and before long, the car started to shake as if it would fall apart. Mark reached for the seatbelt but found nothing.

"No Safety devices here!" Jack bellowed, followed by an evil laugh.

Fast approaching in the distance was another wall sealed with a gate. "What's that?" he asked, his voice shaky and frightened.

"That is the employment sector," Jack shouted over the sound of the roaring engine. "It houses the offices and white collar torments."

Mark looked at the speedometer where the indicator sat at zero. "Shouldn't we slow down?" The panic overcame him and cracked his voice.

Jack looked mockingly offended. "I know I am the bad guy here, but how about a little trust?" In a panic, Mark braced his legs against the floor board and pressed his body against the seat as the gate approached. He closed his eyes and prepared himself for impact, but it never came.

Opening his eyes, he saw what looked like a desert town. A single road stretched out before them, filled with tall buildings and chain restaurants. Mark looked behind them and caught a glimpse of the gate as it closed.

Breaking into a cackling laugh, Jack said, "That gets people every time!" The car started to slow as he pulled into the parking lot of one of the large office buildings where he stopped and put the car in neutral before getting out and handing the keys to a man wearing the outfit of a Soul. Mark exited the car and followed Jack up the steps as the valet behind them entered the car, revved the engine, and quickly drove off around the corner.

The lobby of the building was modern and empty with the exception of a single desk, a fern, and an elevator. An attractive middle-aged woman with reddish-orange hair sat behind the desk wearing the outfit of a Soul and reading what appeared to be the same book Jack had been reading at Mark's new apartment.

"Good morning Doris!" Jack roared as he offered a friendly wave. The woman behind the desk responded only by sticking her arm up with her middle finger extended without looking away from her book. Jack entered the elevator and Mark followed. Leaning in, Jack said in almost a whisper, "We use to be an item. She never got me out of her system," and offered a wink.

From the lobby, Doris shouted, "Fuck you Jack!" as the doors slid closed.

"So sex is allowed here?" Mark asked, figuring the information would be nice to know.

Without looking from the closed elevator doors, Jack replied, "Your shell is equipped the same as you were in life, and fraternization is accepted as long as it does not distract from your employment duties. It is all in the handbook."

Mark found it difficult to balance. The elevator ride was absent of the normal weight shift he was used to. Leaning against the wall for support, he asked, "You keep saying that? What's the handbook?"

Jack dismissed the question, saying, "You will learn about it in orientation."

It wasn't until the doors opened that he was convinced he had moved at all. Jack smiled and said, "This is where you get off," while extending his arm to lead the way.

With hesitation, Mark took his first step off the elevator into a dark corridor with a single door at the end. He turned back to Jack, looking for a sense of reassurance, but only received an impatient look from his piercing blue eyes. The elevator door closed, and Mark was left alone in the hallway. It reminded him of every nondescript office environment he had ever been in. Each step echoed until he finally reached the oak door at the end of the hallway where a bronze placard read "Mortal Resources."

Through the door, Mark found a large room that was painted in bright colors and resembled the waiting room at a pediatric doctor's office. On the opposite wall, he found a glass partition with a metal circular grate in it so the woman behind could be heard. On the wall to the left of the woman was a single door with a keypad but no doorknob. The room seemed strange when compared to the hallway leading to it, as if the rooms did not belong next to each other. From behind the glass, the woman who wore the outfit of a Soul called out to Mark. Her bright and cheerful face and voice fit perfectly with the décor and gave the impression that she was genuinely happy to help.

"Welcome, you must be Mark," she said through a round metal grate in the window. "Please, come fill out some paperwork and we will get you processed."

Mark made his way to the window, passing the rows of sofas and coffee tables holding assorted magazines. "I'm still a little confused…"

The woman quickly cut him off in an authoritative tone, which cut through her overly polite demeanor. "Please hold all your questions until after the onboarding process." Through a small opening at the bottom of the window, the woman slid a clipboard with a pen and some papers attached. Returning to her overly sweet voice, she followed with, "Please take a seat and let me know when you are finished!"

As Mark backed away, the woman continued to stare forward through him as if she was expecting someone else to come through the door, but nobody ever did. He took a seat on one of the couches and found himself sitting across from a creature in a Soul's outfit with no face, only a blank slate where a face should be. At first, he assumed it was a doll of some kind until it started to move using human mannerisms, crossing and uncrossing his legs, folding his arms. Mark did his best to ignore the faceless man and focus instead on the paperwork. It was fairly straightforward for the first several pages, asking for information about previous employers and job responsibilities before moving on to personal questions regarding interests and habits. The last five pages came as a questionnaire with bizarre questions that read half like a personality test and half like riddles.

Question 3:

If John has 3 apples and Jorge has 9 oranges, how many vowels do their names share?

Question 7:

On a scale of one to five, how would you rate the number seven.

Question 11:

John is taller than Mat. Mat is taller than TJ. What is John's race or ethnicity?

Question 18:

If Sally sells sea shells down by the sea shore, where does she sell her body?

Question 23:

If a man goes into the woods with a bear, what kind is it?

Question 31:

Can you read well enough to answer this question?

Once he had completed the paperwork, he brought it to the window and slid it through the opening where the woman was quick to grab it. Without breaking eye contact from the task of separating and sorting his paper work, the woman said, "Please come through the door to your right and down the hall. Take your first two lefts and then your third right until you come to a four-way intersection. Once there, take a right and then an immediate left until you come to a T-junction where you will take another right. Pass three doors and then enter the door on the left where you will find the onboarding room." Then, with a snide and condescending stare, she finished with, "And please don't get lost."

The door opened with an electronic buzz. Mark tried to follow the directions that had been given to him as he navigated the maze like hallways of Mortal Resources. The walls were painted much like the waiting room, and it became hard to focus as each open door he passed showed him more and more of the inner workings of the office. Doorways to offices littered the walls, some led to rooms that looked completely normal, a meek looking man or woman sitting behind a small desk typing away at some report, the occasional fern or small office plant. Others housed men and women dressed in horse saddles and nothing else being ridden by one the Fallen. He had often made jokes about decisions being made by throwing darts at a poster and was not the least bit shocked to find it actually happened here.

Eventually, after several wrong turns and dead ends, Mark found and entered the room with the plastic placard that read "Onboarding" and was surprised to find that he was not the only one going through the onboarding process.   Two others, both wearing Souls outfits and sitting in uncomfortable looking chairs, turned to look at him as he entered. The room was painted white and only held a total of three chairs. In the left sat a younger looking man, younger than Mark at least, who looked on with a sense of confidence. His hair was short and spiky, and his light brown skin was covered in dark tattoos that climbed the back of his neck and looked out of place poking out from under the oversized white button-up shirt. The man on the right was a large black man who appeared to be struggling as his bald head and face started to tint red from his overtight white button-up. After seeing that this was but another Soul, the two men both returned to looking forward and stare at the wall.

As soon as he sat down, the projector sprung to life, and a movie started on the wall in front of them. Mark turned to see where the image was coming from but found nothing. What started was a black and white training film that began with the title screen "Welcome to Your Afterlife!" that faded into the image of a Fallen who shared the same 1950s handsome looks as Jack. Through clever editing, his eyes seemed to focus on Mark as the man said, "Greetings and welcome to your eternity! You are here because you have been offered a chance to serve in hell rather than be punished."

As he started walking to the right, the screen started scrolling and revealed a heavyset man in a skin-tight Soul's outfit just off screen. The Soul carried a large boulder along a track until he reached the end, where he put it down, picked up a different one, and struggled to carry it back the way he came. "This is Joseph," the man said he passed the track. "Joseph here spent his living days in a life of Sloth, so here he is forced to constantly move. Hundreds of people like Joseph are arriving daily, people who have lived in a life of sin. As you would expect, the work load to manage, track, and recruit is just too much for the Fallen to handle on their own. It is because of this demand that the work assignment program was created."

The screen transitioned to an animated short of a city being built as his voice continued, "The Employment sector was originally built to house both Souls and the offices created to perform their assigned job duties, but as we grew, an alternate housing solution was needed, and so the Complex was built."

The screen transitioned back to a picture of the man. "This is a program where the skills you held in life could be used in your afterlife in lieu of an eternity of torment." In the background, the heavyset man fell to his knees in exhaustion, and as he did, cuts started to form in his shirt and flesh as he screamed out in pain. He struggled to stand and pick up the rock, and as he did, he was washed in a wave of relief as the wounds and clothing tears mended themselves. "In each of your living quarters, you will find a book of regulations and explanations to help you adjust to your new life. In the event you are found unfit to perform the task in which you have been selected, then your offer will be revoked and you will be sentenced." As the camera followed the Fallen, the tormented man moved off screen to the left as a background piece resembling an office breakroom entered from the right.

"Next, I would like to talk to you about approved and acceptable interactions with your coworkers. As people work together, relationships and bonds form. Such has happened between Derek, Sheila, and Roger."

He continued to walk right as the camera stopped and focused on three people, two men and a woman who sat around a table in the breakroom set. As the lights came up, the taller of the men looked at the others and said, "So do you guys want to hang out tonight?"

The woman looked at the shorter man, and both nodded in unison. She said, "We could go get a bite and cruse around the Wastelands!" to which the two men both looked excited and nodded.

Finally, the shorter man said, "Sounds great, guys. We just have to remember to be careful out there. Well, let's all head back to work!" Then the lights dimmed while the demon stepped back onto the screen.

"We understand that Mortals are social creatures and encourage you to mingle and find friends. Please keep in mind that you are required to work your assigned shift, and failure to do so could void your contract. That being said, before and after your assigned shifts, you are free to do as you please." He again started to walk right as the camera followed, and as before, when the last scene started to disappear to the left, a new scene started on the right.

The new scene showed a row of adjoined desks that mimicked a call center environment, complete with people dressed in Soul's outfits wearing headsets. "Your exact job duties will be described by the leader you will meet today. Remember, work does not have to be all work, and eternity is what you make of it!"

As the call center scene passed to the left, a single door appeared on the right. "We have found that most people in your situation feel that their afterlife can be almost identical to their living life. If you do what you are told and follow the rules, then this can be a fulfilling and rewarding experience. This ends the video portion of your onboarding. I do hope you have found it entertaining as well as informative. Please remain seated, and you will be collected shortly." With that, the demon turned and walked through the door as the screen faded to black.

The lights came up and the three sat in silence until the door opened behind them. In unison, the three men turned to find a tall woman wearing a Soul's outfit and holding a clipboard. Her pants were short on her, causing a three-inch gap between her ankle and pant leg and accentuating her already lanky and unfeminine figure. She wore her blonde hair with bangs covering her brown eyes and the rest pulled back into a tight bun.

"Good morning gentlemen." Her voice was weak and mousy, which contrasted the confidence her stance and body language portrayed. "My name is Rebecca. Please follow me."

Mark and his fellow on-boarders stood and followed her through the door. As they headed through the maze of Mortal Relations, Rebecca said, "I'm from Acquisitions and Recruiting, and I'll be taking you to your individual leaders. Through the MR offices, they prefer we be a little quiet, but as soon as we hit the elevator, I'll be more than happy to try and answer any questions you have."

As the four of them walked through the hallways, it became harder and harder for Mark to remember where he was. Aside from the redundancy of the maze, the offices seemed to run like any he had ever seen. Unsure about the previous experience of his fellow on-boarders, it was hard to speak on their behalf, but as they moved deeper into the building, Mark could understand what the Fallen had meant when he said Souls found this life not much different than their previous.

In what seemed like a considerably shorter time than it had taken him to get in, Mark found himself back in the waiting room, which was now empty. Rebecca offered a polite greeting to the woman behind the glass, who smiled and offered a nicety in exchange before resuming her blank forward stare. Once in the elevator, after the doors closed, Rebecca looked at her clipboard and asked "Who's David?"

The larger bald man spoke up. "That's me, ma'am."

Rebecca smiled. "Southern hospitality is rare around here; you're going to stick out."

His face turned to one of defeat, and she assured him it was in a good way, explaining, "Demons love having their ego stroked. You can get away with a lot of you treat them like royalty."

She looked equally to all three men in an effort to make sure they all understood. The elevator door slid open, revealing a large call center floor.

Rebecca stepped out of the elevator and asked Mark and the short Hispanic man to wait.

As the door slid closed, an uncomfortable silence took over until the stranger next to him asked Mark, "So what did you do?"

Mark thought about the question for a moment, but the only reasonable answer he could think of was "I guess I was just a shitty person." The two men laughed. Curious, Mark asked "What about you?"

Without missing a beat, the short man responded, "After years of being screwed over, I strangled my boss to death with his own necktie." An awkward silence again filled the empty space until he continued. "Year after year, he held me down because of my race, and finally I just snapped, you know?" He was taken aback at the casualness of the conversation. Mark had never heard someone talk about murder so nonchalantly. The Hispanic man continued, "For years I watched the man steal my ideas and take credit for my work, and I couldn't take anymore."

The elevator doors slid open and Rebecca joined them again. As the doors closed behind her, she looked at her clipboard and asked, "Which one of you is Pedro?" Not sure how serious she was, both men offered a confused look to the other. With frustration peeking through her meek voice, Rebecca said, "I'm not stupid, you guys. I have to ask," and she rolled her eyes. The door slid open, and Pedro followed Rebecca off the elevator, leaving Mark alone with his thoughts. It never occurred to him that people who had done terrible things, real terrible things, would be offered the opportunity he was. In his mind, he imagined this would be the equivalent of a minimum security prison.

The elevator slid open and Rebecca entered again. "So that makes you Mark, right?" she asked while looking at her clipboard. Mark smiled the polite smile you give strangers on elevators and nodded. "Good deal, you are going to Acquisitions and Recruiting with me. Our leader is Cedric. He's not bad for a Demon. Mention how great his hair looks, and he becomes putty."

Confused, Mark asked, "Why do you call them Demons? I thought they were the Fallen?"

Her face scrunched as she spoke of what she clearly thought was a delicate subject. It's best if you just call them demons. Some of them take offence when we say the Fallen; it's kind of like their "N" word. Most of us use biblical terms, Heaven and Hell, Angel and Demon. The Demons understand that most of us know these terms and prefer it to the familiarity that comes with using theirs."

Her face returned to normal as the elevator door slid open a final time and they both exited. "Overall, ours is a pretty sweet gig." Rebecca voice became harder to hear as the noise from the office surroundings took over. "Everything just kind of works, you know? The elevator takes you where you need to be, any computer you sit at knows who you are. Depending on the task you are assigned, you will either research new prospects or review current prospects for change."

Confused, Mark asked, "Prospects?"

The two of them stopped at an oak door, much like the one in Moral Resources. "Yeah, prospects. We are the wheeling and dealing department." Behind the door was a dark hallway also similar to the one he had previously seen that led to a single oak door with a placard that read the single word "Offices." Through the next oak door, Mark found a hallway filled with offices on each side, each housing a large metal desk and computer, but otherwise all originally decorated and different from the rest.

"Everybody wants something," Rebecca continued, "and we weigh the cost of giving what they want verses their value to Hell. Say a goody two shoes off handedly says they would sell their Soul for a candy bar. The information is fed to us by our scouts and with the who, what, when, and where, a researcher, one of us, will find it and bring it to a recruiter, a Demon, and they draw a contract and try to get them to sign it." Mark had the sudden realization that one of these offices belonged to Jack and wondered who it was that had brought his file there.

At the end of the hallway, the two came to a set of wooden double doors. Rebecca knocked lightly and from behind, Mark could hear a man's voice bellow, "Enter!" The doors opened under their own power, and behind them, a slender, effeminate Demon sat behind a metal desk. His office was large and cozy in the style of a wood cabin, making the metal desk look out of place. To the left, a crackling fireplace caused shadows to dance on the right wall, which was filled with pictures of famous actors, all men. The Demon asked, "What can I do for you, Rebecca?" without looking away from the mirror in front of him. He looked different than every other Demon Mark had encountered. Instead of the golden age of television, when actors were brawny and masculine, this Demon appeared to take his inspiration from popular culture throughout the new millennium.

She responded, "I've got the newbie here, thought you would like to meet him."

A gasp of impatience and disgust escaped from behind the desk as the Demon accepted that he would have to stop what he was doing. He pointed at Mark from behind the desk. "What, is that him? Well come on, sit down, let us get this over with."

Mark took a seat in front of the desk as Rebecca closed the door. The two stared at each other in silence until Mark finally said, "I like your hair."

The Demon raised a single eyebrow and then stood up and started pacing behind the desk. "Do you know what my department does?" the Demon put a lot of emphasis on ownership in the statement as he did his best to mimic the scene portrayed in many movies of an authority figure behind his desk.

"Yes?' Mark answered as more of a question than a statement.

Ignoring his response, the Demon continued, "There is a joke that I made up that has become pretty popular among the living. Would you like to hear it?" Before Mark could answer, he continued, "A man asks a woman to fuck him and she says no. The man offers the woman a million dollars to fuck him, and she says yes. Finally, the man offers the woman twenty dollars to fuck him, and she yells at him, asking if he thinks she is a whore, and he replies, 'we have established what you are; now we are negotiating.'"

Mark offered a small smile at the joke, a courtesy that Cedric clearly appreciated. He continued, "What we do here is find prospects. Everybody wants something, and it is our job to determine if giving it to them is mutually beneficial. If they have offered their Soul, then it is our job to try and take it from them." The Demon stopped and sat back in his chair, checking his appearance in the mirror as he did so. "We are basically looking for the innocent and the extreme. The extreme allow us to remind the living world that evil exists, so when they offer their Soul, even though they are pretty worthless as far as stock goes, we help them out. The innocent, on the other hand, are very valuable but are hard to get, so when they make mistakes we pounce." Cedric leaned back in his chair with a sense of accomplishment and Pride at his explanation.

"What about the 37.9 percent rule?" Mark asked.

A half-smile crossed Cedric's face. "So I take it you are a Special Case?" The Demon's body language suddenly changed from relaxed to serious. "The 37.9 percent rule is monitored by another department; you will not have access to those files. You will also not have access to files of people who have already passed. We only deal with the living in this department." He checked his hair in the mirror again and then turned to the computer and started typing. "You know what? I like you. You seem like a smart guy, and I believe you will do well here. I'm going to assign you to updates. I'm sending an email to Rebecca so she can find someone to train you." In an over exaggerated motion, he pressed the final key and announced, "Sent! The update position is the easier of the areas in our department, less stress, more down time." A knock at the door made Mark jump. "Enter!" Cedric called out as the door again automatically opened.

Turning back to the mirror, he then said, "Now if you have no other questions, you can leave."

Mark stood, "I do have one last question." Cedric responded with a full-body sigh, mimicking a teenage who was being asked to perform chores. "Where can I get a better set of clothes?" The Demon responded only with a puzzled look, and Mark followed up, "A set of clothes that actually fits?"

Cedric let out a loud, howling, exaggerated, laugh, and when he had composed himself, through tears rolling down his face he replied, "This is the Underworld, everything here is kind of inconvenient. Did your recruiter not go over this with you?" Without waiting for a response, the Demon turned back to the mirror.

Walking through the hallway, Mark found that many of the office doors that were previously open had been closed. "How'd it go?" Rebecca asked. "You must have done something right; he assigned you to Updates, which is a cushy gig."

With a small sense of satisfaction, Mark replied, "Yeah, I took your advice and commented on his hair."

Rebecca smiled as they entered the call center floor. The area was the size of a football field and filled with rows of four interlocking desks with waste high walls separated by a walkway for easy access. Sporadically spread out through the center stood slightly larger desks. Mark followed Rebecca though through the maze of desks to a slightly larger one where she sat down and pulled a list of names on her computer. "I don't know how other departments work, but we are a pretty tight group. You've seen our leader. He's kind of self-absorbed, and that's great because he really just leaves us to our own devices. In fact, even getting him to meet new people can be kind of a pain. I'm going to assign Tony as your mentor. It looks like he is your carpool driver anyway, so he has the same shift assignment." She then stood up and started walking again through the maze.

Tony's desk was filled with hand-drawn pictures of dragons and knights battling. As Mark and Rebecca approached, he was hunched over his desk with headphones on paying careful attention to the scales on his latest creation. His dark hair hung over his eyes and covered half of his round and pale face.

"Tony!" Rebecca attempted to shout with her meek voice. Tony looked up with and smiled when he saw his visitor. "Tony, this is Mark."

Tony pulled off his headphones and shook his head to get the bangs out of his eyes before extending his hand, which Mark took. "It's good to meet you, Mark."

Rebecca leaned again the wall of his cube. "Tony was one of the first employees here, so I'm sure he can show you the ins and outs. You don't mind being a mentor again, do you?"

Tony offered a friendly smile. "You know me, always ready to help."

"Great! I'll send you Mark's details," and with that, Rebecca excused herself and made her way back through the call center maze. Tony pulled the rolling chair from the empty cube next to him and offered it to Mark. "So the good news is that our day is almost over." Confused, Mark looked around for a clock. It felt like he had just gotten here and was shocked to find it was almost 2pm. Sensing his confusion, Tony explained, "We run on seven six-hour days, 8am to 2pm. No rest for the wicked, you know?"

"What do you do with the other 18 hours of the day?" Mark asked.

A large smile crossed Tony's face. "Pretty much whatever you want. If you know someone with a car then Hell is your oyster. Just stick with me."

Mark rode the elevator down with Tony and once outside, found a tall and round man with bright red face and a bushy Santa-est beard. He stood next to a young and short teenage girl disinterested teenage girl with pale skin waiting for them in the flood of others dressed in similar Soul outfits. The juxtaposition of the two made them hard to miss even in the crowd, and when Tony stood between them, it looked like a staircase made out of people. "Mark, this is Jessie and Laura. They both share our carpool."

The teenage girl rolled her eyes and muttered, "Great, now I have to share the backseat."

Tony laughed. "Never mind Laura," he explained. "Her hormones followed her to the afterlife." Laura responded with a mean face and a middle finger.

Tony walked to the valet while Jessie introduced himself. "Nice to meet you, Mark. Guess this means I'm not the new guy anymore!" He let out a jolly laugh, and Mark couldn't help but notice that it made his belly shake like a bowl full of jelly. A blue compact sedan, similar to the one Jack had that morning, rounded the corner, and another creature in a Soul's outfit with no face exited the car and handed Tony the keys.

Mark followed the three to the car and entered the passenger side backseat. He found Tony's driving habits mirrored Jack's. As the car pulled from the office building and onto the road, he accelerated quickly until the car was keeping up with other traffic. The only difference from the morning's ride was the increased amount of cars. With so many going just as quickly as they, it became easy to forget just how fast they were going.

"Dinner tonight?" Jessie asked the car. Laura provided her sigh of indifference, which she used to express almost every emotion, and in this case, was accepted as a yes. "What about you, Mark?" Tony asked.

"Thanks, but no, I think I need to spend some time and process everything."

From between the seats, Jessie's arm found Mark's knee, and as he patted it, he offered in a reassuring voice, "We understand. We've all been there. It's lucky for you that you found us. My first group was terrible." Strangely, Mark felt better.

Mark kept to himself for the remainder of the trip. It wasn't the strange things he had seen or heard that bothered him, but how well he was adjusting. Climbing out of the car, Tony called to him, "Find your handbook and read Chapter 5. It's going to make tomorrow a lot easier to understand." Before speeding off and he leaving him alone at his new home.

He opened the door and walked in, taking time to look at everything he missed that morning. The living area was smaller than he remembered, and exploration didn't seem to take him as long as he would have thought. Much of his original assessment was correct. It was a single bedroom connected to a small living area by a hallway. The only closet was in the bedroom, which also held the only clock. 4:18pm. Where did the time go? Mark stumbled back out to the living area and plopped on the couch, where he wished he would have gone with Tony. On top of the old TV, Mark spotted the book that Jack had been reading that morning. He thought back to the orientation video. That must have been the book everyone had been referring to. He retrieved the book from atop the TV and returned to the love seat, kicking his shoes off in the process. The book was deceptively heavy considering its size and appeared to be wrapped in a thick, dark cloth. Opening the cover, Mark saw the title page:

An Introduction to the Underworld
By Phelix Utengard

As he turned the page, dust clouded from the rustling of the page. Mark read over the chapter topics:

Chapter 1: In the Beginning
Chapter 2: The Life of a Soul
Chapter 3: The Complex
Chapter 4: The Employment Sector
Chapter 5: The Wasteland
Chapter 6: Prophecies and Things to Come
Index

As Mark flipped through the book, he found the pages were filled with crude drawings etched out in sloppy lines and shading that accompanied many of the topics. With each page turn, he found that more and more of the book was built up not around information, but these drawings, which felt ominous and triggered a sense of dread.

In Chapter 5, Phelix writes:

"The Wasteland is defined as any place outside of the
Complex and the Employment Sector. It is modeled after
the barren and desolate plains many Souls know as deserts."

Well, that was pretty obvious, Mark thought to himself as he skimmed down the page.

"The Tormented travel in groups and are scattered
throughout the Wasteland and can become hostile to Souls
who cross their paths. While they are social creatures,
humans also tend to be irrational (especially the
Tormented). If you choose to travel the Wasteland, you
should be sure not to draw unneeded attention to yourself."

Mark continued to skim through the handbook until he found a sub-chapter titled "Sins."

"All sins are categorized during Judgement.
Pride – Any sin where the offender performs an action
with Prideful intent. Offenders are typically sentenced to an
empty shell and work in the Employment Sector.
Sloth – Any sin performed because of the inaction of a
Soul. Offenders are typically sentenced to move and
perform constantly and are punished if they stop.
Envy – Any sin performed in an effort to take what
others have. Offenders are denied a shell and sentenced to
roam the underworld seeing the small luxuries others have.
Greed – Any sin performed for personal gain or status
change. Offenders are typically sentenced to carry their
weight in gold and are punished if they put it down.
Lust – The sin of causing pain in others in an effort to
cause pleasure to oneself. Offenders are denied the ability to
feel and sentenced to the Employment Sector.
Gluttony – Any sin performed in an effort to keep
others from gaining. Offenders are typically sentenced to
give of themselves, providing a day of relief for another
random Soul and taking their punishment for those 24
hours.
Wrath – The sins of taking a life (including your own)
or acting in violence to benefit oneself. Offenders
extremities are confined within cages and all pain generated

through any direct action by any Demon to any other Soul is re-lived by them.

For more information, please see individual entries for each sin.

Mark put the book down and thought back to the orientation. He had seen someone who had been judged of Sloth, but even then it wasn't until now that it really hit him. It wasn't until now that he understood that he was in Hell.

Day 2

"So the idea is that you just listen to recordings and update the account. It's all pretty straightforward." Tony clicked an icon on his computer and volume sprang to life in the headset.

"Week January 8th through January 14th. Year 2001. Subject: Bobby McDonald."

Tony hit the pause button. "So now we pull up Bobby in our system." Tony started typing the name, and within seconds, Bobby's profile was listed on the screen with the options UPDATE, DELETE, and CONTRACT. "To show you how easy this is, you see how the only option not greyed out is update?" he asked.

"How do we know we have the right profile?" Mark asked.

"The computer does it all." Tony shrugged before saying, "I'm not really sure how it works. If we open up his record we see that Bobby is a pretty bad boy. He's got two counts of Greed, two counts of Lust, and three counts of Wrath. See, Bobby is rated 70; the scale goes from 10 to 90. Chances are he would never get a deal, as he is probably coming here anyways, but we still have to update his record."

Tony hit the play button and the recording started again, "January 10th, 7pm. Subject Macdonald sins in an effort to garner personal gain. Greed. End log." Tony clicked a small plus sign that created a new line where he entered the date and one count of Greed before saving his work and closing the window.

"Does the 37 percent rule mean anything to you?" Mark asked.

Tony cocked his head slightly and thought for a moment before shrugging and offering, "Doesn't ring any bells," as he opened the next email in the queue and clicked the play button.

"Week January 29th through February 4th. Year 2001. Subject: Bobby McDonald."

Tony hit the pause button and typed the name Bobby McDonald back into the system, generating the same account. "It's important to always do a new search even for the same name. Just always trust the system."

Mark nodded before asking, "Why is it from so long ago?"

Tony turned and offered a confused look. "How do you mean?"

"Well, I lived until the year 2015. Why are we listening to things from the year 2001?"

Tony's eyes drifted off to the side for a moment, and when he returned he said, "You know, I honestly don't remember how long I've been here."

It confused Mark how someone could forget their living life. "How did you die?"

Without a pause, Tony casually responded, "I was eaten by a dragon," Before turning back to the computer.

"So what happens if they die before we've updated their information?" Mark asked.

"Not sure," Tony responded. "From what I understand, the Demons see a clock on people, and that determines how quickly things are updated. I asked Cedric about it one day, and he told me he hates it because it takes up too much screen space when he's watching his stories."

At 10am, Tony lead Mark to a breakroom, one similarly designed to the one of in the training video he had watched. Tony poured himself a cup of coffee and offered one to Mark, who declined. "So what's the 37 percent rule?" Tony asked as he took his first sip.

Mark let out a long sigh. "When I was recruited, I was told that it was because of the 37 percent rule. I was told that if someone has wasted 37.9 percent of their life, then they are seen as un-savable, and they are just punished with no trial. I was told that I am a Special Case."

Tony nodded along. "I've heard the leaders talking about Special Cases and met a few who claimed the status here and there before, but I'm not totally sure what it means."

Mark stood and started to pace as he felt the excitement might overflow from him. For a week he had nobody to talk to about this, and now that it was considered a normal conversation, he didn't know how to handle himself. "The fourth time the recruiter met with me…"

Tony cut him off. "You had a recruiter try to sign you four times?" Mark shook his head. "No, I signed after the third time, I think."

Mark could hear the shock in Tony's normally calm and low voice. "That's crazy, I've never heard of a Demon spending that much time with a prospect!"

Mark thought back to that fourth time. Jack had said most people only meet him once. "The fourth time we met, he told me that he could see most people's clocks but not mine."

Tony shrugged. "I don't know, man. Maybe it has something to do with your Special Case status. Honestly, the only people who could answer the question are the people in that department." Feeling dejected, Mark sat back down.

After their break, Mark took the seat next to Tony and shook the mouse to his computer, bringing the screen to life. He clicked the email icon and found that he had already received work items and a few personal messages. He clicked on the one from Rebecca, which read:

Mark,
I wanted to take a moment to make sure you were all set up
and ready for your own workload. Tony's a great teacher and
the job really isn't that hard to begin with, you know? Anyways,
let me know if you need anything.
Rebecca

He clicked the reply button and typed the simple message:
Thanks Rebecca, will do.
and clicked send.

The next email came from Cedric and was the single word "Welcome"
followed by his elaborate signature and a photo of himself. Mark looked to
Tony, who was already hunched over with his headphones on and drawing.
He opened the first work item and clicked play on the audio message.

"Week June 6th through June 12th. Year 2005. Subject: Christina
Snyder." Mark typed the name in the search box as Tony did and a profile
appeared. Mark selected the update option and continued. "June 9th, 3pm.
Subject Snyder sins in an effort to garner personal gain. Greed. June 11th,
3pm. Subject Snyder sins in an effort to garner personal gain. Greed. End
log." The recording stopped and as Tony had taught him, Mark created new
entries in the log, saved the changes, and opened the next work item. "Week
April 8th through April 14th. Year 2002. Subject: Adam Teegan." Mark
typed the name in and received the following error:

Error 439

Mark looked over to Tony, who was distracted in his own work, and
thought it best not to bother him. He pulled up his email and sent an email to
Rebecca:

Rebecca,
I'm not totally sure what to do here. I have a work item and
when I search for the record I get an Error 439, any ideas?
Thanks, Mark.

Within minutes she had replied:

Mark,
When you come across any 400 errors it means that it is
either something you do not have access to or it's in the wrong
department. You can disregard these work items; they must
have been routed to you in error. It happens from time to time.
Keep up the great work!
Rebecca.

Mark did as he was told and pulled the next work item. The recording started, "Week October 8th through October 14th. Year 2001. Subject: Grant Wetsker." The rest of the day passed with relative ease, and before long, the day was over.

"So how was it?" Tony asked as the elevator door closed.

Mark shrugged his shoulders. "I got a 400 error. Do you know what those codes mean?"

Tony scrunched his face as he shook his head. "Nope, all I know is that they are another department. It's either they don't have a record or they have already sold their Soul, or maybe they are already dead, we just skip them and go on to the next."

Mark nodded. "Yeah, that's what Rebecca told me."

Jessie and Laura were waiting outside, doing their best to distance themselves from other gathering groups, when Mark and Tony exited the building. Jessie greeted both men with a sturdy handshake while Laura leaned against the wall and rolled her eyes at the display. "How was it?" he asked.

Mark shrugged and said, "I think it's something I can handle, nothing too difficult." Jessie let out a rolling laugh as he patted Mark on the shoulder.

After the car pulled around, the four entered as they did the previous day. As the car pulled away, Tony announced, "I think we should take a detour and show Mark the wastes. What do you guys think?"

In contrast to the previous day, Jessie offered an indifferent response while Laura sat up straight and excitedly Greed.

"Is it safe?" Mark asked. "Doesn't the handbook say not to do that?"

Laura offered a disgusted sigh. "Don't be lame!" she shouted as she playfully pushed Mark. "The Wastelands are the best part of this place! Can we go, please?" Laura noticed Tony's smile through the rearview mirror and quickly reverted to her mopey self.

The radio played "Comedown" by Bush as they passed through the gates and into the Wasteland. The three talked of the day's events and evening's plans while Mark leaned his head against the window and thought of the long bus rides he would take, which only led to other things he left behind, which eventually led to thoughts of Julie. He hadn't thought about her since arriving, and he felt guilty because of it. He remembered their last night together on the swings. He remembered the strange feeling of being content, the same feeling he felt now.

Tony veered the car off the road and into the vastness of the open and empty Wasteland. Laura pressed her face to the window with a newfound sense of excitement. "The last time we came out here we saw a Sloth group within minutes. It was so cool!"

Tony added, "The tormented are usually too busy with their punishment to really bother with us. As long as we don't run into a Wrath group, we should be fine."

Before long, even the walls of the employment sector had faded from sight. Laura bounced around the car, looking in all directions for something interesting to look at. Tony's eyes met Mark's through the rearview mirror and he commented, "Don't worry man, a lot of us come out here just to break up the monotony. It's something different, you know?"

The silence was suddenly broken by Laura's excited shouts as she did her best to climb through the front car seats and point out the windshield. "There, there, there!" she shouted as she pointed towards a lone figure in the distance.

Tony slowed the car as the figure got closer. "Calm down! I'm not sure what he's out here for. He doesn't look like a Sloth."

Laura squinted her eyes and Jessie chimed in, "It could be an Envy."

Laura added, "This far out? Ha, who's he going to be envious of out here?"

With a sense of concern in his voice, Jessie said, "Is it a Greed?"

From the back seat, Mark spoke up, "I thought they were supposed to carry a shitload of gold on their backs?"

The car rolled to a stop as the creature continued his approach. He wore the outfit of a Soul, but each of his hands were incased in a separate square metal cage. As casually as he could, Tony reached down and slid the car into reverse. "That my friends," he started, "that is a Wrath." And with that, Tony slammed on the gas petal, forcing the car to speed backwards. The creature broke into a jog as Tony slammed the breaks and pulled hard on the wheel, causing the front end to spin forward before changing to drive and again stomping the gas.

Laura and Mark spun around to look at the action from the back window, and Jessie shouted, "Go, go, go!" The creature fell out of his jog and returned to his casual walk as the car sped off in the opposite direction.

"That was so cool!" Laura cried out as she returned to her sitting position. "I don't even remember the last time we saw a singular Wrath!"

In an attempt to add some context for Mark, Jessie added "Normally, the Wrath travel together and stick to their own kind. Usually, if you come across a Wrath group it is very clear from a distance, and most of us would leave before they noticed us."

A sly smile crossed Laura's face. "And by most of us, he means lame people."

Jessie attempted to resort to her level by making a face and sticking out his tongue, only to have the action returned by the young teenager.

Mark asked, "If they usually stick in a group, then why was this one out wandering alone?"

Looking through the rearview, Tony responded, "So I guess you didn't read the whole hand book?" Mark looked at Laura, who shared the look of parental disappointment that Tony offered.

Defensively, Mark responded, "You said read chapter 5! That's the only one I've read so far. I've only been here for 2 days guys. Give me a break."

Day 6

Wayne Douglas
Error 418

Each day it was a different error with no explanation other than the one provided to him by Rebecca. Mark had taken to searching for friends and acquaintances in his down time. It started with Julie whose profile appeared the same as it had been for the past four days.

Julie Monroe   Birth: 1984/6/16   Death: _____
42%   Cause of Death: _____
Assignment: _____
2005/5/13 Lust
2005/5/15 Lust
2005/5/15 Greed
2005/5/16 Lust
2005/6/20 Lust

Fourty-two percent. He thought back to what Tony had said about the numbers and what they meant. Compared to what he had seen, 42 percent wasn't really that high, but if he was dammed for 37.9 percent, then what did it mean for her?

But every time he searched for Wayne, a new error came up. He considered the options. Sure Wayne was a nice enough guy, but to be completely without sin? Could it be that he just didn't have a record? The reasoning was better than the alternative, that he had already had a deal or that he was already dead.

"So nobody has ever found it?" Mark asked as he took a seat in the breakroom.

Tony started to pour himself a cup of coffee. "No, people don't even know if it exists. Shit, people don't even know if Phelix Utengard ever existed. Some people say it was just a pen name to put on the book for mortals to adjust. Makes sense, right? Would you rather have a handbook written by a Soul or a Demon?"

Rebecca entered the breakroom and overheard the last part of the conversation. "What are we talking about guys? Any juicy gossip?"

Tony joined Mark at the table with his coffee. "New guy just finally got around to reading through the handbook."

Rebecca laughed as she poured her own cup of coffee. "Good old Phelix Utengard. So I guess this is about the prophecies then?"

Interested in getting another opinion, Mark responded, "Yeah, the one about there being a stairway in the wastes."

Rebecca took the last chair at the table. "I don't know, a lot of those prophecies are kind of farfetched but Tony's actually seen one or two come true."

Mark turned to Tony, who let a long sigh from being thrown under the bus. "Look, let me start by saying that nearly everybody who comes down here reads those stories and looks for meaning. I personally think that's why they were written, to give us something to do and keep us focused." He then leaned into the table, prompting both Mark and Rebecca to do the same. "That being said, I know a single prophecy that most people witness as coming true. It said

Born in a year that a new land is born
On his 37th year, his world would be torn
At night, the shadows is where he must stay
The world must not know who he is in the day
On his 37th year, his world would be torn
His 38th year, a king would be born"

Mark looked between Tony and Rebecca anxiously waiting for the next one to speak until Tony continued. "Now I don't know it for sure and really only Phelix could tell, but a long time ago, there was a Demon named Isaac Lanson who people claimed to be this man. The Demon himself was mostly quiet and reserved and looked like no other Demon. He chose to look human but not flashy or handsome. He spent time with Souls and spoke to us like he was one of us. It all started in this breakroom, when someone was asking him about his life and he told his story. He said that he was born the year the country of America gained its independence. He said that he was a moral and upright man, a preacher, until his wife was killed. The loss caused him to seek vengeance on the men who committed the crime, and the following year, when he was caught, he had taken 73 lives. He said he was sentenced for execution at the age of 38, and as he died, he was given a trial between heaven and hell. He said that due to most of his life, heaven wanted him spared, but due to the later part of his life, hell demanded that he would serve. A compromise was made and he was given the choice of his fate, and he chose hell to be punished for his sins. Unhappy with his choice, heaven made him an angel so that when he arrived in hell, he was not a Soul, but a Demon. Upon learning his fate, he became outraged that he was not given the chance for redemption."

Mark sat back in the chair as both Tony and Rebecca took sips of their coffee. "So what happened to him?" he asked.

Tony simply offered a shrug and said, "Nobody knows. They say that one day he just walked into the Wasteland but nobody has seen him since."

Rebecca stood and said, "Alright guys, enough filling the new guy's head with stories."

The three headed back out into the call center. Mark sat down at his desk and put his headphones on. He looked over to Tony, who had already started his next work item and was mindlessly typing away. Mark opened his next work item and continued to work.

Day 10

"You wanted to see me, sir?"

Cedric sat behind his desk admiring himself in the mirror, and without looking away, he replied, "Yes, come in."

Mark entered the office and closed the door behind him before taking a seat in front of the desk. He sat in silence and watched as Cedric ran his hands through his hair while admiring the way it fell as he waited for the conversation to start. "Sir?" he finally asked, only for the Demon to throw his hands in the air and slouch back in his chair like a child.

"What?" he bellowed before remembering he had made this meeting. Sitting up and attempting to act more like an authority figure, he said "Yes, I remember. I was asked to follow up with you and see if you had any issues or questions."

Mark thought it a strange reason to have a meeting after what Rebecca had told him about Cedric and his lack of connection with the department he led. "No, I think I've got— before Mark could finish, Cedric cut him off.

"Good, Great! Ok, that will be all." And then he provided a condescending smile, which looked awkward on his feminine face. Mark sat in silence, slightly confused, until Cedric followed up with, "You can leave now," and continued to smile.

Rebecca was waiting for him by his cube. "What was that all about?" she asked.

Mark took his seat. "Honestly, I'm not totally sure. He just asked me if I had any issues or questions."

Rebecca nodded thoughtfully. "Yeah, that's strange. He hates having to meet with us, so actually making a meeting is kind of out of character."

Mark thought back. "He said he was asked to follow up with me, but he acted like it was a huge inconvenience."

Tony pulled his headset off and said, "Looks like someone made a friend in management!" before singing, "Mark and Cedric sitting in a tree, F-U-C-K-I-N-G. First come's oral, then what's next? Everybody's favorite, it's butt sex!"

Mark raised a single eyebrow. "How could you possibly know that song?"

In unison, both Rebecca and Tony said, "Laura." Mark rolled his eyes.

Speaking of Laura," Tony continued, "she wants to get dinner tonight on the way back to the Complex, says she's got some big news."

Rebecca added, "Yeah, she invited me too. She's been running around here telling anybody who would listen about some mind blowing secret she has uncovered."

"I'm telling you, it's going to blow your minds!" Laura's energy and enthusiasm was even higher than when they found the Wrath. "Seriously you guys, you're going to be amazed!" Mark, Tony, Jessie, and Laura sat around a booth in what looked like a movie version of Applebee's.

In chapter 4, Phelix writes:

Because of the Greed of humanity, many deals are less beneficial to the mortal than they are to Hell. During a time of excess, one Demon offered success and prosperity to a restaurateur in exchange for not only his Soul, but also franchising rights. Seeing the benefit, the same Demon made similar deals with other restaurateurs, leading to the boom is chain restaurants. These franchise opportunities were placed in the Employment District where some Souls where assigned to serve their sentences. These Souls have been often been found guilty of Gluttony or lesser offences of Wrath and are given positions in which they not only have to provide but also must take the verbal abuse they have offered throughout their living time.

The waitress arrived as the group waited for Rebecca and others and offered an indifferent greeting and prepared for the worst. Following the suggestion of the handbook, both Laura and Jessie laid into the waitress with verbal assaults and insults regarding her timeliness and ability. Tony politely ordered a ribeye steak and Mark ordered the same. Rebecca joined the group as Laura seemed she was going to burst if she did not spill her news.

"Ok, I've waited long enough. Screw all them other fucks who didn't show up to have their minds blown!" Mark had been excited all day, and only found out from Jessie before entering the restaurant that Laura was known to do this frequently, and it was usually a letdown. Laura brought a handbook to the table and continued, "So the other day, I was reading the handbook, and I know I've said this before, but I seriously found a prophecy about me!"

A collective sigh came from the table as they all knew it was coming.

"I'm serious, you guys!" Laura persisted. "It all makes sense! This prophecy talks about a woman who was taken early in life with dark hair and who works in recruiting will cause a revolution, and that's totally me!"

Skeptical, Jessie said, "What exactly did it say. Let's see the actual prophecy?"

Laura rolled her eyes and muttered "Non-believers." as she flipped through the pages.

The food arrived, and Mark took a sip of his drink, which was watered down and warm. He thought back to his first meeting with Cedric. This is hell, after all. Laura continued to flip through the pages, reading a line of text every so often in an attempt to find the passage she was looking for when from across the restaurant, a woman caught Mark's attention.

He stood and excused himself as he made his way and met her halfway there. "Holy shit," She said, "I never thought I'd see you here."

Nicole stood before him in a Soul's outfit. She was exactly as he remembered her. For a moment, all the problems and issues and drama that filled the final days of his life vanished, and for that single moment, he was happy to see someone he knew. Mark opened his mouth, but before anything could come out, she cut him off.

"I never got to say it, but I'm sorry. I was kind of a crazy bitch. I had been hurt before, so I was looking for something that showed you were going to hurt me too."

Mark asked, "How are you here?"

Shame washed over her face as she told the story. "After I left that night, I overdosed. I was so upset and was so lost that I needed something to make me feel better, and before I knew it, I was here. I had so much to live for. I was getting my son back, but I needed instant gratification, and it cost me my life."

She wrapped her arms lightly around him as Mark whispered, "I'm so sorry." The restaurant noise died down at the display of affection, something not often seen there. Noticing the attention they had gathered, Mark led Nicole outside.

"Where have you been sentenced?" Mark asked as they took a seat on the curb.

"I'm working in Reinforcement. We sit and watch videos of the tormented all day and report when they are not complying with their punishment. What about you?"

Ignoring the question, the novelty of the reunion wore off, and Mark was overcome with the desire to tell her everything about the week of his death. "You have no idea what I was going through that week." He became fueled by the anger and frustration that he had no outlet for. "I was recruited by a Demon to work in Hell. He kept popping up in my dreams almost every time I fell asleep! And then, after days of not knowing if I'm crazy or not, you pushed me down the stairs!"

Mark took a long breath, and during the pause in his rant, Nicole spoke the words, "But I saw you with her."

Julie. A sudden realization washed over Mark as he realized that he had done to Nicole what he had done to so many women. Maybe not in her actions, but in her reasons she was justified. He never acted on feelings for Julie, but he couldn't honestly say he wouldn't have if given the chance, and the whole time he was lying to Nicole.

"I'm sorry, Nicole. I never meant to hurt you." As Mark spoke the words, he couldn't tell if it was something he meant or not.

The door to the restaurant opened, and Laura exited in a huff. "I'm telling you guys, I'm going to lead a revolution! I'm going to be queen of the Wastelands!"

The group exited behind her with Jessie still looking through the handbook. "I don't know, this is pretty vague. It could be anybody."

Tony followed up with, "It can't be you. It says whoever it is has to be beautiful."

Rebecca let out a laugh that ended with a snort as Jessie agreed, "Yep, it says so right here. Beautiful. Can't be you."

With a sense of new found nobility in her voice, Laura rolled her eyes and said "Peasants, I will remember this when I rule."

Mark stood as the group reached the curb and introduced Nicole. "We actually use to know each other in life," He explained as the group all said hello back.

"Well, I guess I should get back to my group. It was nice meeting you all," Nicole said before excusing herself and reentering the restaurant.

"What did I miss?" Mark asked.

"I'm going to be queen of the Wastelands!" Laura announced while taking a bow.

Jessie shook his head and, showing Mark the page, said, "Nope didn't change. Still says you have to be beautiful."

Laura responded with a swift kick to the shin before shouting, "Fuck all you guys!" and stomping back to the car.

Day 15

Mark started spending more time with Nicole if for no other reason because it made Hell feel more normal. They started with emails back and forth at work, dirty jokes and fond memories. They talked about the things they missed the most and the places they wished they had gone. Sure, Tony, Jessie, Rebecca, and even Laura were people Mark felt comfortable with. None of them had the familiarity of Nicole. None of them had the history like he had with her. Even with the history, it felt like they were meeting for the first time. In life, everything was very superficial and always about physicality, but now they were actually getting to know each other.

Coming back from break, Mark found a new email from Nicole:

Hey babe,

I got approved as a carpool! Wanna come with me tonight and take these wheels for a spin?

Mark typed the response:

Depends if take these wheels for a spin is a euphemism or not.

Nicole's next email came through shortly thereafter.

Have Tony drop you at Friday's, see you tonight!

During the elevator ride down at the end of the day, Mark asked Tony to drop him to meet Nicole, to which he graciously agreed. As the blue sedan pulled away, both Tony and Laura where shouting "Mark and Nicole, sitting in a tree!" while Jessie shook his head in confusion.

> In Chapter 3, Phelix writes:
>
> As with other steps taken, artificial light was added to the Complex and Employment Sector with a desire to increase productivity in mind. The decision was made after similar changes produced positive results. This artificial light would simulate the change from day hours to night hours and is used as a way to comfort Souls and provide them the sense of normality that they so desired.

Nicole worked a later shift and wouldn't leave work for another two hours. The artificial light had started to dim, and Mark had no desire to be out alone after dark, so with some time to kill, Mark decided to have a whiskey and a burger. He sat at the bar and politely ordered from his waitress, who was clearly pleased that she was not being yelled at.

> In Chapter 2, Phelix writes:
>
> While the poisons of the living world are available in great quantities, they are no longer lethal and pose no threat to Souls. Stimulants and depressants also fall into this

category, and while some Souls take pleasure in reenacting old habits, the drugs and alcohol you find here will have no effect upon you.

Mark sipped his whiskey, and while the taste was familiar, almost comforting, he quickly realized that without the desired after-effect, the bitter taste was hardly as appealing. He flagged down the nearest waitress, who reluctantly moved closer to him and prepared herself for the worst. He picked up the glass and turned to the waitress, who had flinched at the sudden movement, and said, "Could I have a glass of water instead?"

She hesitated as her eyes darted between him and the glass until she finally took it and backed away slowly until she was no longer within arm's reach, where she turned and moved away quickly. Within minutes, she had returned with a glass of water and offered it to him as one offers a sacrifice to a deity. As he grasped the glass, she quickly stepped away and muttered, "I'm sorry, I'm so sorry. I was gone for far too long. Please forgive me," Before she turned and rushed away. Mark thought back to the people he had seen in restaurants acting horribly to the wait staff and understood the intent behind the punishment, but couldn't imaging the physical and mental torture these people went through. After all he had seen in his short time here, in his opinion, this was the worst sentence when considering the crime.

"It is not often I agree with a Soul," a familiar voice spoke from beside him, "but you are right. We treat those Souls so badly."

Out of habit, Mark attempted to take a deep breath in and count backwards but came up empty. "Really?" the Demon asked. "Did that ever really work for you in life either?"

Mark turned in his seat to find Jack sitting next to him. "People think it's strange that you've talked to me as much as you have. Shouldn't you be on to the next contract or something?"

Jack snapped his fingers. A waitress appeared between the two and placed a colorful drink in front of him. "Just like a mortal to think it is always about them. We are the vain ones, remember?"

Mark looked around and found that the restaurant seemed bare compared to only a few moments ago. "You know, it occurs to me that I've never seen demons outside of the office buildings."

The Demon smiled. "Well, it sounds like you are not too observant. Just because you have never seen us, does not mean that we are not there."

Mark hated to admit it, but the Demon was right. He had no idea what they were capable of, and the idea that they could be secretly spying on the Souls made perfect sense. "Ok, no bullshit. Why are you here?"

Jack raised his glass. "I'm here to toast to my favorite Special Case." Mark raised his glass and clinked it against Jack's. "Sure," he continued, "I like to come in for a bit for lunch and do some light reading." The Demon patted the handbook, which appeared next to him on the bar. "This thing is fascinating. I am sure you agree. But it looks like I have another appointment after all." Jack took a final sip of his drink before standing and picking up the handbook. "It was nice catching up with you. Do try to keep in touch." And then he was gone.

With a strange but noticeable kind of casualness, the area started again to fill up with customers and servers. Before long, Mark felt a hand on his shoulder, only to spin around and see Nicole.

"Been waiting long?" she asked as she took the seat next to him.

It was clear that he was deep in thought, and with a concerned tone in her voice, she asked what was wrong. Mark opened his mouth but stopped when he thought of what Jack had said. What if they were everywhere? Instead, he took Nicole by the hand and led her outside.

In an effort to act normal, he said, "So show me the car."

The distraction worked, and overcome with Pride that she had been chosen, Nicole weaved through the lines of cars until she stopped at a black compact four-door sedan.

"Did they tell you why everybody drives the same car?" Mark asked as he climbed into the passenger seat.

Nicole replied, "You really need to finish the handbook," before starting the car and pulling out of the spot. "They made me watch this video about unwritten rules of the road and how to navigate the Complex and the Employment District." The radio played "Ace of Spades" by Motorhead as she pulled out into the road and quickly accelerated the way Tony did. "It even goes on and on about not going into the Wastelands, but everybody does. Hey, you wanna go?" Mark's mind was lost trying to understand Jack's appearance and the words he said. Was it some kind of message? "Mark? Mark!" He focused back on Nicole who, suddenly realized he was acting strange. "What's with you?" she asked. "You've been acting strange since I picked you up."

Mark debated if he should tell her. "I had a strange conversation with someone at the restaurant. Just kind of weirded me out, you know?"

The explanation seemed to satisfy her because she re-asked her original question. "So you wanna go to the Wasteland?"

Mark did his best to offer a confident smile and said, "Doesn't matter where we go." And he took her hand.

Day 16

He rolled to his side and saw that she was still sleeping. Even with the darkness, he could make out the curves of her face. She was still pretty, pretty enough anyway. She still had the look of a woman who had seen the best and the worst of life and lived to tell the tale. Now that they were here, now that he had had her, it didn't feel the same as it once did. The satisfaction or the sense of achievement that normally followed was absent, and it made him feel empty. As quietly as he could Mark, climbed out of bed and walked to the living room. He took a seat on the loveseat and picked up the handbook and opened to the table of contents. He looked over the names of the chapters, as he did frequently when he couldn't sleep, and thought about what Jack had said. There had to be something in here Jack wanted him to see.

In Chapter 3, Phelix writes:

The Complex is the first of two areas that are guarded from the Wasteland. Maps of the Complex are given to those who have been chosen to be worthy enough to manage a car pool. Without a map, most people find the Complex too difficult to navigate. Throughout the Complex are a variety of house styles that can be rewarded or revoked depending on performance.

Mark skipped ahead.

Each Living Quarter is equipped with a sleeping area and a living area. Some Living Quarters are also equipped with other rooms, such as kitchens, bathrooms, and closets. If you are assigned a Living Quarter that has an additional room, please remember that it is not functional as Souls do not have the need for such functions.

Mark skipped ahead.

Because we understand that humans are social creatures, we realize that the desire to spend time is your living quarters with people you meet may arise, but please keep in mind that you are contracted to perform, and failure to do so could result in the termination of your contract.

Frustrated, he flipped to Chapter 1 and thought best to just start at the beginning. The book was so factual and difficult to read. Mark found himself struggling to remain engaged.

In Chapter 1, Phelix writes:

In the beginning, when a Soul moved on, he would be given a trial to determine his worthiness to enter Heaven. When a Soul was determined unworthy, he would then be judged and sentenced before being sent to the Afterlife. Over time, this system would falter, and with the change of a millennium came a change in values which caused a higher than average number of Souls to be deemed unworthy. Because of the work load, a change was made, and sentencing would be done by the Fallen.

Mark skipped ahead.

The employment sector was created to track and file the arrival of new Souls. Originally, a single building was created, and as the offices grew, the sector grew as well.

Mark skipped ahead.

With the increase of offices, the recruitment efforts evolved into what it is now. With the inclusion of technology came the need for qualified employees. The training required for an average Soul who had paid his debt and would be moved up was considerable and was often deemed impractical.

Recruit; — the word stood out to him. Curious, Mark flipped to the index to search for the word and found references on over seventy pages. He started with the earliest references, most of which he had already read.

Page 5: Recruitment efforts are allowed by Paradise to test Free Will.

Page 18: Recruitment started in an effort to gain valuable Souls in exchange for earthly desires. A recruit is given something in their life in exchange for their Soul in the afterlife.

Page 22: Recruitment expanded to fill the need for experienced roles within the Employment sector.

"Hey babe, couldn't sleep?"

Nicole stood in the entrance to the hallway wearing only her white button-up shirt. Mark folded the corner on the page he was reading before putting the book down beside him. He still had not told her or anyone about his conversation with Jack, but he knew that people were starting to take notice of the toll the subject had taken on him. Nicole crossed the living area and picked up the book, taking its seat next to Mark.

"You know, I tried to read through this thing when I first got here and couldn't make it past the first chapter." She flipped through the pages, causing small clouds of dust to rise.

"Yeah, it's so dry and hard to read," he commented. "Honestly, I don't know what I'm looking for in it, but I think there's something I need to know and that the answer is in there."

Nicole's eyes squinted slightly as she asked, "What kind of answers are you looking for?" Mark let out a deep sigh, but before he could answer, Nicole followed with, "You know you can't leave, right?" The thought had never occurred to him, and the realization that the thought had never occurred to him left even more of an impact. He had accepted this change so quickly, so easily, and wondered if trying to escape was something others thought of.

"Yeah, nothing like that," He responded without admitting that it would be something he would be thinking about and researching later. "I just feel there is something in there I should know."

Nicole turned her attention to the book and flipped through before saying, "Maybe it was this?"

In Chapter 3, Phelix writes:

Souls living within the Complex are permitted to take
part in sexual relations as long as those relations do not
interfere with contracted assignments.

Mark took the book from her and read the passage out loud. "Yeah, we know this," He responded, but as he looked up from the book, Nicole had moved to her knees and positioned herself in front of him. In that moment, he wasn't sure if he was happy to have her here, to not be alone, or if he was just feeling the excitement he would have in the same position when living. She started to kiss his knee while fumbling with the button on his boxers. Mark placed the book down on the empty seat next to him and watched Nicole in action. it was hard not to appreciate the artistry with which she worked. All too often, this was a rushed experience seen more as a chore than an act of love, but it was clear that Nicole meant to leave an impression. As she worked, he thought about when they had first met and their relationship. He thought of the first drink and drug fueled conversation that led to her fondness for oral sex. It was almost a year before he would experience it firsthand, but that kind of admission is still something that is hard for any man to forget. She was becoming more aggressive, just her style. Start slow and soft, building anticipation with some light teasing while creating lubrication. Speed up slightly and wait for a reaction before pulling back so the act can go on; lather, rinse, repeat. Mark thought about their first time. They were sitting on his couch and passing a bowl around when she took the initiative, leaned in, and kissed him. Up until then, it was all oral and hand stuff. The first kiss felt strange. It felt strange to think that they had been so intimate but had never kissed. He pulled her on top of him and they made out while grinding against each other like teenagers before heading to his bedroom. He remembered being more excited over the act than who it was with. As they tend to do, one memory opened to another. Their first time led to their last time which led to the attack, and before long, right as he came, he was thinking of Julie.

The alarm sounded as they lay on top of each other on the couch. Neither could sleep, so they both sat in silence and watched reruns of *Happy Days* on the television.

In Chapter 3, Phelix writes:

Each living quarter is equipped with a working television as a way to help Souls adjust. We came to understand that television has begun to play a large part of everyday life for mortals, and most Souls find it comforting. Because of restrictions set upon us by Paradise, we can only air programs that existed or flourished thanks in part to a deal with us. This rule applies to music as well.

Mark had only watched a little television, only recently when he was unable to sleep and usually only as background noise while reading the handbook. He had found that most of the options were reality shows, CNN news, and Lifetime made-for-television movies, but occasionally he would run across a sitcom. The biggest surprise was the full series run of *Who's the Boss*.

Nicole stood and said, "I've gotta get back to my living quarters for my carpool," before leaning down and kissing him. As she walked down the hallway to the bedroom to gather her clothes, Mark picked up the handbook and thumbed through it. Maybe it wasn't a message. Maybe Jack wasn't trying to tell him something. He continued to flip through the pages until Nicole came back from the bedroom dressed in her Soul's outfit. "Will you get your nose out of that book?" she demanded before taking it from him and tossing it in the corner. She kneeled in front of him so that they were eye to eye. "Look," her voice was strange. Her tone sounded genuinely concerned. "I don't know what's going on with you, but sitting around here and focusing on that stupid book is going to get you nowhere." She took his hands. "This is a second chance for us. We could be out in the wastes being tormented, but instead we have a bed and a purpose and each other." He offered her a half-smile, which she took as acceptance. She stood up and said her goodbyes before leaving him alone holding the handbook. She was right. All things considered, it could be worse. Then he remembered what his father told him. Everything happens for a reason.

Error 481

A new error. Mark had started compiling a list of the errors he received when looking up Wayne. Every attempt brought a new error, 439, 426, 445, 447, 418, 432, 401. Mark had completed his work items with about an hour to spare and decided to do some snooping. He looked for his mother and was surprised at the lack of information. He thought back to his youth and all the men that came and went. He guessed by the definition in the handbook that wouldn't count as Lust. She wasn't trying to hurt anybody; she was just looking for someone to love her. He looked up Miles Trubuck, the owner of Loans4you, and was surprised that he had not made a deal. He seemed like the kind of person who would sell his Soul for personal gain, but all he had were several counts of Greed. That old saying that you can never judge a book by the cover felt exceptionally meaningful. He finally he typed Julie Monroe only to find the same profile as usual, no change at all.

"What are you doing?" Mark failed to notice Tony's head poking over the side of his cube.

He quickly closed down the profile. "Nothing, I was just checking up on some people."

Tony made a stern face. "I would be careful with that if I were you," he offered. "Just because you don't see someone doesn't mean they're not watching." Jack's words spoken in another voice.

The two closed down their computers and made their way to the elevator. "Are you all right?" Tony asked. "Jessie thinks you're not adjusting well. Even Laura's noticed that you're a little distant, though admittedly she said she likes you better like this."

The two men shared a laugh, and when they finished, Mark replied, "I don't know man. It just... Have you ever seen a Demon outside of this building, like in a restaurant?"

Tony made a confused face as he thought for a moment before answering, "No".

"Yeah, me neither," Mark lied.

Outside, Jessie and Laura were waiting in their usual spot. Jessie offered his usual greeting, but Laura looked more upset than usual.

"What's with her?" Tony asked as he shook Jessie's hand.

"Not sure," Jessie replied, "Met her at the elevator and she looked like that. Hasn't said a thing since."

Laura stood and crossed her arms. "I'm right here. You don't have to talk about me like I can't hear you."

Tony met the valet and took the keys as Jessie asked, "Fine, what's with you?"

Laura offered a disgusted grunt and stomped to the car without answering. "When did teenagers start acting like that?" Jessie asked as he and Mark walked to the car.

Mark shrugged. "I don't know, in the late 90s I think."

Jessie stroked his Santa-like beard. "The 90s, as in 1890s?"

It occurred to Mark that he had never asked Jessie about his story. "How long have you been here?"

Still stroking his beard, Jessie replied, "I died in 1862. What year is it now?" Before Mark could answer, Tony honked from the car, interrupting their conversation.

From the driver's seat, Tony asked, "Anybody up for dinner?" but received no responses. Mark's questions had preoccupied Jessie, Laura remained poutier than usual, and Mark only thought about what Jack had told him. The group sat in silence during most of the ride back to the Complex, accompanied by "Unbelievable" by EMF.

In chapter 2, Phelix writes:

> Because of the many deals made within the music business, popular music is widely available to all Souls and is another thing used to provide comfort during the transition as well as a sense of community. Popular music has even helped contribute to productivity as many mortals are inspired to make deals thanks to the successful songs written by artists who made deals for their souls.

When both the employment sector and the Complex became just specks on opposite horizons, Tony pulled off the road and slowed the car to a stop. Turning to the side so he could address the whole car, Tony asked, "Ok, we need to figure this shit out because you guys are depressing the fuck out of me."

Jessie, Mark, and Laura all exchanged glances until Jessie spoke up. "Mark just reminded me that I've been here for over fifty years." He began to stoke his beard again. "It's like just yesterday I was alive but... Shit, has it really been over fifty years?"

From the back seat, Laura rolled her eyes and said, "Geez, you guys have stupid problems. What about me?" her voice started to rise in frustration. "I'm just a nobody! There's not a single prophecy about me!" She slouched back down and muttered, "I'll never be special."

Tony turned forward and placed his hand on his head. "I carpool with idiots."

He started the car and pulled back onto the road, heading back to the Complex. "I was contacted by a Demon," Mark said.

"What, at work?" Tony asked.

Mark shook his head. "No, at a restaurant." The car jerked forward as Tony's foot slipped on to the breaks.

"What do you mean?" asked Jessie. Even Laura had sat at attention for the gossip.

"The Demon who recruited me, Jack, he showed up at a restaurant the other day," Mark explained.

"Didn't you tell me that he met you four times before you signed?" Tony asked.

Before he could answer, Laura added, "Four times? That's crazy! I'd never heard of someone getting so much attention!"

Mark began to blush. "Well, the last time was after I'd signed the contract."

With this, Tony again pulled off the road and slowed the car to a stop. Jessie chimed in, "I've never seen a Demon at a restaurant."

Mark nodded. "That's what I said too, and he told me that just because we can't see them, it doesn't mean they aren't there. What's even stranger is that when he said it, everybody around him seemed oblivious to him being there, like they couldn't see him either. The only person he interacted with was a waitress, and even then he didn't talk to her. He just snapped and she appeared with a drink."

The four of them sat in silence, and it was clear to Mark that they had never considered that they were always being watched either.

"You're fucking with us," Tony announced from the driver's seat, but his tone betrayed his false sense of confidence. "I've been here for almost 600 years. Shit, I was here when there was nothing but a single building in the middle of the wastes when we worked constantly. In all my time, I've never heard of anybody talk about Demons meeting them over drinks."

In an uncharacteristically small voice, Laura asked, "What did he say?"

Both Jessie and Tony turned and waited for Mark's response. "He said he was just there to toast to his favorite Special Case and that he sometimes goes there for some light reading."

Jessie and Laura exchanged glances, as if each of them was waiting for the other to speak first. "You're a Special Case?" Laura finally asked.

Mark offered a confused nod. "What's so special about a Special Case?" Tony asked.

Jessie started to stroke his beard again. "We knew a couple of Special Cases. Laura and I, we use to work with a woman named Rachel and... what was the man's name?"

Laura added, "Jackson."

Jessie slapped his knee. "That's right, Jackson. Rachel was there when I started and Jackson came in a few years before Laura and then one day they were just gone. We asked around if anybody had seen them, but nobody knew a thing. It was like they were just gone."

Mark had given up on sleeping entirely and dedicated every moment to reading the handbook. The days started to run together as his mind ran on auto-pilot. Each day was a mirror of the previous. He would go through his work items, but his mind raced with the words that he had read. The nights that Nicole had stayed with him, he would lay in bed waiting for the cue of heavy and breathing before excusing himself to the living room, returning only minutes before her alarm would normally wake her. After days of searching and coming up empty, the distraction that normally accompanied his mind had turned to frustration, and it showed. The group had not discussed the topic of Special Cases, at least not in his presence, but he secretly thought they were just waiting for him to disappear when talking behind his back.

He wasn't sure if his assigned work was decreasing or if he was just getting better at doing it. He understood why Tony was always drawing. He would break up the day by searching for people he knew in between work items.

Julie Monroe.

No update.

Wayne Douglas.

Error 472.

Miles Trubuck.

No update.

But even then, work never lasted the shift. A notification of a new email from Rebecca popped in the corner of Mark's screen. He paused the recording he was listening to and opened the new email which read

Got a minuet?

The casualness of the message felt strange. He had never before received such an informal email from Rebecca. Mark's reply was equally informal:

Sure, what's up?

Within minutes, he received her response:

Can you come by my desk?

Mark quickly finished his work item before taking off his head set and standing. Tony took notice and gave him an inquisitive look. Mark explained, "Rebecca asked me to come by her desk."

A goofy smile stretched across Tony's face as he said, "Well, look at Mr. Popular."

Mark found Rebecca at her desk skimming over her email. "Knock knock?" he announced as he came to her cube.

She spun around with her trademark smile and said, "Hey, I wanted to ask you some questions."

Curious and slightly worried, Mark leaned against the wall of her cube the way she often did to his and said, "Nope, that's no good. I'm the one who asks questions here."

Over the past weeks, Rebecca had become a valuable and trusted resource. The insight she had given him not only for work but for adjusting to life always paid off, and with that trust, a strong friendship had formed. "Look," she started, "I don't know all the details of what brought you here, but I see some strange things going on, and I want to know more. Knowledge is power around here, and if something is fishy, it's going to be in our best interest to find out what first."

Mark thought back to something Jack had told him: knowledge is power.

Rebecca continued, "Cedric hates meetings, but when someone told him to have one with you, he did it. You have no idea how strange that is. In all of hell you manage to find someone who you knew on earth and who just happened to die around the same time as you?"

Mark had never considered it before and internally fought with himself as he knew she was probably right. "I just kind of assumed everybody would eventually run into someone else they knew. How big could this place possibly be?"

He felt good about his justification only to be let down by her response. "You're right, but this isn't meeting someone you grew up with, this was meeting someone you knew who also died and was offered a deal around the same time as you." Another shocker, it made sense, she was far from a saint, but he had never considered that Nicole had been offered a deal. Rebecca could see the realization on his face. "You guys never talked about your deals?"

Mark shook his head. "I don't know, it just never came up." His mind was racing as he fought to understand this new information. How could he have missed such an important fact? It was too much, too fast. He thought about telling her about Jack, he thought about telling her about being a Special Case, but in the end, he stood quietly and waited for her to speak. He was afraid of her reaction. He thought of what Jessie had told him. He thought of Rachel and Jackson.

"You still with me?" she asked with concern in her voice, snapping him back to the conversation. "I want you to keep your eyes open, Mark. I want you to tell if anything out of the ordinary happens, ok?" Mark faked a reassuring smile and nodded.

Back at his desk, Mark stared at his computer screen, zoning out for several moments. He pulled up his email and sent a message to Nicole:

Hey, can we get together tonight?

Her response came almost immediately:

Sorry babe, going to dinner with some friends and then hitting the wastes. Rain check?

He would never admit it, but he was kind of glad. With no idea of what to tell her or talk to her about, this gave him the opportunity to avoid her without causing suspicion. He looked to Tony, who was busy with his head down paying careful attention to the fine lines on whatever fantastical creature he was working on.

"Hey, Tony?" he asked, causing Tony to lift his head and pull back his headset. "Have you ever met someone you knew in life?"

Tony shook his head as he leaned back and returned to his work. "I died during a religious movement. the only ones of us to end up here were people who died suddenly. Most people confessed and were forgiven on their deathbed."

Mark turned back to his computer screen and focused on the green flashing underscore, waiting for the next record to look up.

Julie Monroe

No change.

He struggled to focus but could only think of the handbook and the lack of answers he found within. Unable to think of anybody else, he typed a new name:

Phelix Utengard

Error 418.

Mark opened the document he kept to track errors and found that he already had 418 when searching for Wayne. Confusion clouded over him, how could Wayne be in the same category as Phelix Utengard? His interest was piqued. He had never considered it before, Cedric told him he wouldn't have access to people who had passed, but he searched for his own name.

Error 499

It wasn't on his list. He searched again.

Nicole Palmer

Error 499

He marked his discovery. 499 was assigned to people who had passed and accepted deals. He searched again.

Phelix Utengard

Error 426

It was on the list. His mind rattled trying to find what Wayne and Phelix had in common. He thought about what Rebecca had just told him. Did this count as out of the ordinary?

He then thought back to something Jack had said. Just because you don't see them, doesn't mean they aren't there. Was Jack just fucking with him?

The moment before the paranoia would have driven him crazy, Mark felt a hand on his shoulder and spun around to see Tony packed up and ready to go for the day. Mark did his best to hide his anxiety and lied to himself about the success of his actions. The look on Tony's face said that he knew something was wrong, but he was also afraid to ask what, so they instead just walked silently to the elevator.

The ride down was tense with both men knowing there was something they should say, but neither having the balls to do so, and when the elevator stopped, the doors opened not to the lobby, but to a dark hallway that led to an oak door with the plaque reading "Mortal Resources." Mark looked to Tony, who shared the same confusion written on his face. Cautiously, the men stepped off the elevator and made their way to the oak door. Tony spoke lightly, "I've heard horror stories about this place. It was put in place after I had started. so I've never been here."

Mark confessed. "I searched for myself and for Phelix in the system. Do you think they know?" Before he could answer, the door opened and the light from the waiting room flooded the hallway.

The waiting room was exactly as Mark had remembered it. The room was empty of Souls save for the same woman as his first visit, still behind the glass partition. The only other occupant was a Demon in a black suit who was leaning on to the counter and talking to the receptionist. From the distance, Mark couldn't make out their conversation, but it was causing the Soul to giggle and laugh, like a woman who was being flattered. The Demon stood and turned to reveal Jack's over confident smile and bright blue eyes.

Jack walked to the nearest couch and took a seat, leaving the receptionist to focus on her job. "Mark?" she asked.

He took a step forward and responded, "Yes?"

The receptionist offered Jack a smile, no doubt an inside joke, which he responded to with a wink. "Mark, we have a reassignment for you. Tomorrow, please report here and you will be taken to your new leader for reorientation." Mark looked first at Tony and then back to the receptionist and started to speak but was cut off by her preemptive response in the same authoritative tone. "You will maintain your current carpool. Please hold all additional questions until after the reorientation process." She then smiled coldly as if waiting for him to leave. He turned to Jack, who again only offered a smile.

Mark followed Tony through the door, closing it as he went. Before the final click, he could hear the same giggle and laugh he did when they entered and he pictured Jack leaning back against the counter. Grabbing Tony's arm, Mark quietly said, "I have to tell you something," causing Tony to turn. "That was Jack. That Demon was Jack. That Demon was the one who recruited me." A look of intrigue washed over Tony's face. "Rebecca told me that she thinks something strange is going on here. She told me that the things she is seeing just don't add up." Tony stood speechless as Mark let out a long sigh. "Just don't tell the group. They have already been acting weird towards me."

Tony's response was interrupted by the door to Mortal Resources opening behind them. Jack confidently walked to the elevator, and once inside, spun around as the door closed with enough time to offer a wink.

Mark's plea went ignored as Tony recounted the event in the car. Jessie and Laura both sat attentively and listened to the story told from his perspective, including an exaggeration of the Demons presence (complete with a detailed description of fiery wings and translucent skin) and an unflattering description of Mark shaking in fear at the sight of the Demon.

While trying her best to look tough, Laura said, "I would have stomped my foot and demanded answers from that hag!"

From the passenger seat, Jessie added, "I've never heard of someone being transferred, and why would they keep you with the same carpool? I mean, don't they assign carpools based on your department?"

Mark thought back to the handbook.

In chapter 3, Phelix writes:

Carpools allow transportation from the Complex to the Employment Sector. Because of the high volume of Souls, it was more feasible to organize carpools than to give every Soul the opportunity to drive. Originally, carpools were based only on living proximity, but in an effort to provide the social interaction that many Souls crave, they are now organized based on both living proximity and assigned division. Because of a deal made with the Chevrolet Company, all company vehicles are Cavalier Sedans. Unlike in the living world of their origin, vehicles do not require maintenance or fuel.

The day's events smothered Mark as the rest of the group discussed office politics and policies and the radio offered "Semi-Charmed Life" by Third Eye Blind for the soundtrack. Words of disbelief and sentiments of fighting the system floated through his consciousness, and on some small level that would never matter, it made him feel welcome for the first time in days. Once inside the Complex, he was dropped off and watched as the car disappeared around a corner. In that moment, his mind gave way, and he sat on the lawn in front of the tiny building that was his assigned living quarters for what an onlooker would consider a considerable amount of time. His mind sent signals to his body, but it refused to listen or move; he had the intent but the mental block stopped all thought and action. With too much to choose from, his mind decided to shut down and not think of anything. The artificial light started to dim, and a new crop of Souls returning from the employment sector started to roll through the streets of the Complex. Before long, the artificial light was completely off and then only lights came faintly from behind windows and the occasional headlight beams. Later, he would describe how he felt as broken, and that the feeling would make him think of Julie.

Day 23

It was several hours before he felt like he could move, and it was only as far as the love seat in the living area. On the empty seat next to him sat the handbook, the item that had occupied most of his time for the last several days, but the possibility of discovering previously overlooked information could not provide the motivation or energy required to act on the impulse. Instead, Mark sat on the loveseat and watched a reality show where a man had to choose one of 10 women, knowing that one of them secretly had a penis. It was down to the final three when the familiar honk of Tony's carpool arrived. Sluggishly, Mark made it to the car and took his spot in the backseat. He was vaguely aware of the others in the group greeting him, but it came through like voices and sounds underwater. Instead of responding, he rested his head on the window as Tony pulled forward. Watching the small buildings turn into slightly larger buildings and then vanish into nothing as they entered the wastes gave him the familiar feeling of riding the number seven bus uptown. The memory made him want to smile, but nothing came out.

Tony rode the elevator up with Mark. The small talk he attempted in the car had been met with silence so he now decided to just keep to himself, offering only an encouraging "Enjoy the new assignment," as Mark exited the elevator into the Mortal Resources hallway.

He shuffled through the door and was greeted by the same woman behind the glass. "Good morning!" her bright and cheery voice rang out. "Please take a seat and someone will be by to collect you shortly."

Mark sat on the couch in the same spot he had when he originally did his paperwork and tried to collect his thoughts. He told himself that enough was enough and that it was time to focus, but the pep talk yielded minimal results.

"Marky?" a soft voice called from the doorway. The name brought back painful feelings, and he was unable to explain such a reaction. Mark turned to see an older woman standing in the doorway. She wore the outfit of a Soul that seemed to fit her perfectly. Her face was kind, grandmotherly even. Her hair was gray and short, not neat but punky, cut in a style that seemed inappropriate for her generation. Her expression was one of infinite patience, which showed when she politely asked again, "Are you Mark?" The only response he could offer was a simple nod. A warm smile spread across her face. "Alright then, please come with me." Mark followed the woman back into the hallway where she stopped once the oak door closed. Cautiously looking back to the door, the woman said in a loud and hushed whisper, "These hallways, they are actually portals. That's how this place works." She leaned in close. The calm and matronly look she expressed before had been replaced by one of paranoia. "Any hallway like this is unmonitored because the Demons don't see them as relevant. Most of them don't even use them." Mark thought back to the previous day. Jack used this hallway. Was she lying? Was this all a trick? Sensing his suspicion, the woman offered, "My name is Ellis and I know your father."

In Chapter 5, Phelix writes:

> Those sentenced to punishment because of Wrathful actions wander the wastes. They are seen as outcasts and do not typically associate with other Souls. Like all Torments, they tend to travel in groups in order to fulfill the mortal need of companionship. All Wrathful sinners are marked with the symbol of Wrath, and depending on their Wrathful actions, they are often fitted with cages surrounding as little as their hands and as much as their torso. In extreme situations, Wrathful sinners will be held together with other Wrathful sinners in a large cell. Some lesser offenders are without cages, but still bare the mark of Wrathful sinners.

The adjacent page held a crude drawing of a faceless man with a jagged and crooked Z on his chest.

Mark asked, "What do you mean you know my father?"

Ellis unbuttoned the middle four buttons and pulled open her shirt to reveal a jagged Z similar to the one in the handbook etched in her skin between her breasts. "We don't have time now, but I will explain what I can." She started to re-button her shirt. "You have to promise me to keep your cool, ok? You don't know who you can trust. For now, follow me. You have to meet your new leader."

Ryan was less like Cedric and more like Jack. He looked and acted like a gameshow host, striding around his office with a hop in his step and far too much enthusiasm. The office itself was very minimalistic with only a sturdy desk and three chairs, one behind and two in front. "So I am not sure why you are here. It was handed down from above, and we are but servants." His voice was a perfect mix of friendly and condescending and showed his contempt for both his job and mortals. "I understand you were assigned to Acquisitions and Recruiting under Cedric." As he said the name, a falter in his voice showed his disgust. "You will find that here in Verification, we follow similar practices, though the job is quite different." The Demon's eyes narrowed and focused on Mark, making him uncomfortable, like a child in an authority figure's office. "Ellis will explain more. You are dismissed."

Mark stood and cautiously exited the room, making sure to not lose sight of the Demon with a friendly smile. Outside of the office, he found Ellis patiently waiting. The woman standing there was the same one who met him at the door of Mortal Resources and looked nothing like the woman she became in the hallway.

As they made eye contact, she asked, "All done?" The casual nature of her voice infuriated Mark, who did all he could to hold back thinking of the promise he agreed to.

The system Ellis showed him was identical to the one he had used previously. "Here we track and report people who are not fulfilling their contracts or assignments. We receive work orders with their names and search here to find their assignments." Mark was only half paying attention and half waiting for her to turn around and finish telling him what she knew. Every few words from her mouth he understood as "I will explain when I can" until the word "contract" floated past his filter and caught his attention. She continued, "Once we have information regarding their assignments, we can search in the Locator tool to see their whereabouts and location history. When someone reports abuse of the system, it generates a work item and we check it out." As she typed the name in the space provided, Mark saw an itemized and time stamped list appear, some lines blue and others grey.

6:15am : Exit Assigned living quarters
Enter Car
6:20am : Exit Complex
6:40am : Enter Employment Sector
Exit Car
6:55am : Enter Office
Elevator
6:57 am : Enter Floor 32
7:00 am : Enter Break room
8:54 am : Exit Break room
9:00 am : Terminal sign on

"The blue entries are entry and exit points while the gray items, like where it says enter and exit car or elevator, these are places that can't be tracked." Her speech was casual, but he now understood why she knew at least part of what she claimed to. Ellis circled her mouse around the 7:00am to 9:00am entries. "This was the reason it was reported. Someone saw this person sitting around in the break room for 2 hours in the morning and was most likely upset that they were getting away with it." She continued to scroll down to midway down the record.

3:00 pm : Terminal sign off
Elevator

3:05 pm : Exit Office

"See," she said while circling her mouse over the 3:00pm record, "This person worked their 6 hour shift, but their car pool seems to be off their schedule. Most likely they are riding with someone there are not assigned to, it happens pretty often. No doubt someone will get a work order for someone sitting in the break room for 2 hours from 1:00pm to 3:00pm." Ellis closed the tracking system before going back to the work order where she replied with the word complete and opened the next.

Mark asked, "Do you ever get any of the 400 error codes?"

Ellis's face contorted in confusion as she responded, "I have gotten one or two, but I can't remember how long it's been. It's definitely not common." For the first time in days, Mark's mind focused on a single topic, believing that he may be able to answer at least one of his many questions.

After several more examples, Ellis set Mark off on his own. The clock on his computer showed just after noon, meaning that at least the day was almost over. He pulled up his email and had received one from both Rebecca and Tony as well as two from Nicole. Starting with the most recent, he opened Tony's email.

Mark,
Hope everything is going well with your new assignment. I'll meet you in the lobby at 1. Let me know if you need anything.
Tony

Mark replied
Ok.

The next email was from Nicole and read:
Hey Babe, plans tonight?

Mark closed the email without responding and went onto the next from Nicole:
Everything all right? I haven't heard from you.

He replied:
Yeah, sorry, I was given a new assignment and have been training all morning. No plans but not feeling great, come by tonight.

She replied almost instantly with a smiley face. He opened the final email, the one from Rebecca, and found her concern comforting.
Hey Mark.

Tony told me about the new assignment. I just wanted to check on you and make sure everything is ok. Remember what we talked about.
Rebecca

Mark closed the email without responding, focusing instead on doing a little searching before it was time to go. He searched himself and instead of the 499 error, he received his record.

Mark Waters   Birth: 1983/3/28   Death: _____
29%   Cause of Death: Loss of blood___
Assignment: Acquisitions and Recruiting_____
1992/5/13 Envy
1998/7/02 Lust
2008/4/28 Greed

It looked similar to the ones he had seen previously. He reviewed his information, finding his date of birth and his assorted sins. Under his assignment, it still listed Acquisitions and Recruiting. It showed his number as 29, which would have drawn more of his attention had his date of death being not been blank. The cause was there, loss of blood. Just reading the sentence caused soreness in his stomach. In every example Ellis did, there was always a date of death, and the lack of information seemed odd. The clock now showed 12:45. The time had passed too quickly. He cleared the screen and searched for Nicole and again found her record instead of the 499 error.

Nicole Palmer   Birth: 1980/12/17   Death: 2015/8/15
72%   Cause of Death: Suicide_____
Assignment: Reinforcement_____
1989/6/02 Lust
1990/3/12 Greed
1990/3/12 Lust
1990/5/26 Lust
1990/8/19 Lust
1992/1/1 Envy
1993/7/4 Sloth
1995/11/20 Wrath
Continue…

Nicole's record was complete and showed the date of her birth and death as well as all her sins and her assignment, Reinforcement. With what he knew now, it seemed to reason that her department was the one that submitted the work orders to his new department. He continued to scroll down her report, which was considerably longer than his. Her list of sins ran the gambit from Lust to Envy to Wrath to Sloth. He scrolled back to the top and found the reason for death marked as suicide. He thought back to when they met and recalled her saying she overdosed. Was that the same thing? His moment of contemplation was interrupted by the feeling on a hand on his shoulder, causing him to jump. He turned to find Ellis standing behind him who, in a cheerful voice, said, "Its 1:00pm, let's go."

The air was tense as the two rode the elevator down to the lobby. It was clear to Ellis that Mark had questions but did not know how to start, and equally clear to Mark that Ellis wanted to answer his questions but didn't know if she could. Feeling their time coming to an end, Mark started to speak, but was interrupted by Ellis with the single word "soon".

The door slid open to the lobby, and they both made their way through the crowd to their respective car pools with nothing more said. As he stood and waited for the group to join him, Ellis's motherly and calm voice echoed her single word in his mind. Jessie and Laura arrived next, followed shortly after by Tony, who went to request the car.

"They call it Verification." Mark did his best to think of what he had been shown about his new position and not the information he was given by Ellis. "It's similar to A&R. We get work orders and we do research."

Laura coughed the word "Narc," causing Jessie to quietly ask what a narc was and Tony to only shrug his shoulders.

Mark continued, "We have a tracking software that logs whenever a Soul goes into or out of a building or area and basically when other people narc..." he emphasized the word and glared at Laura, as a rare smile to spread across her face, "it generates a work order and we look into it."

Tony offered a worried look in the rearview mirror and asked, "So they really do track us? Do they listen in?"

Mark knew exactly what he was asking and wished he had a better answer. "I don't know. I do know that places like in the car or in an elevator or in the dark hallways in between offices are marked as places not tracked, but who knows what that really means." A slight look of relief crossed Tony's face.

"Did you find anything out about why you were transferred?" Jessie asked.

Mark considered telling them about Ellis and what she had said. It was all he could think about, after all. How did he know he could trust anybody in the group? How did he know he could even trust Ellis? The fact was that the only thing he knew was that he needed to know what Ellis meant by knowing his father. "No," he responded, not sure if it was a lie or not. "My new leader said that he doesn't even know why I was transferred." The sentence brought the conversation to a sudden stop. Each of the group suddenly realized that the mystery had not been solved and nobody wanted to be the next to bring it back up.

In an effort to remove the tension, Tony took the group through the wastes, where they came across a group of Torments assigned to Greed.

In Chapter 5, Phelix writes:

Those sentenced to serve punishment because of greedy actions wander the wastes. They are seen as outcasts and do not typically associate with other Souls. Like all Torments, they tend to travel in groups in order to fulfill the mortal need of companionship. All Greed sinners are marked with the symbol of Greed. Typically, they are sentenced to carry with them physical items that represent the items gained by their sins. As time moved forward and physical currency changed from coin to paper, the decision was made that all monetary Greed sins will be represented with Gold.

The adjacent page held a crude drawing of a hand with a perfectly circular ring emblazoned onto it.

Mark had never seen someone sentenced to pay for the sin of Greed. The handbook did not do the punishment justice. Instead of carrying items symbolic of their Greed, the items were pulled by straps attached to a collar around the sinner's neck. Even from the distance at which the group sat, he could see the pain and suffocation that came with each step as the collar choked the wearer.

"I would be all 'Fuck this shit!' if I was them!" Laura suddenly shouted, causing the rest of the group to jump.

"They can't," Jessie explained. "they only keep going because if they stop, the pain is worse. Going forward chokes them and standing still burns them. They choose the one that hurts the least." His words were more than factual. He spoke with experience. The group sat in silence, waiting for him to say more, waiting for an explanation which came only with "I've done my time; I've paid for my sins. I hurt a lot of people and I can't take that back, but now my slate is clean." The group continued to watch the Torments for a short time before Tony turned the car and headed back to the road.

Upon arriving home, Mark headed straight for his bed. Both Jack and Phelix had told him that he wasn't really tired, and this feeling of exhaustion was mental and not physical. He knew that this body did not require sleep, but it didn't change the fact that the simple act of lying down and closing his eyes relaxed his racing mind. He had forgotten that he asked Nicole to come over and wasn't sure how long he had been asleep when she woke him. He only knew that seeing her made him feel better, made him feel normal. Two people had cautioned him against trusting, but the good times washed the bad times from his mind when she said, "Hey babe, are you all right?" The two sat on his bed and he explained everything to her, starting with the several meetings with Jack and what he had told him in the restaurant. He told her about being a Special Case and the 400 error codes and then seeing Jack again in Mortal Resources before ending with Ellis and the elevator ride. She showed a supportive look as he unloaded all the thoughts, fear, and paranoia he had experienced recently, and when he finished, he fell exhausted to the bed where she curled into his arms and he fell asleep again.

Day 24

Mark woke and saw a green 3:18am when he turned and looked at the alarm. He sat up in bed and was surprised to find he was alone. He checked the living room but found nothing as well, no trace of Nicole. Had she been there? Was it a dream? He dressed and then sat on the couch and turned on the TV to find the season of Roseanne where they won the lottery. Before long, the artificial light started to come on and simulate a sunrise. Tony arrived at his usual time, and the group headed from the Complex to the Employment Sector. Morning conversations were never as eventful on the afternoon ride home, but something about today felt different. Everybody was standoffish and distant. They all felt like strangers to Mark, and the radio only emphasized the fact with the song "Suspicious Minds" by Elvis.

They all went their separate ways inside the office. The Acquisitions and Recruiting floor came before Verifications, leaving Mark alone on the elevator for part of the ride. At his computer, Mark found only five work orders, a considerable difference from his time in A&R. Before opening the first work order, Mark wrote a short email to Nicole:

Hey,
Did you come by last night? I remember seeing you but you were gone when I woke up and wasn't sure if it was a dream.

He waited for several minutes, expecting the usual immediate response, but it never came. In order to occupy his mind, he searched for Julie Monroe, but found that her profile had not changed. He searched for Wayne Douglas and received Error 403 and added it to the list. He searched for Phelix Utengard and received error 447, which he verified was already on the list. Frustrated, he pulled the first work order and found the name Terrence Micks. As he did in his previous assignment, Mark searched for the name, but before he could click the update option, he noticed that the contract option was now available. It made sense. Ellis did say they were to verify if people were fulfilling their contracts and assignments. Mark clicked on the contract link in the search results and was given access to a lengthy document that he recognized as having much of the same wording as the one he signed. He found the portion of the contract he was looking for on the second page:

Signee offers (1) one eternal SOUL in exchange for an additional 15 years of life. Upon death, Signee agrees to serve in Department of Transportation in lieu of sentence.

Mark closed the document and searched for his own name, where again he found that the contract option was accessible, but unlike the lengthy document he received when searching under Terrence Micks, when he clicked on the contract option, he received only an error:

Error 418

He recognized the error from the list he compiled from Wayne's and Phelix's errors and made a note next to it.

"How's it going?" a voice asked from behind him, causing him to jump. Ellis leaned in and read the error on the screen. "418? What were you searching for?"

Mark closed the search window and lied. "I must have typed the name wrong. Not feeling myself today."

He looked at her eyes for a sign that she bought it, but found that much like her motherly voice, her motherly face was hard to read. She smiled as she held up a keyboard and said, "I've been given a special assignment that needs to take priority. Can you come help me for a bit?"

Mark followed her to the elevator, the whole time unsure what exactly he expected to happen. Did she know what he was looking up. Would she report him?

"So what's the assignment?" he asked, trying his best not to let his worry show.

"Ryan said there was some issues down in Reinforcement. it's the department creates work orders for us."

Mark thought back to Rebecca saying, "Anything out of the ordinary." He had gone so far from ordinary at this point that it was getting hard to tell what ordinary was anymore. What were the odds that he would be chosen to go to the department where Nicole was assigned?

The air was tense as the elevator moved to the floor it needed to go to. "The thing about elevators is it's still possible that they can open anywhere at any time. People sometimes use the elevator to hide when they figure out its not traceable, but you would be surprised by how many people get caught by a roaming Demon."

Mark smiled and nodded but couldn't decide if she was making idle conversation or if she was trying to tell him something. "How long have you been here?" he asked.

She slightly cocked her head and smiled. "Do you mean here, or do you mean here?" she asked. Mark was unsure how to answer the question, and lucky for him, Ellis didn't wait for a response. "I died a long, long time before you were probably even born. I killed a man because he raped me, and for that offence, I was stoned to death." Mark tried to remember when stoning women was a punishment for a crime, but came up empty. "When I arrived, I was sentenced, and after I had paid for my sin, I was assigned here. As far as when that happened, I honestly could tell you. After you've been here long enough, it all kind of runs together. A leader once told me that time is a luxury of the living."

Her story ended as the door slid open to reveal a large room full of computers and rows of desks. It looked exactly like the Verification and A&R departments. Ellis made her way around the room to a solid oak door in the far corner of the room. The door seemed out of place, and he had trouble remembering a similar one in any of the other departments he had been in. As the door opened, he saw a room that looked like the hallways that connected offices. an untraceable room. On the far side of the room sat a man in front of the single computer in the room. He was tall and wore the outfit of a Soul. He wore his long bright red hair in a ponytail. The neatness of his hair was contrasted by the unruly facial hair that covered the majority of his face.

"Mark, this is Nathan. Nathan here was kind enough to report an issue with his computer." Mark turned to Nathan, who reached down and yanked the keyboard out of the computer, breaking the connecting wire before dropping it and walking out of the room. As the door closed, Ellis started, "Nathan owed me a favor, and I think I owe you some explanations." She took a seat in the now empty chair and started to plug in the new keyboard. "I met a man, your father, when I was serving my sentence. The tormented tend to find each other, and the Sinners mostly stick to their kind, so one day we met each other and decided to travel together." Mark was in shock; he had so many questions but couldn't ask any of them. She had completed the repair and powered the computer back on before continuing, "We only have a short time, so let's get to the point. We eventually met up with others. at first we only sought out those who were like us, those with a small cage on one hand or none at all." Mark thought back to the handbook. Phelix talked about the size of the cages being related to the sins. "I had a single small cage on my right hand, the hand I used to commit my sin. Your father had no cage. that's pretty usual for suicides. Over time, our group grew and grew and we accepted more and more. Before long, we were one of the largest groups in the wastes. Your father is a good man; he directed us and stopped the internal bickering. When there was an issue, he was the first with a solution. Many people looked to him as a leader."

Mark's mind and heart filled with emotion. Ellis had described his father's personality to the letter, and he wanted to believe that in death, he was at least respected for the great man he was.

"How do I know this is real?" he asked.

Ellis smiled. "He talked about you often, especially in the beginning, when it was just us. He told me about the last time he saw you. He told me about sitting on the concrete in the middle of nowhere, when he lost his legs. He told me his final words to you were that everything happens for a reason."

Mark lost all control and broke down. He felt the release that comes with crying uncontrollably but nothing came out, another side effect of having a shell instead of a body. Ellis came to him and wrapped him in her arms. "How did you find me? I don't understand. This can't be a coincidence."

Being this close to her, Mark could feel the slight body shift and sigh that came from wishing she knew the answer. "One day I woke up, and my cage was gone. I stayed with the group for several days but no longer felt the pain and torment. On that day, I knew that I had paid for my sins. Shortly after, I was contacted by a Demon and assigned to this position." She released the hug and returned to the computer. "Ten more minuets are all we can spare. As word spread around, the group started to act hostile towards me. Knowing that there was someone among them that was not in constant agony made me an outsider, and your father could only protect me so much. I told you father about the offer I received, and he encouraged me to go, but before I left, he made me promise to look for your name. He knew that one day you would pass on, and if you came here, he wanted me to find you and tell you his story. He wanted me to tell you even though you are here to remember that everything happens for a reason." She turned back to the computer to check the clock one last time. "And now we've got to go. How you got here, how you were assigned this department, I don't know, but I've been around enough to know that your profile isn't like others I've seen. You're special. I don't know how, but if I were you, I'd watch my back."

Right on time, Nathan entered the room and took his seat at the computer. Mark followed Ellis back to the elevator where he tried to process what he had just been told. He didn't tell her that she was right, he was a Special Case. He doubted she would know any more what it meant than anybody else. Back on at his desk, Mark checked his email, looking for a response from Nicole but received nothing. He opened the email from Rebecca but couldn't think of anything to say that would help. To ask her to meet would be pointless as they had no access to an untraceable room and neither of them drove a carpool.

The group still felt disconnected after work. Laura was never a social butterfly but now both Jessie and Tony seemed pre occupied. Mark felt a sense of guilt. had his problems caused this tension? Tony asked if anybody was up for a bite, and while the consensus was unenthusiastic, there were no objections. Their regular Applebee's was uncharacteristically busy for the midafternoon, but the group was quickly seated. Both Laura and Jessie yelled at the waiter, a large man with a bowl cut, while Tony and Mark talked.

"Did she say where he is now?"

Mark shook his head. "I didn't ask, but I'm not sure I really want to know either. I think he wanted me to know that I shouldn't worry about him, you know? I'm more concerned with the coincidences adding up."

In tears, the waiter left to go place the table's order, causing the others to take notice of the conversation. "Yeah, it is pretty strange the number of people who know you," Jessie said before taking a sip of his drink. "I thought I knew this guy I saw in the lobby one day, but it turns out it wasn't him."

"And things are starting to get strange with Nicole. She was supposed to come by last night, and I think she did, but I don't know if I was dreaming or not."

Laura interrupted, "Souls don't dream. something to do with free will or whatever."

In Chapter 1, Phelix writes:

As the need for Souls grew and they became more than just the Tormented, some privileges were revoked. Originally, when passed out from exhaustion or pain, a Soul had the ability to dream, as they would usually dream only about the torment they were assigned to endure. With Souls serving in the Employment Sector instead of being assigned torment, their dreams were those of hope. In an effort to prevent encouragement of free will and the desire to hope, the ability to dream was removed.

Mark remembered now reading that somewhere, which means she had to have been there. He continued, "Today at work, I sent her an email but got no response."

Tony asked, "Isn't your new job all about verification?"

He didn't have to respond. The answer was written on his face. It had never even occurred to him to search for her. That afternoon, he completed the few work orders he had and then, desperate to keep his mind occupied, he searched for other people he knew in life. After he had run out of friends and family, he started searching for famous people and was surprised to find that Adolf Hitler was assigned to Gardening & Maintenance.

"I've never seen a garden here," Laura interjected.

Jessie responded, "They are forced to mow patches of dirt and gravel. So did Ellis tell you why you were transferred?"

Mark shook his head. "She said she didn't know, which only adds to the coincidences. I can buy someone knowing my father, and I can even buy him asking her to keep an eye out for me, but to be suddenly transferred to her department for reasons nobody can tell me is a step too far."

Laura's eyes went wide with excitement. "Hey!" she shouted in an effort to get everybody's attention. "What if this is one of the prophecies? What if that's what Special Cases are?" Tony and Jessie offered a groan, but Mark took interest as Laura continued. "What if that's what happened to Rachel and Jackson? What if the reason they just disappeared is because they fulfilled their prophecy? It totally makes sense!"

Jessie took a sip of his drink before saying, "I told you before that nobody has ever seen any of those prophecies come true. Phelix Utengard probably wasn't even real! He was probably a Demon or something who wrote that stupid book so when someone screwed up, then the Demons could say it was their own fault for not knowing!" Mark had never seen Jessie this worked up before. the friendly and thoughtful face started to turn red and stuck out because of his Santa-like white, bushy beard.

In an effort to control the situation, Tony attempted to calm the man by placing his hand on his shoulder and saying, "Its ok man, let's step out and get some fresh air." In a frustrated action, Jessie pulled his arm away before pulling his chair back and walking to the entrance. "I'll check on him," Tony said as he excused himself and followed through the front door.

By the time Mark and Laura had exited, Jessie was calmed down and sitting on the hood of the car. Even his posture and body language felt different from the man Mark had grown to know over time. As the two approached, he hopped down from the hood and took steps toward them.

Addressing Laura, he said, "Look, I'm sorry. I didn't mean to snap at you. I just think all this talk about coincidences and prophecies is getting to me." He turned to address the whole group. "Why can't we just accept that we are here and it is what it is? Why do we have to torture ourselves with the idea that things will change?" He looked out at the horizon where you could slightly see over the tall wall that separated the Employment sector from the Wasteland. "I spent a lot of time out there, and now that it's over, I just want to focus on now because the office and the Complex is so much better than out there."

The four of them stood in silence and reflected on what Jessie had said. Though she would never admit it, even Laura took away the message. The ride back to the Complex was as quiet as the ride into the Employment Sector that morning.

Not a word was said until Mark got out of the car and Tony called out, "Goodnight."

Mark sat on the love seat next to the handbook and stared at the black television screen. He thought about the things his father had tried to teach him and the idioms that never made sense to him. As the artificial light started to dim, he looked out of the window at the changing skyline and wondered what his father was doing right now. The words "everything happens for a reason" rang through his head. The idea seemed silly to him, and he found it hard to believe that he wasn't in control. It was because of this that he had flat out ignored the last chapter of the handbook. He shared the same belief as Jessie that the prophecies were silly things and in reality meant nothing. He picked up the handbook and flipped to the last chapter.

In chapter 6, Phelix writes:

After the Great War and the fall from greatness, when the defiant army of the Fallen accepted their loss and retreated to the depths of the Underworld, a single Messenger followed with the words of what was to come. The Messenger rode a white steed and embodied everything that the Fallen warriors had lost. fearing a backlash, the Messenger announced from above that it had not come on a mission of war, but one of pity. It announced that as a servant, it was honor bound to deliver its messages and asked for permission to do so without retaliation. The Fallen allowed the Messenger to place foot on the ground with the understanding that once he did, he could not leave and must spend eternity with the Fallen. Honor bound to deliver its message, the Messenger agreed and sacrificed itself in the name of duty. The Fallen gathered round the Messenger as it spoke, taking in every word that one may benefit them, but they were taken by surprise by its words. The Messenger told that the warriors uprising and eventual loss was foretold by a prophet and was inevitable. It explained that long ago, before the Great War and before humanity, a being that knew all wrote the unforeseen events of the world. These texts were given to the Court of Paradise as a gift where they were kept in secret to be used only in events of dire urgency. A single being would be given the honor of deciphering the knowledge and choosing when, if ever, to act, a choice the being never made. After watching the events unfold as predicted, the being decided that nothing would stop what is foretold, and when the Great War came, he choose his side based on the information within. After the Great War, the being came to the Court of Paradise and explained that a second and third Great War would come, and Paradise would always prevail. With this admission, the Being denounced the honor of guarding the secret and instead insisted that the knowledge be shared. If the knowledge was available, then perhaps the Fallen would see that a Great War was pointless. It is because of this that the Messenger was sent.

What followed were pages of cryptic text that spoke in metaphors. Mark flipped through several pages reading excerpts as he went but found nothing he could understand. Phrases like 'A Dragon's Cycle' and 'Eyes of Time' offered few answers and more confusion, but his research was interrupted by a knock at the door. Without waiting for a response, Nicole opened the door excitedly. The smile on her face spread wider than any he had ever seen on her before.

Dropping next to him on the loveseat, she said, "I'm sorry, I'm sorry, I'm sorry!" her voice was rushed as if she would explode if she didn't get out everything she needed to say. "I left last night to go get ready for the day, and today at work they told me that I was approved for a bigger living quarters and check this out!" She grabbed the hand book from him and flipped around to the front before forcing it back into his hands. "See right here in the Complex chapter! Cohabitation is permitted under the condition that both parties adhere to their contracts and assignments. We can live together!" He found her enthusiasm infectious, and for a moment, a smile spread across Mark's face before he was pulled back to reality. Nicole noticed the change and asked, "Aren't you happy? I did this for us... Don't you want to live with me?"

Mark stood up in an attempt to distance himself before asking, "What were you offered?"

The shock and rejection still covered Nicole's face when she asked, "I don't know what you mean."

"Your contract, why are you in the Employment Sector? I've seen your profile..."

Nicole stood as she cut him off. "You looked at my profile?" Her voice was heavy with anger and distrust.

He knew she was trying to change the subject. This tactic was nothing new. "Tell me what they offered you, Nicole." The statement came as more of a demand, something he had never done to her.

She fell back on the loveseat and crossed her legs and arms. "What does it matter? I agreed to come here to be with you."

The moment she said it, they both caught the lie. As she tried to backtrack, he demanded an explanation. "What do you mean you came here to be with me? You said you died before I did. Tell me what's going on here!"

Feeling helpless, she decided that silence was the best response, another tactic Mark was well aware of. He tried a softer approach and asked again. "Tell me what your contract was for."

Nicole stood back up and slapped him, making Mark stumble backwards. "Fuck you, Mark, that's what my contract was for. This is bullshit. I don't know why I even bother with your lame ass. All you do is bitch about your life and that stupid little girl you met and whine about how you don't understand what's going on. Can't you see that we are in paradise here? We have everything we need or could want. We never get old, we never get sick. You go to work and do your fucking job and after you are free in a way you never were when you were alive!" She then shouted, "And you can't figure this shit out!" emphasizing each syllable with a swing of her open hand, which he caught on the last swing.

Now holding her arms and only inches from her face, he asked a final time, "What was your contract for?" His voice was low and menacing, a voice that even he was surprised he was capable of.

Nicole responded with a knee to his crotch. Mark released her arms and buckle over, landing hard on his knees. Nicole followed with a kick to the side of his head, causing him to fall to the ground. Mark had not been in a fight since he was a teenager, and aside from the Nicole's kick to his side and the stabbing that ended his life, he was a relative stranger to such immense pain. Nicole took the opportunity to grab the hand book and started to tear the pages from the book, again emphasizing each pull with her words. "And how do you keep getting copies of this fucking book! How many times do I have to hide and destroy this stupid thing?"

Mark lay there partially covered in pages from the handbook. Nicole sat back on the love seat and let out a deep sigh. "This could have been fun, you know?" her voice was calm, completely different from only a few moments prior. "We could have explored and cuddled and fucked for eternity, but instead you had to keep going. You couldn't just drop it." A knock at the door drew his attention, and she left the love seat to answer the door. "We are doing this the hard way," she told the large silhouette in the doorway, who nodded as he entered the house.

The look on Jessie's face was one of remorse. It was clear that he did not agree with the decision made. He bent down to pick up Mark and carried him over his shoulder to the car where Nicole was waiting. With a single swift motion, Jessie dropped Mark into the backseat of the compact car through the passenger side. Nicole opened and then leaned into the back driver's side door to make eye contact before saying, "We are going to go for a little ride into the wastes, and tomorrow you will be just another Special Case that one day disappeared."

She backed away from the door and Jessie took her place. His eyes were watering as he said, "I really am sorry," and landed a punch to his forehead. He could feel his head pressing down into the seat from the force generated as the punch connected, and then there was nothing.

Part 3

From his laying position in the back seat, Mark couldn't see anything. The dim lights that came from the artificial stars provided just enough to create silhouettes. From the front seat, he could make out the low sound of the radio playing the top forty hits from the eighties and found a strange satisfaction in the coincidence that he was listening to "The One I Love" by R.E.M. He could feel the cloth of the seat on his skin and assumed that at least part of the gag in his mouth was his shirt. From his inability to move, he would correctly guess that another part of it was binding his hands behind his back. The car felt motionless, had they arrived at their final destination, or was this a pit stop?

"Fireeeeee! Fireeeee!"

The thoughts in his head were interrupted by the sudden outburst from the front passenger seat as Jessie started singing along. Mark attempted to sit up, but found it difficult because of the restraints in his positioning, but the shifting around was enough for Jessie to take notice.

"Oh hey, you're up!" he loudly whispered before cautiously checking out the front of the car. "I don't know how much time we have. She's talking to some Demon out there, but I wanted to clear the air between us." The polite tone of his voice was confusing considering the situation. "I'm not a bad guy," he reasoned. "I'm just doing what I was told. I can't go back to the torment. I did my time and paid for my sins. They told me that if I didn't help, then I would be resentenced." Even through the anger Mark could see his point. Even if he had not experienced it first hand, from what he had been told and witnessed about the Wastelands and the Tormented, it was easy to see why people would do anything not go to back. Jessie started to unbutton the top of his shirt as he continued to speak. "I was a conman, a kind looking older man who took advantage of young widows. It was a different time than what you knew. a windowed woman had few options and often looked for a man who was more like a father figure to protect them and their money." With the first 3 buttons on his shirt undone, he pulled the left side down past his shoulder to reveal a ring seared into his skin. The ring had a faint red glow to it, making it impossible to miss even in the darkness. "I had stolen a small fortune when I decided to retire. I traveled south through the States posing as a retired lawman in an attempt to cross the border into Mexico. I thought that nobody would question or dare to mess with a retired lawman, but I was mistaken, and right before the border, I was attacked by a group of men who didn't take kindly to men who enforced the law." Even with only the dim light as a source, it was easy to see the painful honesty on Jessie's face. It was clear that he did not tell that story to many people, but Mark couldn't tell if the shame was from the sins or from the poor decision that had led to his death. His tone changed from one of quiet reserve to frustration "I never hurt anybody. Sure, some of those women may have lost some money, but I never left them destitute. I wasn't a bad guy, not compared to some of the people here! The sentence did not fit the crime, and even if it did, I paid for it threefold." The toll the story had taken on him was clear as he turned again to avoid any eye contact with Mark.

The radio changed to "Everybody Hurts" by R.E.M as Nicole opened the door and took the seat behind the wheel. "Ugh, I hate this music," She muttered as she reached for the radio and found "You're so Vain" by Carly Simon. She looked to Jessie and said, "So we are close, apparently it's just up ahead. He said it's marked with the sign of Wrath."

His response was nothing more than a somber head nod. Mark laid as still as he could in an attempt to not draw attention to himself. He wasn't sure if it was guilt or indifference, but Jessie had not mentioned that he was now awake, and Mark wasn't anxious to announce it.

"Will you cheer the fuck up?" she demanded. "It's almost over, and tomorrow it all goes back to normal for you. It all goes back to normal for us."

The car started and took off. Each bump and hill of the wastes echoed and vibrated through the car in a way that would be acceptable sitting up. They sat in silence with only the radio for sound, and after a short time, the car started to slow until it again was stopped. Nicole peered in the backseat and smiled when she saw Mark was awake. "Good morning Babe!" she announced. If she was feeling remorse or regret, it didn't show in her face or voice. "Get him out of the car," she ordered, and Jessie obeyed. The radio started "Paint it Black" by the Rolling Stones as Jessie opened the back driver's side door. His pull was gentle as he took extra care not to hurt or cause any discomfort as he again threw him over his shoulder and carried him to the front of the car.

From the kneeling vantage point, he could only see a large rock with the symbol of Wrath carved into it, the same symbol he saw both on Ellis and in the handbook. Outside of the cone of light provided by the headlights was total black. He looked up and saw that not even the artificial stars or moon would witness his demise.

"Well, here we are," Nicole started as she paced in front of him. "You know, Mark, for what it's worth, I really liked you. From the moment we met, I liked your devil-may-care attitude, your total disregard for authority. What can I say, I like bad boys. I have a type." Mark looked away and avoided giving her the satisfaction of eye contact. At the sign of disrespect, she stepped forward and brought the back of her hand against the side of his face, knocking him off balance and causing him to fall. He felt the familiar light grab of Jessie, who must have been standing behind him, waiting for his cue. Mark was placed back on his knees as Nicole continued. "You know, you're not the only one who's been reading that book. You have just been focusing on the wrong chapters. There's a prophecy that talks about Broken Windows and Broken Shells and Windows to the Soul. I don't remember it word for word. But it turns out that was written about destroying the shells we are given. Yeah, some Wrath figured it out. If you destroy a Soul's eyes then the spirt leaves the shell. From what I understand, it's kind of what happens to people sentenced to Envy."

Mark started to struggle, causing a fake sympathetic "awe" from Nicole. "Go ahead, take out the gag. It looks like he's got some last words." Jessie did as he was told and removed the shirt from Mark's mouth, causing him to cough and stretch his jaw. "Did you have something you wanted to add?" she asked mockingly.

Torn between the desire to ask questions and denying her the satisfaction that would come with her no doubt snarky response, Mark sat in silence, debating his words. "Why?" he finally asked.

Nicole cocked an eyebrow and repeated the question, "Why? What do you mean why?" She walked towards and then circled around him as she spoke. "Do you mean why me? Or are you asking why here?"

He interrupted her monologue with the question, "Why are you doing this?"

She stopped in front of him and placed her hands on her hips as a sign of frustration. "Are you on about this again? Does it matter? You're about to be vaper. You're about to be forced to wander Hell for Eternity with no ability to touch and speak. Why does it matter?"

Jessie spoke from behind him, "Quit being a bitch, you betrayed the man. He he at least deserves to know why."

Nicole's eyes burned as she glared at Jessie and asked, "Did you tell him why you betrayed him? Did your explanation offer him piece of mind? You are here to do the heavy lifting, nothing more. If I want your feedback, I'll ask for it."

Mark didn't want to say it, but the answer to her question was yes. He didn't agree with the motivation, but he understood it and that realization made him uncomfortable.

"Look," Nicole started, "we all have something we want, and we all do what we can to get what we want. I'm not different. You can call me a bitch all you want, but I was given the opportunity to get what I wanted and I took it."

"What did they offer you?" Mark asked again, causing her to scream in frustration.

"I get my kid back if I got you here. Is that what you wanted to know? What does it matter? They told me to keep you away from that stripper bitch so you would end up here. I keep you here and I get my son and I get to go home."

Julie. Mark struggled and attempted get to his feet but was stopped by Jessie's hand on shoulder. "What has this got to do with her!" he demanded.

Nicole rolled her eyes. "I don't know, I don't ask questions. I was told to keep you away from her so you would end up here. He told me that if I couldn't convince you to stop looking around and just accept it, then this is an alternative."

Jessie interrupted, "What do you mean you get to go home?"

Her face beamed with Pride as she explained, "I'm a Special Case. I get go back up the stairs from that stupid prophecy. We kill this loser and I wake up."

Mark's mind raced at the thought that being a Special Case may mean that he could leave, but how did she know? Not even Jack knew for sure what it meant. She continued, "Now I'm going to finish it and go home to my son. Goodbye, Mark."

She stepped towards him and extended her hands towards his face, causing him to struggle against the force of Jessie holding him down. "Wait, wait, wait!" he shouted. "You can't go back home, you killed yourself!"

Nicole laughed, "You think you know everything."

Mark thought back to her profile. "But you had a date of death!"

The statement caught her off guard. "What are you talking about?"

Jessie seemed confused as well, and the grip on his shoulders eased. "Your profile had a death date. Your profile says you died on September 15th. I'm a Special Case, and I don't have a date of death on my profile."

Nicole took a step back. "No, you're lying. I get to go home. They told me I get to go home. He said if I overdose, then I'll go into a coma and I can wake up at the ER."

Mark felt a sudden surge of compassion for her. "They lied to you, Nicole. When you overdosed, you died."

She fell to her knees as the realization hit her. "But I was getting my son back... We were going to start again..."

As he watched her fall apart, he could remember being told that he wouldn't see his father again. Nicole slumped over onto the floor as Jessie removed his hands from Mark's shoulders.

He attempted again to stand when he noticed Nicole launch at him. She screamed as she lunged for him with hatred in her eyes. Her hands were extended, and he closed his eyes and bent his neck to in the only action that he could use to protect himself. Time felt as if it slowed, and he waited for the attack and was shocked when it never came. Cautiously, he lifted his head and slightly opened his eyes only to find that he was inches away from her chest. As he lifted his head more, he found that her arms had fallen to her sides and that a pair of large hands were wrapped around her skull with their thumbs pressed firmly into her eye sockets.

Jessie held his grip long after she stopped moving, long enough for Mark to maneuver away from the scene and make it to his feet. Jessie stared at her and didn't look away even after he finally released the grip, causing her to collapse in front of him. When he was finally able to look at something other than the lifeless shell, it was only to his hands, which trembled in the light from the headlights. "Jessie?" Mark finally asked, causing the large Santa-like man to look up.

"If they lied to her, then maybe they lied to me." His face was torn with regret and conviction. "She deserved it. She was a bad person."

"Bad is a relative term." The familiar voice sent chills down Mark's spine as he turned to see Jack leaning against the rock with the Wrath symbol carved into it. He smiled as their eyes met and continued, "People call me bad all the time. Was she really doing anything more than trying to protect her family? All she wanted was to see her son."

Jessie fell to his knees and started begging incoherently as Mark spoke. "You're the one behind this? You're the one who set this up?" his voice rose with every word until he was screaming as Jack calmly smiled on as if it didn't bother him. Jessie, who had always feared the Demons because of his time in the wastes, stood and walked towards Mark in an attempt to stop him, but was halted by a simple stop gesture from the Demon.

"You have been through a lot, and your frustration is understandable. That being said, please understand that the only reason you continue to stand is because I want something and I need your help." The Demon's voice faltered as he said the word need as if it caused him personal pain. "In a short time, this area will be covered with Wraths, and it is best that none of us are still here. I am sorry Jessie, but you cannot come with us. Please untie him, give him your shirt, and take the car back to the Complex."

Doing as he had the whole night, Jessie complied without question as Mark demanded answers. "I'm not going anywhere until you tell me what's going on!" The determination in his voice hid the fear of the answer he might receive as the car they arrived in pulled backwards before turning and heading in the opposite direction.

Jack smiled. "I guess now your options are come with me or wait here for the Wraths that migrate this way." Jack walked around the large boulder, and after a moment, the sound of an engine started. Mark looked back at the silhouette of Nicole's lifeless shell as he weighed his options and found them considerably lopsided. Reluctantly, he followed Jack's footsteps around the boulder to a dark colored compact sedan.

Jack drove with the lights off, causing the already bumpy ride to be even more so. Mark clutched the arm rest and the dash board while bracing his feet firmly against the floor. He noticed that Jack at least looked like he was paying careful attention to the pitch black surroundings. He had so many questions that he was sure would only end with a snide response or, even worse, an answer he didn't want to hear, so he let his mind wander but found it circling back to what Nicole had said. He tried to think of the many prophecies he had read in an attempt to decipher any of them. He thought that if he could only find one that was true then, he may find comfort in her ramblings about going home.

They drove until the artificial light started to rise before anything was said. Mark looked through the windows of the car at the vast and barren Wasteland which spread in all directions before being startled by Jack's words. "You will not be missed in the office today. I have taken care of it and given you an excuse to be out. This will only give us a one-day head start before they start looking." For a second time, his words seemed uncharacteristically kind and sincere. Not since their first meeting had Mark not seen him show the signs of the calm and confident gameshow host that he normally portrayed.

They drove in silence until they came across a pack of Tormented beings punished for Greed in front of a large rock with the familiar Ring symbol carved into it. "What's going to happen to Jessie?" Mark asked as the Tormented shuffled towards the car. In their eyes he could see the blind desire for something new as the weight of their Greed slowed them and caused them to struggle.

The Demon signed, "I guess it all depends on how smart whoever it was who sent him on the suicide mission in the first place is. If he signed a new contract, then he will be found in breach of that contract."

The sudden realization struck Mark that he would never see Tony or Rebecca or Laura ever again. He wondered if they waited for him in the morning for the carpool, or if Jessie had told them he wouldn't be going. How would he explain that, tell the truth? "Yeah, Mark isn't going to make it to work today because his girlfriend and I took him out to the wastes last night to kill him, only I had a change of heart and killed his girlfriend instead, and that's when I left him there in the middle of nowhere with a Demon." Was this what happened to all Special Cases?

As the artificial light reached its peak, Mark asked, "So where is it exactly we are going?"

Instead of an answer, Jack replied, "Let me tell you a story. A long time ago, there was this Great War over Mortals of all things. The Creator favored the Mortals over all his creations and some Angels grew resentful."

Mark interrupted, "Yeah, yeah, I know. I read the book. The fallen warriors were sent to Hell and the Messenger delivered the prophecies."

Jack laughed a quiet laugh and slightly shook his head. "Mortals are always so headstrong. The problem with your race is that you are unwilling to listen. You assume that everything you read is correct and tells the whole story."

He was right. It was hard for Mark to admit, but he was right. Even in a world where things are edited for time and content, he still took most of what he saw at face value. "I'm sorry," He offered. "Please continue."

The Demon took the offer of respect and wore his approval on his face. "You only know one part of the story, the part that Phelix decided was relevant. What is not told in the book is how the war was started. It does not tell that some of the Angels grew resentful of the love and attention that was given to Mortals and suggested an uprising. Not all Angels were in favor of the uprising, but when the Great War started, we all were forced to pick a side, and some of us were sentenced and punished for simply choosing the one."

Mark asked, "Were you one of the ones that was forced to pick a side?" but the Demon ignored the question to continue the story.

"The war was brutal, brother fighting brother when neither really knew what they were fighting for. As the battles waged, the creator would not be seen, some say in fear of a double cross. Most of us never believed that reason because we never believed that one of us would attack the creator, which in turn only further caused us to question what it was we were really fighting for." Jack started to slow the car, causing the bumps to become more noticeable until the car eventually stopped. The Demon turned off the motor and continued the story. "Eventually, the war ended and the fallen were sentenced. This is where the handbook picks up. The Messenger came to down and gave the book of prophecies, but another thing that the book gets wrong is that the Messenger was not forced to stay in order to deliver the message; he was forced to stay because he too chose the wrong side."

As the Demon spoke, he became more and more passionate. With each word, the volume in his voice rose and turned his voice into one formed by years of pain and neglect.

"The Messenger did nothing more than voice his opinion that the punishment given to the Fallen Warriors was too harsh. He did nothing more but to stand up for those he saw as being unjustly sentenced and because of that, he was branded a trader and given the book to deliver on his way to serve his punishment."

Jack looked nothing like his normal self. As his story unfolded, the bright blue eyes faded and the perfect wavy black hair fell flat. The Demon's face had contorted to become gaunt and grotesque, which made Mark uneasy. Noticing the look on Mark's face Jack, checked his reflection in the mirror and explained, "Fallen wear a lot of their emotions on their faces and use much of their energy maintaining the illusion." With great effort straining across his face, the Demon focused, and his face restored to its former state.

"So you were the Messenger?" Mark asked.

"I was the Messenger. For over a millennium I have served dutifully as sentenced, and now you are the key to going home." Jack's eyes looked strange. They looked hopeful. For the first time, he looked like a human and not just something trying to look like a human.

"What do you mean I'm the key? I don't understand what any of this has to do with me."

Jack smiled and said, "All in due time," before exiting the car. Mark did the same and hurried to catch up as the Demon was already walking away. Mark was thankful that the Wasteland only looked like a Wasteland and did not come with the unforgiving conditions found in the places for which it was modeled. The two walked until the artificial light started to dim when the Demon said:

Out of place in space and time
Only some can stand the climb
An entry, an exit, made of stone
Hidden where no lights are shown
Wrath and Greed show the way
Envy, Sloth, and Pride by day
Follow Lust and Gluttony
Only then the way you see

Mark spoke the words again to himself while trying to think of where he had heard them before. It was something Laura had said when she was talking about prophecies. "You're looking for the stairs?" Mark asked.

"Nope," the Demon responded as he raised his hand and pointed into the distance. "I am looking for him."

In the distance, Mark could see what could be a man moving in their direction. What started as a speck on the horizon quickly turned to a figure in the distance, and before long, Mark found himself standing face to face with a man in a Soul's outfit. His face was kind and showed the wrinkles of time and wisdom. He smiled at the sight of Jack. "Greetings, old man," the Demon said as the two shook hands. Mark was taken aback by the sight. He would have never imagined a Demon being this familiar and friendly with a Soul.

The old man replied, "Am I getting that easy to track nowadays?" before laughing a cautious laugh.

Jack smiled, "Actually no, I knew this was one of your old haunts and I just got lucky, I guess."

The old man's distrusting eyes shown through the friendly banter. "Yeah, you always seem to get lucky. Why did you find me, Jack?"

The Demon returned to his polished gameshow act as he said, "I think you know why I'm here. The word is you are the only one who knows where it is."

The old man rolled his eyes. "You know you cannot use it. Revealing its existence would only give false encouragement to Souls and cause millions to try."

Mark had watched his parents play the pronoun game growing up and had even played a few rounds with several of the women he had been with over the years. His only question was why? Everybody knew they were talking about the stairs, so it was not for Mark's benefit, meaning that it could only be for the old man's. The realization came with another question: why would Jack hide that he had already told someone about the stairs unless it was out of respect for the stranger, and more so, why would the Demon respect the old man so much?

Interrupting his train of thought, the old man said, "I wish you would tell your Mortal to stop thinking about us."

"I do not think he knows that we can tell when we are thought of," Jack responded in a playfully teasing way.

Mark added, "You were the one who drug me out here with no explanation, so forgive me if I've offended you by having an internal monologue about your motives!"

The old man's smiling face changed to one of patience and understanding, and as they made eye contact, Mark felt a sense of warmth and love he had not known since he was young. "Forgive me, being alone often makes me forget why I had chosen to be alone. You understandably have questions that this Demon has not or cannot answer. Walk with me, gentlemen, and I will answer what questions I can." The old man placed his hand on Mark's shoulder and turned him to walk back the way they came.

Mark asked, "Who are you?"

The old man introduced himself. "My name is Isaac Lanson."

Mark remembered finding the prophecy in the book after he was told the story.

Born in a year that a new land is born
On his 37th year his world would be torn
At night the shadows is where he must stay
The world must not know who he is in the day
On his 37th year his world would be torn
His 38th year a king would be born"

Isaac explained, "Yes, I am that Isaac Lanson," making Mark feel sheepish and foolish. "Jack and I met long ago, longer than I can remember. He was at my trial and he was there when I first arrived."

Jack added, "I was the one who taught him how to change his appearance, a trick he refuses to use."

Isaac laughed, "Not true, I am wearing a disguise now!" causing Jack to snort in disgust. He continued, "Jack thinks I should be more like him and the others. He thinks I should adopt an image that is more pleasing, but it serves no purpose for me out here, so I choose to look like my former self. But I digress. Jack told me his story, one similar to mine. Never did either of us think that we would find someone in a similar situation. Jack moved on to recruiting and overtime became more like the fallen warriors he surrounded himself with while I decided that I would instead distance myself in an attempt to retain some part of my lost Humanity."

"So the prophecies are true then?" Mark asked.

The old man looked at Jack and they both smiled. "Nobody really knows," He finally responded. "Souls read the prophecies and assign them to anything they can to look for meaning and hope. I can tell you that many of the stories are true. the rumors that Souls talk to each other about are often based in fact."

"Like the staircase?" Mark asked.

"Yes, like the staircase. After I decided to leave, I understand that people had found a passage that could be associated with my life, but I have not read it. Was my coming prophesied? I would not say so, but only the person who wrote the prophecies could tell you."

Jack added, "Even some Fallen think that the prophecies are true," as he and Isaac exchanged playful glances. "It is a frequent argument between several of us. But enough about the prophecies. Isaac, we need to know where the staircase is. This Mortal is a Special Case and can use it."

Mark thought back to the previous night and what Nicole said. She was right, but how did she know that only Special Cases could use the staircase? When did Jack find out?

Isaac stopped in his tracks and surveyed Mark, looking him up and down in a judging manner. "He is not what I would have thought a Special Case looked like." Mark was unsure if he was proud or offended. Turning back to Jack, he continued, "So even if he is a Special Case, what is in this for you? Why do you care so much about getting this Mortal to the staircase?"

Jack's charm seemed to amplify as if he was trying to be persuasive or avoid the question. "This Mortal was my contract, and if this is not his time, then this is a black mark on my record, and I will not have that."

The Demon's words seemed too genuine, a sign that he was likely not completely honest with his answer, but the reasoning seemed enough for Isaac, who sighed and relented. "I will tell you the location, but you must never reveal it to anyone."

Jack held his hand over his chest where a human heart would be and said, "Would I lie?" causing both the men to laugh.

As the three reached the sedan, Jack turned to Mark and said, "Please give us a moment. I will be right behind you."

From the passenger seat of the car, Mark watched as Jack and Isaac shook hands again and exchanged more words, which caused a look of concern on the Demon's face. They then embraced and walked their separate ways, Jack heading back to the car and Isaac walking alone back into the wastes.

As soon as the door closed, Mark asked, "What was that all about?"

The confidence in Jack's face was betrayed by the fear in his voice. "It is probably nothing," he offered reassuringly. "Isaac thinks that people other than me have been tracking him. I knew there was another player in this game, but I did not think that they were as smart as I am." Jack turned the car to the left and headed off through the Wastes as the last bit of artificial light disappeared from the sky.

The Demon now kept the headlights on through the night, a sign Mark took as the Demon did not know exactly what to expect. The car slowed and sped up when sights of bonfires in the distance came into and disappeared from view. Seeing the Demon be vulnerable made Mark look at Jack differently. Understanding that he did not have the answers to most of the questions in his mind, Mark took a different approach and asked, "How long have you been a recruiter?"

A confused look crossed Jack's face, and it was clear nobody had ever asked him about himself before. "It was assigned me to from the beginning, although it has changed considerably over time. This place, Hell as you Mortals call it, has always been, even before the Great War. As a Messenger, it was my duty to inform the damned of their status. Once they had passed, they were then sentenced. After the Great War, the decision was made that we must increase our numbers, and mine changed from a role of supplying information to gathering Souls."

From his tone, it was easy to see that he had fond memories of before the Great War, which probably only made it hurt more to think about what he had lost. The two spoke of life in Paradise and the beginning when the all-powerful became the Creator, and before long it started to feel like a road trip with an old friend. As the artificial lights started to come up, Mark felt comfortable enough to ask, "What exactly are Special Cases and why can only we use the stairs?" The question had been with him since Jack told Isaac that it was a black mark on his record.

The Demon considered the question, and as he did, all the pleasantness drained from his face. In a serious tone, one that Mark had never heard from him before, he said, "I was wondering when you would start with the questions. Know that if I had the answers, then I would give them, but the truth is I do not know much more than you." Mark could hear the frustration in his voice as he admitted his lack of knowledge. "I do not know what exactly a Special Case is, and until Isaac confirmed it, it was just a rumor that you would be able to use the stairs. You may ask any question you want and I will tell you what I do know, but understand that it will likely only lead to more questions."

"Why was I transferred?' Mark asked.

Though his voice remained serious in tone, Jack smiled and said, "I am surprised you have not worked that one out for yourself."

"You mean Ellis?" he asked, causing a confused glance from Jack. "You mean it wasn't Ellis?"

The smile vanished from his face, and with concern in his voice, he replied, "I am not aware of anyone named Ellis. This could be a new wrinkle. I felt that someone in your carpool group would betray you and attempted to limit their access. Who is Ellis?"

Ellis' words rang in his head, "Don't trust anybody." Advice that he had clearly not followed so far. "She said she knew my father and that he asked her to give me the message that everything happens for a reason."

Jack considered the words and asked, "Did she tell you anything about prophecies?"

Mark shook his head, "No, she only told me that there were some places that Souls were not tracked. I'm part of a prophecy, aren't I? That's what this is all about."

The Demon shrugged his shoulders. "Nobody really knows who or what most of the prophecies refer to, but it is possible that someone else thinks you are the subject of one. That would explain the actions against you. As far as I am concerned, you were in the right place at the right time. If it had not been you, I would have found another Special Case. If for some reason you are not supposed to be here and I get you out, then hopefully it will reflect positively on me."

Mark was surprised by the selfish and simple rationale. He would never admit it, but he wanted this to mean more. He wanted more than a simple explanation and he felt cheated with the knowledge that being a Special Case was simply being an error.

With the artificial light on full, Mark could see a great wall that seemed endless on each side approach in the in the distance. The idea that there was an end to the wastes was something that had never dawned upon him. Phelix described it as an endless ocean of nothingness filled with only the Tormented and the occasional large boulder that was left by a Sloth when his sins had been paid for. Jack veered the car left and pulled next to the wall without decreasing in speed, creating one less direction for Mark to stare off into.

"Look," Jack called out as he pointed forward past the hood. "Tire tracks."

Mark sat up in his seat and saw what Jack had noticed. They were driving in the impressions of tire tracks that had previously been left. "I can't imagine there being any adventurous Souls this far out. We've been driving for days."

Jack nodded his head without response. They rode in the existing tire tracks until the artificial light had started to dim, then they noticed the tracks turn and head back out into the wastes. Conflicting feelings arose in Mark. He was glad that they were not following someone, but knowing someone else was out this far did little to calm his nerves. The artificial light went off, and Jack turned the headlights on and continued to drive. The sense of familiarity Mark had felt vanished with Jack's confession of motives and left a tension between them that he could not confront.

Hours had passed in silence when the car started to suddenly slow. The jerk caused by the change in speed snapped Mark back from his thoughts as he looked to Jack for an explanation. "Isaac told me to follow the wall until I found the sign of Envy marking the turn back into the wastes." Mark thought back to the handbook trying to think of the sign of Envy, but lost focus at the sudden turn of the car. Jack pulled hard to the left and pointed the car back out into the wastes, where he again pulled hard left as he applied the brakes, causing the tail end of the car to swing the car around until it was facing the large wall. Jack pointed forward, and through the headlights, Mark could see a large "V" carved into the wall. He suddenly remembered the entry from the handbook.

In Chapter 5, Phelix writes:

Those sentenced to serve punishment because of
Envious actions wander not only the wastes, but also the
Employment sector. Due to their lack of shells, most people
do not realize that the Envious are everywhere. Unlike other
Torments, they tend to travel separately as the need of
companionship is often fulfilled by the voyeurism found in
watching others. Often times the Envious will gather around
the symbol of Envy found in the Wasteland.

The adjacent page held a crude drawing of the wall with a large "V"
carved in it, the same wall that was now in basking in the headlights of the
car. Jack turned the car and headed back out into the wastes as he mumbled
to himself:

Wrath and Greed show the way
Envy, Pride and Sloth by day
Follow Lust and Gluttony
Only then the way you see

The prophecy. Suddenly, Mark understood what Jack was doing. The
rock where Nicole had taken him had the Wrath symbol and the Tormented
Greed they found were by the Greed symbol and now the symbol of Envy.
Pride, Lust, and Gluttony must have been the remaining signs. Mark thought
back to the handbook and said, "I don't remember Pride or Gluttony having
symbols or even being assigned to the Wasteland. What are we looking
for?"

"I do not think we are looking for just symbols. I was never one that
believed in the prophecies," He admitted. "But I think we are on the right
track here. Isaac told me to look for the wall and then for the symbol of
Envy, but it wasn't until then that I realized we had also seen Wrath and
Greed. For eons I had watched as people struggled to decipher the words in
that book while I assumed they were ignorant and simple minded but now,
to see them unfold in front of me, I think I may be a believer."

Mark reclined the chair, lay back, and stared out of the window at the
darkness above while considering Jack's words. He was right, it was so easy
to disregard the stories as nonsense when others are looking for meaning,
but to see one unfold right in front of you gave you a certain sense of awe
and wonder. It made him want to believe. He could finally understand why
Laura clung to them so, but the realization only made him question if that
was their purpose. All his life he had watched as people assigned meaning to
horoscopes and palm readings and fortune cookies. Was it possible that he
was the one that was wrong? For a moment, he wished he was the optimist
and more open-minded; he wished he was like Julie. As the name crossed

him mind, he was weighed down by a sense of guilt. He had not thought of her in days. He tried to justify it by telling himself it was because of all that was going on, but his mind wouldn't let it rest.

The two drove through the night, and as the artificial light started to come on, the car started to sputter and lose momentum. Jack watched on in confusion as the car rolled to a stop in the middle of the barren wastes with nothing as far as the eye could see. He turned the crank, but the engine would not turn over. He slammed his hands against the steering wheel and said, "Well, that is not good."

Mark thought back to the handbook. Phelix wrote that cars shouldn't need maintenance or fuel, but the car had acted like it was out of gas. "What do we do now?" he asked.

Jack leaned his head back and closed his eyes before letting out a sigh. The frustrated look on his face said all it needed to. "I think this is a clear sign that whoever Nicole and Jessie was working for knows what we are up to, and that means they are on their way as well, which means we need to move." Abandoning the car, the two started off into the wastes.

Driving at top speed did little to give an accurate impression of the distance they had traveled. For days, small signs had come into view and gone just as fast. The occasional rock or roaming Tormented would be a sign that they were, in fact, moving. On foot, the vastness of the waste really showed, and by the time the artificial light had reached its maximum, it was easy to still see the Cavalier in the distance behind them. In an attempt to pass the time, Mark asked, "So what happened to the car? I didn't know Demons could do that kind of thing."

Jack shrugged but said nothing.

It was clear he had no interest in talking, but that did not stop Mark from trying to provoke him. "I didn't know that some Demons were stronger than others."

Jack's mouth twitched slightly at the comment. "We Fallen do not vary in strength of ability; however, some have more knowledge than others. Everything can be traced and tracked, and if someone was looking for us, then it was only time before they found us." His voice was low and soft but clear and menacing, as if he were whispering in Mark's ear. "Right now, we need to focus on moving, because before long, we are going to have company that we do not want." Mark felt nauseous as a chill ran up his spine. He had witnessed both the charming and charismatic gameshow host and the casual and friendly persona, but neither had the intensity the Demon now showed. The twitch in his mouth moved throughout his face as Jack continued, "I have come too far to be stopped now."

They walked in silence until, in the distance, Mark could make out large blurs moving on the horizon. Moving toward an object made the trek feel more productive, and before long, the blurs formed into a group of Tormented Sloths pushing large boulders, much like the one Mark had seen in the orientation video what seemed not so long ago.

In Chapter 5, Phelix writes:

Those sentenced to serve punishment due to Slothful actions wander the wastes. They are seen as outcasts and do not typically associate with other Souls. Like all Torments, they tend to travel in groups in order to fulfill the mortal need of companionship. All Sloth sinners push boulders and large rocks that are marked with the symbol of Sloth.

Following Jack's lead, they walked perpendicular in the opposite direction until they could pass behind the group, which seemed more preoccupied with their endless task than the visitors anyway. Alone with only the Demon to distract him, Mark let his mind wander and found himself thinking more and more of Julie. He admitted to himself that thinking he wouldn't be able to see her again is what made the transition easy, and now, knowing that he might made his time there even more unbearable. As they walked in the dimming light, he thought back to the last time he had seen her and their time at the park. He thought about holding hands and walking home and her kiss goodbye. Before long, the light had gone completely. His eyes adjusted slightly, giving him sight for several feet in front of him but nothing past that. With defeat in his voice, he asked, "How do we know where we are even going?"

From beside him, he heard Jack's familiar voice say, "I do not think we do."

Afraid to stop moving for fear he would lose Jack, Mark continued his pace as he broke down and shouted, "So we are wandering around in the dark while in the middle of nowhere with no idea of where we are going? I think it's over. I think at this point we've lost." Suddenly, he felt a tug on his shirt, causing him to fall to the ground where he was straddled and a hand was placed over his mouth.

In the dark, it was hard to tell, but he thought the person pinning him down was Jack, a thought confirmed when the Demon leaned in and whispered, "I need you to shut up and not say a word. There is someone out here with us." Without speaking, Mark nodded his head, which was good enough for Jack. He removed his hand. Mark felt the weight lift off him but heard no sound, as if the Demon had turned to smoke.

On instinct alone, Mark tried to take a deep breath, breathe in on the evens and out on the odds, but like the last time he tried, nothing happened. He tried to be as still as possible but still heard every small movement he made through the sand and gravel beneath him. He listened for any sign through the darkness but came up empty. His mind raced with questions that he would never get an answer to. Could Demons see in the dark? How long did Jack know they were not alone? Is this why he had been silent and avoiding conversation?

"Ugh!" the brief noise came from behind him and caused him to sit up.

He tried to focus his eyes to peer through the darkness in the direction the sound had come but to no avail. "Jack?" he called out but received no answer. In the distance, he now could hear a faint dragging sound that seemed to be getting closer. "Jack?" he called again. "Is that you?"

"What part of not say a word do you not get?" Jack responded in his normal voice, causing a wave of relieve to wash over him. A sudden thud sounded from in front of Mark as Jack explained, "I don't know what happened to this guy, but something is wrong with him." With a snap of his fingers, a small light appeared at the end of his fingertips, causing a dim light to wash over the shell of a man wearing a torn and shredded Soul's outfit.

"Are you telling me you could have done that at any time?" Mark asked.

The Demon nodded. "Yes, but why would I? I can see in the dark."

"Unbelievable," Mark muttered to himself before asking, "So now what? You knocked him out. What are we still waiting for?" Jack pointed down at the Soul's left arm where a jagged Z was burned into his forearm. "What, do you think there is a group around here?" The Demon shook his head, and he then pointed through the tears in his shirt to a symbol of a broken heart on his chest.

In Chapter 5, Phelix writes:

Those sentenced to serve punishment due to Lustful actions are assigned to the Employment sector unless their sins are deemed violent in nature. They often hide their marks and are rarely noticed among the Souls who have paid their debts or otherwise been assigned to the sector. Unlike Torments in the waste, they tend not to travel in groups as the mark is often seen as shameful to those who are no longer being tormented.

Mark recognized the symbol from the handbook but had never seen one in person. Jack explained, "This symbol is fresh. See how it looks red compared to the other? This Soul has paid for his Wrathful sins and has now been assigned to pay for his Lustful ones. Follow Lust and Gluttony, only then the way you see."

The shell started to stir in the dim light as his eyes opened only to be greeted by a Demon. The Soul attempted to move himself backwards in fear as Jack smiled. It was clear he enjoyed the power trip.

"I'm sorry, I'm sorry, I'm sorry," he muttered almost incoherently. The Soul shook his head in an attempt to avoid looking directly at the Demon when he finally saw Mark, who generated an even greater reaction of fear. Lacking options, he curled into a tight ball and continued to mumble to himself.

"I like him!" Jack announced.

Mark walked to the Soul, who had moved far enough that he was only barely visible in Jack's light. "Hey, we're not going to hurt you." He did his best to keep his voice calm. "We're just travelers."

The Soul continued to rock back and forth saying, "Don't lie to me! He's a Demon and nobody just wanders around the Wasteland. This is a trick! You're one of them, aren't you?"

"I've had enough of this." Jack said as he stood and made his way to the Soul. With each step, the light extended farther until the Demon was standing over the cowering man. "You will answer our questions, either out of fear or respect, I do not care which." The Soul nodded his head in agreement. "Where did you come from?"

The Soul trembled, causing his words to stutter. "I was p-placed in t-this shell as it was b-being beaten."

"Placed?" Mark asked.

The Demon smiled. "He is a glutton. This was his assignment."

The Soul nodded again. "I've n-never been p-placed outside of t-the Employment Sector. When t-the Wraths left I-I-I just s-started walking unt-till it got dark and I heard him sh-shouting."

"Which way did you come from?" Jack asked in his calm and confident voice. "Did you see or pass any landmarks?"

He pointed in a direction and said, "Right b-before it went dark I c-could see a large stone in the middle of nowhere in the d-distance. I hear that the T-tormented use them as m-markers so I tried my best to avoid it. C-can I go?"

Jack smiled at Mark, who offered only a confused look in exchange. "You can go, Soul, but do not cross my kind again!" The Soul crawled to his feet and ran in the direction opposite of where he came.

"Was that really necessary?" Mark asked, as if his objection would make any difference.

The Demon smiled as the light on his finger slowly went out. "Probably not, but it was fun."

They had traveled until the lights started to come up when they saw it in the distance. "There it is," Jack said as he pointed to the large rock. Mark's eyes squinted as he tried to see, but from as far away as they were, it looked less like a staircase and more like a random rock in the middle of nowhere.

"Are you sure this is it?" Mark asked.

The Demon's smile was all the answer needed. Like an excited child, the anticipation was written on his face, overtaking the calm and confident swagger. By the time the artificial light had come completely up, the rock formation in the distance had tripled in size and started to look more like a staircase that led to nothing. There appeared to be no second floor or platform at the top, only a staircase to the sky crudely carved from a large boulder.

As they moved closer still, Mark could make out a figure wearing what looked like a Soul's outfit leaning against the wall of the stairs. "Who's that?" he asked. "Is it the people Isaac warned us about?"

The joy and excitement changed to a look of concern on the Demon's face. "I do not know. We are kind of playing it by ear at this point." They continued on until they were in front of the stairs where the Soul moved to greet them. He looked strange, almost too happy to be in the position he was in. The Soul moved with an overly embellished sense of confidence and looked like he was trying to mimic the walk of a Demon. Mark offered a questioning glance to Jack, who replied by shrugging his shoulders.

"I've never seen a Fallen bring someone. This is exciting!" The way the Soul said "Fallen" without fear or contempt in his voice was confusing. It wasn't often a Soul showed such indifference to the creatures, as if their power meant nothing to him. The Soul extended his hand to Jack, who took it cautiously, as he continued his greeting. "It's been longer then I could count since someone has actually made it this far and even longer since there was one who could use them." As he said it, he turned and looked to the stone monolith behind him. It was clear that he held deep respect for this makeshift staircase.

"Who are you?" Mark finally found the voice to ask. Judging by the face he made, it seemed the question caught the Soul off guard.

After a moment, he responded, "Phelix?" as more of a question than a statement. "Phelix," he confirmed with more confidence the second time.

"Phelix Utengard?" Mark asked, a question answered with a simple nod.

"Phelix Utengard, the Phelix Utengard who wrote the handbook?" Mark asked.

"The one and the same!" Phelix beamed proudly.

"I thought Phelix Utengard was a Fallen?" Jack asked as he quickly retracted his hand, causing Phelix to laugh.

"I get that a lot, not totally sure why. I mean Fallen don't really have the reputation for helping Souls if you know what I mean." Realizing who he was talking to, he quickly added, "Most Fallen, you seem like a nice enough guy. But let's get to the good part. You're someone who thinks they can climb the stairs, aren't you? You came to try your luck and get out of the Underworld, didn't you?"

Mark found Phelix's openness alarming and off putting. The time spent in isolation seemed to have an effect on the man's mental faculties, and it showed. His words came fast and jumbled together at times, as if he had forgotten how conversation between two people works. He spoke as if every word might be his last, so it was imperative to get them all out as fast as possible. Words from Ellis saying not to trust anybody came floating through his head. "What is this?" Mark asked in hopes of learning something more than he knew.

Phelix's eyes went wide with the question, and he smiled a broken and twisted smile as he turned and opened his arms wide. "This is my staircase!" he shouted with glee in his voice. "I made them myself you know. Took me a long time, but I carved them with my own two hands!" The Soul beamed with Pride over his creation and took offence at the confused looks passed between Jack and Mark. "You doubt me?" he shouted. "I was prophesized to write the handbook and again prophesized to build the staircase! You cannot judge me. Only he can judge me! I am a chosen one; I am the eyes of the Creator!" As his rant finished, the Soul turned and walked to the side of the monument in disgust.

Mark looked to Jack for guidance. If the staircase was the delusion of a mad man then what was their next step? It was too late to go back. By the Demons own admission, someone knew what they were up to. But instead of answers, he received only an intrigued look from Jack's face.

"I have heard those words before," he said. "When I was sentenced, the angel who came to me said that he was the chosen one, the eyes of the creator." Mark's eyes tuned to Phelix, who was now leaning against the staircase as he had when they approached. Jack continued, "He told me that the Creator sees all. He had seen my deceit and was disappointed." Jack's face again started to contort as it did when he talked about his time in Paradise. The pain of disappointing a father figure made his voice tremble slightly. It was a feeling Mark was well aware of. "Seer!" he called out, causing the Soul to look up. "I know you and meant no offence. Why are you here? Why would you be sentenced with the Fallen?"

Phelix beamed with Pride again, not at his creation, but at the respect and recognition shown by the Demon. He again approached the pair and said, "The Creator's gaze cannot penetrate this place, so I was sent as his conduit. I know you too, Messenger, was told to take your book of prophecies and make them available to all as what is destined to happen is knowledge all should share. Are you here to fulfill your destinies?"

"What do you mean?" Mark asked "It's my destiny to climb the stairs?"

"No," a voice called from behind them. "It is your destiny to make a choice." Mark turned to see a figure wearing a black hooded robe. His familiar voice recited:

An unjust visitor
An unjust choice
The fate of hell
Within his voice
Before the War
Sins must be paid
On the steps
A decision is made

"He knows his prophecies!" Phelix added with a cackle.

Jack shouted, "Why do you choose such dated garb, brother?" The last word coated with disrespect. "Most Fallen have long forgotten that form."

The hooded figure offered a condescending laugh. "Does my appearance upset you, brother? Does it hurt to be reminded of our former glory? I thought it was fitting considering the event, but if you prefer, I can offer a more relatable appearance." The hooded figure started to contort and stretch as his body changed. His dark robes changed to jeans and a button up shirt as his hood pulled back to a twisted face that slowly morphed to a familiar one.

"How is this look?" Wayne asked as he stared at Mark. "Do you prefer this look?" he snapped his fingers and his Jeans and shirt changed to a black suit. "Or how about this one?" he asked Jack.

Jack smiled. "Theodore. You were always one of the strongest believers in the prophecies."

"Please," Wayne interrupted. "I think the Mortal would prefer you call me Wayne."

"This is why I couldn't find you in the system," Mark concluded. "This is why your name always came back with a 400 error. But I knew you for two years. We saw each other daily for two years!"

"You knew what I needed you to know," Wayne responded. "It was extremely difficult listening to you and gaining your trust, but everything about you lined up with the prophecies, so I just had to stick with it. I just had to wait for the right time and then send the right recruiter to bring you here. That Julie girl almost ruined it; love would have given you reason to stay. You Mortals let too much of your life be run by your organs. Not even taking you to see her at her lowest moment was enough. Luckily, Nicole was more than willing to help in exchange for custody of her child. She almost failed. I told her not to sleep with you, told her to stay away knowing it would make you want her more, but Mortals just do not listen sometimes. She believed so much that when I told her to kill herself, she did without question." He made his way to the stairs and stood in front of them. "I knew that keeping you here was the key. Given enough time, you would make the decision."

"And when I started looking for answers you decided to make it so I couldn't leave by destroying my shell?" Mark asked.

"I always knew you were a smart one," Wayne confirmed. "The problem came from my recruiter and his openness about your Special Case status."

"Special Case?" Phelix asked. "You're a Special Case?"

Wayne's voice boomed at the Seer, "It does not matter what he is!" before regaining his composure. "What matters is that he is here to make a choice, and until he does, he will not be leaving."

"And how do you expect to stop him?" Jack asked. "We have no control over free will, brother, or have you forgotten?"

Wayne smiled, forcing his normal mouth into a long and twisted version as he spoke. "Do you think I am the only one who wants a second Great War? Do you think I am alone? When I announced that I had found the one of the prophecy, a number of Fallen pledged their support to me. We are strong and have power that no Fallen could fathom." His face morphed from the Demonic twisted version back to the one that Mark had built a relationship with over the years. In the kind and friendly voice he recognized from the cube next to him, Wayne asked, "What is it you want, Power? We could make you a King. All Souls and even lower Fallen like the Messenger here would bow before you. How about fame and money? We can give you the power to possess and you can go back to earth and take any life you wish. Or how about this," Wayne snapped his fingers and a television appeared in front of them showing a group of Torments. Pointing to one without restrictive cages, he said, "That is your father. We can wipe his debt clean. We can even give you a large home where you could live together while you reign over your minions."

The Demon's eyes became wide as Mark watched his father on the screen. They both knew he had found a soft spot, and like any salesman, Wayne applied pressure. "How long has it been since you had seen him? How many years do you have to catch up?"

"Mark?" Jack called.

"Quiet!" Wayne demanded. "This does not concern you!"

Mark watched the screen as his father walked through the Wasteland followed by a group of Torments in varying levels of confinement. He appeared to be leading the way, meaning that maybe Ellis was telling the truth. His attention only left the screen when he felt a bony hand on his shoulder. In a kind voice, unlike the erratic one he used previously, Phelix said, "Do not let this Demon fool you."

Wayne bellowed, "This is the last time I will warn you, Soul! Stay out of my business or you will regret your interference!"

The Seer's face hardened as he looked to Wayne. Abandoning his kind voice, he repeated his rant from earlier, "You cannot judge me. Only he can judge me! I am a chosen one; I am the eyes of the Creator!"

Wayne offered an indifferent look and sighed heavily as he snapped his fingers. but nothing happened. Confusion crossed his face as he snapped again with the same results. "Foolish Demon, you have no power over me! Only he can judge me!" The Seer raised his hands. and Wayne was forced to the ground by an unseen force.

"How?" Wayne managed to ask under the tremendous weight.

"Quiet Demon!" Phelix shouted before turning to Mark and returning to his kind voice. "This is not your time. You should not be here." Looking into his eyes felt like looking into the eyes of Isaac. "Provide me this Soul's contract." He ordered to Jack, who snapped his fingers and pulled it from thin air. Phelix took the parchment in his out reached hand and quickly unrolled it. "The reason these stairs were built is for people like you. Your contract states that you are here of your own decision. Before you make your decision, consider that you have not passed on, and if you do not sign a new contract, then you are free to leave whenever." The Seer snapped his fingers, and Wayne showed signs of relief as the invisible weight lifted from his body.

"That is why I could not see his clock?" Jack asked. "That is what a Special Case is?"

Jack's face filled with remorse for all the Special Cases he had collected as Phelix offered only a simple nod as his response. Noticing the change, he said, "What you are feeling is good. It means you may still be redeemed."

"No!" Wayne shouted as he returned to his feet. "No, he is staying here!" He marched forward as he spoke, becoming more determined with each word. As he got closer to Mark, he raised his hands and extended his thumbs as Nicole did on her approach. "I will finish what that little bitch could not and destroy the windows to your Soul!" Suddenly, the Demon fell to the ground again as the Seer raised his arms. Pinned beneath the invisible weight, he struggled to yell "If you leave, I will personally make sure your father and your mother and all your loved ones suffer torments worse than you can imagine!"

"Time is not on your side," Phelix said. "You must make your choice."

Mark looked to the screen that still showed his father leading a group through the wastes. Though far away and grainy, he could still make out the familiar smile on his father's face as his last words rang through his mind.

Everything happens for a reason.

Mark turned and placed his first step on the stairs. From under the invisible force, he could hear Wayne strain to yell, "You stupid Mortal! You will be back. You cannot change who you are, and when your life is over, you will be back."

A zebra can't change its stripes.

No point in painting a turd.

Mark looked to Jack, who still wore the regret he was feeling on his face, and then to Phelix, who only offered a smile. Lifting his body off the ground, he placed his second foot on the stairs and was blinded by a white light. As his eyes adjusted, he found that the crude stone stairs had changed and become smooth and off-white. Looking back, he found that the Wasteland was gone and in its place, only more stairs that continued to go down as far as he could see. Looking forward, he squinted through the bright light and took his next step, which sent a warm sensation up through his leg and into his body. With the next step, a sense of calm washed over him and he found himself free of fear and anxiety. He found that with each step, the climb became easier as he felt lighter, both physically and emotionally. As he went higher, he was flooded with memories that came in the form of a new perspective without being bogged down by self-doubt. He watched himself grow from a child to an adult and relived all the success he had as well as the mistakes he had made through the eyes of an objective third party. The memories continued past his death and into his time in hell, ending finally at him putting his second foot on the steps.

Suddenly, his memories stopped and he found it hard to even recall the most recent of events. He looked around and found himself at the top of the stairs, which looked like a park surrounded by a wall of clouds. To the left, he could see a metal and wood playground with slides and places to climb and to the right, a row of swing sets, a young girl with dark hair swinging on one but the rest empty and motionless. At the far end of the playground stood a wood door surrounded by small and maintained decorative bushes. With the exception of the door, the playground looked familiar, like a distant memory. He and his mother moved several times after his father died, and after a while, all parks and playgrounds began to look the same.

"Hello?" he called to the girl on the swing set, who didn't seem to hear him. She kicked her feet forward only slightly, gaining just enough momentum to keep the swing barely moving. He moved closer and noticed that her blue polo shirt had a yellow bobcat printed on the left breast pocket. It was a shirt he knew well; one he was forced to wear every few days as a child for the year he spent in the Midwest. 'It makes you part of a group' his mother once explained to him. 'It gives a sense of belonging. No one can feel bad for what they are wearing if everyone wears the same thing.' The sound logic was disproven when the school board failed to understand that kids will be kids. Instead of excluding someone based on their clothes, people were now being excluded because their low income families forced the cool kids to be denied the cool clothes. At this early age, he remembered learning that people will always find a way to hate because it's the easiest way to feel better about being you.

Mark watched as a small boy came from the clouds wearing a similar shirt, only reversed in color, yellow with the blue logo. He sheepishly made his way to the swing set, to the swing furthest away from the girl while avoiding eye contact. She looked to him as he passed but payed him no mind. The boy pulled a rolled up comic from his back pocket and took a seat, kicking his feet up and starting to swing. He could remember his father always telling him not to carry his comics like that. "It rubs the pages together and makes them hard to read," he would say, a lesson Mark had never learned. He watched his younger self as he pretended to read the comic while secretly glancing at the girl. Small parts of this girl floated in and out of his memories. Insignificant details gave him backstory. She lived across the street from him and they went to the same piano teacher. He often would get there early and listen to her lesson finish, and once or twice she smiled at him as he left. Their lives never intersected otherwise, their social circles and background differed far too much. Sure, he saw her around school, but they never had the same classes, and while he rode the bus, she always got a ride from her parents. He would have never admitted at it at the time, but the only reason he continued the lessons was for the brief moment they would share as he waited in the living room for her to leave.

Young Mark reached the end of his comic and felt he could no longer use it as a bluff. Trying to sound as causal as possible, he asked, "Excited for the next school year?" The girl turned her head and offered a questioning look as if she did not know if he was talking to her. He repeated, "Are you excited for the next school year?"

She flashed a smile, the one he remembered from their times in-between piano lessons. "Not at all. Summer never seems long enough, you know? Besides,

Her openness was comforting as much as it was alarming. Mark could see that his younger self had not thought much past the first line and lacked the confidence to carry on a conversation. He prepared for a train wreck that was avoided as she did most of the talking, letting Young Mark do little more than offer the occasional smile and nod.

She continued, "My dad sells cars, so he's always away, and when he is home, they like to throw parties, meaning I can rarely have friends over. At least during the summer, I'm not trapped at school. Mom likes to sleep a lot during the day, so I can usually get out and spend time with friends, but what I really like to do is come here and swing."

A flood of memories came rushing back to Mark. He remembered this park. It was outside of the school. One weekend day, he and another boy traveled along the creek all morning and ended up here. They spent the afternoon climbing on the playground, which was normally claimed by the big kids by the time his class had lunch. Soon after, he found that cutting directly through the cornfield instead of following the twisting and winding creek shortened the trip by several hours, and on days when he couldn't find anybody to play with, he would take a comic and come to swing.

"What about you?" It was clear the question caught the boy off guard, and the girl could tell by his lack of a response. She stood and moved to the swing next to him. "You go to my piano teacher, don't you?" The boy nodded. "Yeah," she confirmed. "I thought so. I've seen you around. You look familiar."

"I think we're neighbors," He managed to say, causing both her smile and eyes to widen.

Kicking her feet off the ground, she said, "Yeah, that's where I know you from! So weird that we've lived across the street from each other for who knows how long only to meet here."

From his left, Mark could hear a calm male voice say, "You saved that little girl's life."

The thought of questioning who this was came in only a whisper and was easily ignored. With no desire to even see who he was speaking to, Mark asked, "Why don't I remember this?"

He felt a hand on his shoulder as the voice tried to reason. "Some think it is because Mortals have been conditioned to only focus on the negative. People want justice for when they feel they are wronged and consider the satisfaction gained from vindication better than that of a small act of kindness." Mark found truth in the words as tried to think of the last good thing he had done and, as he did with Jack, came up empty. "For what it is worth, she does not remember either."

Mark watched as his younger self and the girl started a conversation. He could no longer hear their words, only seeing their actions, but they were both smiling, and he told himself that they were happy. Turning to the voice, he saw an average looking man wearing a grey suit. The lines and wrinkles on his face gave the impression of experience and age while his eyes looked bright and young. "Are you the Creator?" he asked.

The man smiled a kind and small smile and shook his head. "Please," he said, "come with me."

With his hand still on Mark's shoulder, he led him through the park to the wooden door. Mark focused on the children as he passed, still unable to hear them. He watched as she started to fall backwards on the swing and he grabbed her arm. The act filled him with warmth.

Through the door, he found a vast white emptiness with only two reclining chairs tilted towards each other with a small round table in-between them. "Please, sit," the man said as he closed the door. Mark took the chair on the left, and as he sat, he found that the door too had vanished, leaving him alone with the stranger who took the chair across from him.

"I'm sure you have many questions," The stranger said as he crossed his legs.

Mark considered the statement and was surprised to find that he didn't have nearly as many questions as he thought he would have once he found someone who could provide answers. Struggling, he asked, "What is this place?"

Through his polite and caring smile, the stranger explained, "This is in-between life and afterlife. This is where you would have come had you not signed your contract."

Your contract, the words hung heavy in the air, and for the first time, the stranger's voice changed from one of acceptance to one of disapproval.

"What is the 37 percent rule?"

The stranger uncrossed his legs and sighed. "The Fallen use many tactics to gain Souls, but I have not heard of this 37 percent rule. It is no doubt something made up by the Fallen. What did your contract say about it?" The question hit Mark like a ton of bricks. It was something he had said to so many people for so long, 'did you read the contract?' His silence was the only answer the stranger needed, and he returned to his polite smile. Mark leaned forward, placed his elbows on his knees and put his head down while trying hard to think through the wall that had formed in his mind. "Come now," the stranger said, "do not be shy. I know there is a question you have."

He shook his head, half in response and half trying to gain control of his thoughts. It strained him to remember anything, and when it felt like he finally would, it felt as if too much information came flooding to him and clogged his mind. It was overwhelming, everything that had happened with Nicole and Jack and the trip through the Wasteland and the prophecies. As the word passed through his mind, Mark looked up and into the eyes of the stranger, who offered an understanding smile. "I was told that there is a prophecy about me that said I have to make a choice that will affect the second Great War." The stranger looked on and nodded his head to show he was listening. "I think I made the right choice. I chose to use the stairs. I just don't understand how that choice is connected."

The stranger placed his hand on his chin and took a deep breath before answering. "Why do you think that was the choice?" The honestly of the question filled Mark with self-doubt. "Surely because that was the hardest choice you had made recently, it is easy to assume it had some great meaning, but how do you know it does?" He leaned back in his chair and crossed his legs again. "Mortals look to things like prophecies in an effort to apply meaning to their actions and choices. Your kind craves validation. It is part of the human condition. When the Seer made the prophecies available to every Soul, he saw it as a way to help people cope and understand that what will happen is what should happen; however, the Souls did not understand that lesson and instead looked for Hope by fitting prophecies to events."

"But I saw one unfold," Mark argued. "The steps we took were just like that of the prophecy!"

"Did you?" the Stranger asked. Mark was amazed that such a simple question could cause so much doubt. Was it him who realized that the prophecy was coming true, or did he latch onto an idea that Jack had? "I do not like having this conversation as Mortals tend to take it personally, but I regret to inform you that there was no prophecy about you. The prophecies delivered by the Messenger tell the story of the second Great War and how it will be futile. They were designed to discourage the Fallen and nothing more." The stranger leaned in and, with heavy sympathy in his voice, said, "I understand how you feel, but know that you are not the first or last Mortal I must share this news with."

Mark stood up and started to pace. "Then what was the point of all this? Why was it so important that I was taken?" The frustration was now showing in his voice. With each attempt, he found it became easier to access his memories, a fact that the stranger seemed to notice.

"You were never taken. How long you stay is up to you. It is your near death experience," the stranger corrected. The sentence stopped Mark's pacing as he again offered a confused look. "As I have said, had you not signed your contract, then you would have come here regardless. This was and always would have happened, a fact that the Fallen fail to understand. It was again one of the Fallen who misunderstood that you were the one of the prophecy. I understand your desire for meaning and purpose, so perhaps you will take solace in knowing that a prophecy was fulfilled with you present."

"What are you talking about?" Mark asked as he retook his seat.

The stranger cleared his throat and recited:

An unjust visitor
An unjust choice
The fate of hell
Within his voice
Before the War
Sins must be paid
On the steps
A decision is made

Mark offered the stranger a confused look as he explained, "The Messenger, the Fallen you call Jack, on this day he made a choice on the steps. He made the decision to take you there and in doing so, he has started in motion what will end in the second Great War. Others will see his sacrifice and side with him. When the war comes, the Fallen will be divided and in the end those who side with Paradise will have been taught why they were punished. They will understand why the defense of their brothers caused them the punishment it has. They will understand that some Fallen truly believe in their cause, and when it is over, they will be forgiven."

"But does the punishment really fit the crime?" Mark asked.

The stranger uncrossed his legs and again leaned forward. "Thousands of years are only a small part of eternity. It is all about perspective."

He spoke with the care and love of a stern father figure that reminded Mark of his own father. "So what happens now?" he asked. "Where do I go from here?"

The stranger stood and pointed behind the chairs. Mark stood to now see a door, similar to the one they entered. Placing his other hand on Mark's shoulder, the stranger said, "If you are ready then, it is time for you to leave and go back to your life. Do you have any final questions before you go?"

"Only one," he answered. "Who are you?"

The stranger smiled. "We have no names as we are not individuals, but one part of a whole. I am a Messenger, and I am but a conduit. The Creator speaks through me."

Mark nodded, though he did not really understand, and then headed towards the door. With his hand on the doorknob, he turned again, but the chairs, table, and Messenger were gone. Alone in the vast white emptiness, Mark turned the knob.

"And then what happened?"

Mark closed the composition notebook and placed it on the stack with the others. It had taken three sessions, but he had told the whole story, and now maybe he would see some results.

"And then I woke up," he shrugged. "I gasped for air and couldn't breathe, but luckily a nurse came running and pulled the tube from my throat. My jerking motions tore twelve of my stitches, but after I was patched up again, they told me I had been in a coma for 3 days after the surgery."

Dr. Julius Wrenford sat relaxed in his arm chair, leaning back with his left leg crossed over his knee and sitting at an angle that gave him the reach he needed to use the small table next to him as a desk. He was the last therapist in town and normally only worked with children, but at the urging of Miles Trubuck, he had agreed to see Mark. Word had it that Mr. Trubuck even paid in advance, an act of kindness that Mark never thought he would see. His drab eyes looked to his notepad and started jotting some notes. Mark assumed they were about how he was delusional. Of all the doctors he had seen in the last six months, he liked this one the most. His demeanor was comforting; he wasn't as uptight or stiff as others.

Looking back to Mark, he stroked his short beard and asked, "When did you start writing all of this?"

Mark did his best to hide his frustration. He had told his story so many times, and it always ended in disbelief and disregard. With a heavy sigh, he said, "The second day I was awake. I asked for a notebook and started writing down my thoughts. The doctors thought it would be a good idea to let my mind start working again, but I found that all my thoughts were about my time in the Underworld, so I asked for a second book and just started at the beginning." Mark looked down to the stack of notebooks in front of him, all of them filled with his story and drawings of anything he could remember. When he was released he took them to St. Luke's in an attempt to see Father Phil, but Sister Shannon would not allow him. He continued, "I don't know if the act of writing it all out helped, but I found that as I wrote, the things I'd already covered just kind of faded from my memory. It makes me wonder if I didn't write it out, would I have simply forgotten it all."

Dr. Wrenford looked back to his notebook and continued jotting notes while Mark braced himself for the worse. This was usually the point where he was politely told that they could not help him or was written off as having a stress dream from a near death experience.

Tapping his notepad several times, the Doctor said, "What happened to Nicole?"

Mark looked down and slightly shook his head. "I found out that she had overdosed and brought into the same hospital as me as a Jane Doe."

Wrenford took notes as he spoke.

"She wasn't identified until after I woke up but the time of death couldn't be determined." Mark watched as the doctor's pen danced across the notepad and defensively added, "They say I probably heard nurses talking and just put it together in my mind but if nobody knew it was her how did I know?

The doctor didn't answer the question, focusing instead on his notes until the silence was broken with by his next request. "Tell me about Julie."

Mark smiled. It was a small action that warranted yet another note from the doctor. "She was there when I woke up. The nurses said she had been there often and called her my wife. When I was released, she told me that Bobby had helped her fake a marriage certificate and even lent her his wife's ring to complete the look."

Wrenford chuckled, "They say that a woman willing to commit forgery for you is a keeper. How are you two now?"

Again Mark shrugged, "As good as we can be, I guess. On Tuesdays I go to the Pretty Kitty and watch her work until Bobby gets off, and then we go bowling. We are a pretty normal couple otherwise."

Mark's eyes drifted around the room, looking at the diplomas on the wall and the pictures of far off countries he would never visit. "And are you falling back into your normal life. Are you back to work yet?" the doctor asked. The question hung heavy in the air as a silence filled the room. Wrenford reviewed his notes. "Tell me about Wayne."

Mark wasn't sure where to start, and his hesitation showed on his face. "This is where you tell me that I'm imagining things," he finally answered with frustration in his voice.

"Why is that?" the doctor asked.

Mark took a deep breath and tried his best to explain. "People say Wayne never existed. Nobody at Loans4you knows who he is, and people say that the desk next to mine has been empty for as long as I've been there." Mark paused when he noticed Wrenford taking more notes. The first time he had told this story, he spoke with the passion of someone who knew without a doubt that he was right, but after months of being told differently, even he had trouble believing it now.

"Go on," Wrenford encouraged.

Mark leaned back in his chair as he recited the same thing he had so many times before. "The people in the Lounge say I never ate lunch with anybody. People even told me that I would occasionally talk to nobody at my desk. I'm not crazy; I know there was someone there." The doctor nodded and looked on interestedly as he spoke. "It makes sense, the Fallen are manipulators, and if he was here to trick me, then why would he leave a trace?"

"If?" the doctor asked. Mark offered only a confused look. "You said if," he explained. "You said 'If he was here to trick me.'"

"So?"

The doctor picked up his notebook and flipped through the last several pages. "The way you tell your story is with such conviction and certainty. There is little doubt in the words you chose when writing it. To hear you question if the 'Fallen' where trying to trick you seems strange. What about the person," he flipped further through his notes, "David, the leader at the meeting?"

Mark shook his head. "He said that he meets so many people. So many new people show up for one meeting and never again, he didn't even recognize me."

"And Julie didn't see him there either?" he asked. Mark just shook his head. The doctor closed his notebook and placed it on the table beside him. He removed his glasses and placed them on top of the notebook and then sat up straight, uncrossing his legs. "You know, we have only been seeing each other for a short time, but I can tell by your body language that you do not have the greatest of expectations for this." Mark, impressed by his honesty, sat up and mirrored his stance. "You have been through something traumatic, that much is clear." Mark shifted uncomfortably, waiting for the same dismissal he had received from others. "The answer you are looking for is if what you experienced was real or not. You are looking for someone to tell you that it was real, and I'm sorry to say that I am not qualified to do that. What I can do is tell you that I think you are asking the wrong question."

Mark fell back onto the couch again and looked to the ceiling as disappointment filled his face. "And just what question should I be asking?"

The doctor picked up his notebook again and flipped to almost the beginning. "Let's assume that it was real. The first 'Fallen' you met, Jack. You were assigned to him, and the rationale he gave you was that you were already sentenced, he told you that there was nothing you can could do to stop what was going to happen. During your conversation, you said that you couldn't remember the last good thing you did, right?" Mark nodded his head. "And even though you were unable to think of the last 'good' thing you did, you still pleaded with him that you were not a bad person."

Mark closed his eyes and tried to remember but came up with nothing. Frustrated, he said, "Yeah, probably, I don't remember."

Wrenford then flipped to the end of his notes. "You said something similar towards the end too. When speaking about the 'Messenger', you said you couldn't remember the last good thing you've done."

Mark again sat up and leaned forward, "Yeah, so?"

The doctor smiled and put down the notebook. "Now let's assume that it wasn't real. People who are fighting with the idea of morality have similar dreams. If it was real or not is not the question. The question is would it have happened if you did not doubt yourself? Tell me, Mark, do you think you are a good person?"

Mark wasn't sure how to answer the question. "I don't know," he finally responded. He knew he wasn't a bad person, but was he a good person? Did everybody have those kinds of thoughts? Wasn't it normal to question if you were a decent person or not? "How can you tell if you are a good person? Is it based only on your actions? Or is it your inactions that count? Do you have to be a saint?"

Mirroring Mark's actions, Wrenford offered a shrug. "I think it's all about perspective. If you compare yourself to a saint, then you're going to come up short every time. Now the good news is that if you are questioning your morality, then maybe subconsciously you want to be a better person. I think by just asking the question, you already have the answer."

"So what do I do now?" Mark asked.

"That's easy," the doctor said, smiling. "You work on being a better you."

Emotion flooded through Mark's face as he felt a tear roll down his cheek. "How?"

With reassurance in his voice, Wrenford replied, "Well, that's what we are here to find out, but it will have to wait. Our time is up."

www.ingramcontent.com/pod-product-compliance
Lightning Source LLC
Chambersburg PA
CBHW032010240626
47153CB00003B/1194